Karen Saunders often gets asked where the inspiration for her character Suzy Puttock comes from. The truth is, she's a walking, talking disaster zone, just like Suzy. She's had tons of ridiculous injuries like a broken nose during a tickling fight and concussion getting into a car. As for her most embarrassing moments, well, she's got *loads...*

Karen graduated with a BA in English Literature from Warwick University and did lots of different jobs, like selling Christmas hampers, answering telephones and working in PR, before completing an MA in Writing for Young People at Bath Spa University. She's been making up stories _____ chaotic casts of teenage

By the same author:

Me, Suzy P.
Suzy P. and the Trouble With Three

Suzy P., Forever me

Karen Saunders xxx

templar

A TEMPLAR BOOK

First published in the UK in 2015 by Templar Publishing,
part of the Bonnier Publishing Group,
Northburgh House, 10 Northburgh Street, London EC1V 0AT
www.bonnierpublishing.com

A CIP catalogue record for this book is available
from the British Library.

ISBN: 978-1-78370-163-6

1 3 5 7 9 10 8 6 4 2

Printed and bound by Clays Ltd, St Ives Plc

In loving memory of Tanneke Doerrleben,
who always walked on the wild side.

CHAPTER ONE

Well, this sucks.

I'm standing on the outer edges of Collinsbrooke School's playing fields, dodging nettles and thistles and trying to avoid any form of participation in the world's lamest rounders match. The drizzle is making my curly brown hair frizz and I'm shivering in my too-small gym kit.

It's my idea of hell.

I can't run. Can't catch. Can't throw, can't bat.

It's fair to say that rounders is *not* the sport for me.

Ugh. I *hate* PE.

And I shouldn't even be here. I dropped the subject as fast as humanly possible when I was choosing my GCSE options and honestly thought my days of hanging around sports fields wearing unflattering nylon outfits were over.

Apparently not.

Unfortunately for me and my fellow exercise dodgers, our teachers had other ideas. Over the holidays there were problems between some kids in my year and some students from St Edward's, on the other side of town. There's always been a rivalry between us but this summer things kicked off, big-style. (Or as much as things ever kick off around here. It's hardly gangland central, let's be honest.)

The rumours all suggest different things happened to start it – someone got off with someone else's boyfriend, someone nicked someone else's bike – nobody really knows for sure, but whatever it was, it got way out of hand. Soon there was a huge fight being organised in the Aldi car park. The police caught wind of it and broke it up, but the teachers went into crisis mode. In their infinite wisdom they decided the best way to smooth things over was this farcical event.

The letters arrived before we got back to school, telling us the date the reconciliation game would take place, informing us that there would be several matches going on so everyone in the year could participate, that our teams would be mixed, that by the end of it we'd all be friends again, blah blah blardy blah.

It finished by declaring it wasn't optional. No excuses.

Honestly, I sometimes wonder if teachers live on the

same planet as the rest of us. I mean, *really*? How did they think a calm-stormy-waters-with-rounders match was going to help?

I tried to get out of it, but Mum was having none of it – she was already freaking that she'd never be able to visit Aldi again without being stabbed – hence I'm here. In a bordering-on-indecent kit, because Mum thought after last term I'd never have to do PE again.

As did I.

I'm grumpy. I'm bored. And I'm properly tired. My big sister Amber had twin girls a few months ago, and they cry *a lot*. Mainly at night. There's not been a whole lot of zeds happening in the Puttock household of late. The tiredness is not helping the boredom any, because even the muddy grass is looking tempting enough to curl up and nap on.

Admittedly, I'm finding things extra boring because I opted to be a fielder, far, far away from the main action, and deffo the safest place for me. Only it's really dull standing around a field for hours by yourself with nothing to do. I should've brought a book along.

Although they've mixed up the schools between the two teams, the rivalry is still way obvious. There's been pushing. There's been shoving. There's been an awful lot of shouting. But still we've not been allowed to bring this whole farce to an end and we're hating each other more as the games go on.

Checking my watch, I see it's not that much longer until this fiasco is over. Thank the Lord and all that is holy for that.

In the distance, I can almost see my boyfriend of forever, Danny, leaping forward to try to catch someone out. I imagine him looking seriously cute as he bites his lip, fringe flopping over his blue eyes as he frowns in concentration. But he fumbles the ball, and the Collinsbrooke watchers groan. Even from here I can see his ears turning red as he rubs his hands dejectedly through his light brown hair. Poor Danny. His sporting ability's on a par with mine.

My best friend, Millie, and her boyfriend, Jamie, were stuck on teams in one of the other matches, the game at the opposite side of the field. I wonder how they're getting on? Millie's always stupidly enthusiastic about everything, so she didn't really mind having to do this, and Jamie's great at sport. He even chose PE as one of his options, the crazy fool.

I'm so busy squinting across the field that I don't notice what's going on. I tune back in to a load of shouting… uh oh. All of a sudden people seem to be trying awfully hard to get my attention:

"Suzy, catch it! Suzzzzyyyyyy!"

Oh God. There's a ball coming this way.

Aaaaah, this wasn't supposed to happen! I'd carefully positioned myself so I wouldn't have to get involved!

It seems Kara Walker was up to bat; she's clobbered the ball crazy hard and is sprinting off round the posts.

I need to catch the ball.

I *have* to catch Kara out.

She's one of my least fave people on the planet.

Only... the ball's coming so quickly. And if it hits me, it's going to smash my face in. My nose will be broken. It'll knock out all my teeth. Oh noooooooo!

The yells are getting louder. I tell myself I can do this and get in position, hands poised, ready to try and catch – but at the last possible minute I bottle it and leap to one side, cradling my head in my hands.

Out of the corner of my eye I see the ball bounce onto the floor then roll into the undergrowth at the very back of the field.

Now all I can hear is booing.

Gnargh, stupid sporty people. Who cares about this stuff, anyway?

When the boos have lessened, I risk glancing up. The guys that aren't on my team are killing themselves laughing; the ones that are seem to want to kill *me*.

"Get the ball, Suzy! Get the ball!"

I can't even *see* the ball, but as it's Jade Taylor bellowing at me, maybe I should make an effort to be getting the blimmin' thing.

Jade Taylor. Otherwise known as Queen Bitch, and best friend of Kara. Stunningly gorgeous, stunningly sporty, stunningly competitive and stunningly mean. Me and my mates kind of have a history with these two – it's fair to say we're not exactly close since Jade and Kara managed to break up Danny and me for a while as part of a bet. I avoid them as much as possible, only now Jade's running towards me at speed, huge norks bouncing hypnotically.

"Where'd it go?" she asks, skidding angrily to a halt next to me.

"Um, in there somewhere," I say, gesturing to the grass and brambles.

"Well, get looking for it, you dozy cow."

I don't dare refuse. She'd make my life hell if I did.

Jade and Kara are best friends but also mortal enemies. They are more competitive than *anyone* else I've ever known, which will be why Jade's so hacked off with me for fumbling the catch. To see Kara get caught out would have made her ecstatically happy, even if it was me who'd made it happen.

It feels like forever until I see the ball. My arm gets scratched to pieces trying to retrieve it, but eventually I've got it in my hand.

I look upfield.

It's an awfully long way. I'm never going to be able to chuck it back to the other players.

Still, I suppose I should at least have a go. Show willing, that kind of thing. Miss Lewis, our PE teacher, wrote on my report last year that I had an 'apathetic attitude'. Which is kind of true, I suppose, but not very nice.

"What are you doing, you utter tool? Stop wasting time," Jade snaps, snatching the ball and lobbing it powerfully up the field

"I... um..."

This is the point where I need a snappy, witty retort to put Jade firmly in her place. Which will no doubt pop into my head later tonight, but right now, I've got nothing.

Total brain-blank.

I watch as Jade jogs away, and kick crossly at a clump of mud.

The game continues for a few more minutes as the last players queue up to bat. The other team wins by a run, and I'm glowered at by most of my teammates as we're made to line up and shake hands. But then everyone seems to be glowering at everyone else, so maybe it's not only my fielding that's the problem.

Pfff.

I'd confidently say the calm-stormy-waters-with-rounders peace mission was a big fat fail.

"Hey," Danny says, grinning as he jogs over and we head back towards the school. Not for the first time, I think how lovely his smile is. It makes his eyes go all crinkly. He flings an arm around my shoulder and pulls me towards him, kissing my temple.

"Hey," I say back. "I'm so glad that's over. I can't remember the last time I had such fun. Possibly when I visited Evil Aunt Loon at the nursing home and trod on those false teeth."

Danny laughs. "Grim. At least it's done now. Seen Jamie and Millie?"

I spot our friends a short distance away, about to come up the steps.

"They're over there. Hi, guys," I say, waving.

"We won!" Millie says, flicking her newly dyed hair triumphantly. She's left the back blonde but dyed the rest hot purple. It looks amazing, if a smidge space-age. Only Millie has the confidence to carry off something like that. "That was so much fun. How'd you get on?"

"Don't ask." My stomach growls loudly. "I'm starving. Got any sweets?"

Millie looks heartbroken. "I haven't. I'm sorry."

We stare at her in shock.

Millie is pretty much 99% fuelled by sugar, with jelly babies being her favourite. She's *always* got sweets within easy reach. This is, after all, the girl who stuffed emergency jelly babies into her bra during a cross-country run, and who took a suitcase of the things with her on holiday in case they didn't sell them abroad. (We were going to Wales.)

"How come?" Jamie says. "Have you eaten your daily ration already?"

Millie sighs heavily. "There were some news reports on how bad sugar is for you and Mum started getting her knickers in a knot that I was going to end up an obese diabetic or something. I've promised her I'll do my best to cut down, but she wants me to go cold turkey. I'd kill any one of you for a sugar hit right now."

"In that case, maybe your mum has a point," Danny says.

Millie shrugs as I hold open the door so my friends can file inside. "She's going to give me an iPad if I can last until Christmas," she says.

"Wow, that's a pretty amazing incentive," I say.

"If you can manage it," Jamie says, smiling wickedly. "I can't see it happening myself."

"Hey!" Millie says, swatting him. "Do you really think I won't be able to do it?"

"You *do* have a pretty strong addiction," Jamie says.

"Do not. And Christmas isn't so far off."

"It's months away!" I say.

"That's not *that* long," Millie says, weakly.

"We'll see," Jamie says. "Catch up with you later."

The boys go on ahead as we turn into the girls' changing rooms.

Urgh. As if doing PE wasn't bad enough, the post-sport showers are worse.

Way, way worse.

Because who wants to parade around naked in front of their classmates?

Um, *nobody*.

So it's somewhat unfortunate that Miss Lewis, our teacher, is completely obsessed with personal hygiene and cleanliness, and makes everyone shower after any kind of sporting activity, even if you haven't broken a sweat because you've been standing on the sidelines. She's physically herded girls into the shower cubicles before. Mortifying.

But maybe today, if I can get dressed fast enough,

she won't notice… it's not like I'm pongy or anything, I hardly moved out there.

I'm about to wiggle into my trousers when Miss Lewis appears in front of me.

"Have you showered?"

"Er… yes?"

Miss Lewis shakes her head. "I don't think so."

"But —"

"No buts," Miss Lewis says, pointing in the direction of the showers. "In. Now. Otherwise it's detention."

Yurgh. As if being humiliated on the playing field wasn't enough, now I'm being humiliated in the changing rooms, too.

I take off my clothes under my towel before scuttling into a cubicle, intending to take the world's fastest shower.

I've just turned the water on when…

Drrrriiiiinggggggggggggggggggggggggggggggggggggggggg!

Heh? What's that?

It can't be, can it?

Oh God. It is.

Fire alarm.

It's a fire alarm.

I am naked in school and the fire alarm is going off.

I seriously don't believe this.

All around me are squeals and yells as girls stampede to get their clothes back on.

"Okay, everyone, file out to the playground assembly point, as quickly as you can. I haven't been warned about a drill," I hear Miss Lewis call.

I switch the shower off, grab my towel and see everyone disappearing out of the door. I run back to where I'd hung up my stuff... which is no longer there.

"Hurry up!" Miss Lewis says, sounding increasingly panicky. "We need to leave!"

Where are my clothes? Wherearetheywherearetheywherearethey?

I know this is my peg, because my bag's on it. And my underwear's shoved inside. And my shoes are underneath. But my clothes – shirt, trousers and jumper – are nowhere to be seen.

The last few girls leave the room, and now there's just me and Miss Lewis.

"Suzy, you need to get out," Miss Lewis says, getting more and more stressed. "I hope it's not a fire, but with the St Edward's team here and all the problems between the schools, anything could have happened."

"Um, my clothes have gone," I mutter.

"Gone? What do you mean, they've gone?"

In the corridor, a male voice is shouting loudly: "We

need everyone out of the building. Everyone outside, as quickly as possible, please."

"Suzy, we're going to have to leave," Miss Lewis says. She seems awfully flustered. Is there really a fire? Seriously?

"But I've got no clothes!" I squeak.

"Well, you'll have to put your kit back on," Miss Lewis says, starting to usher me towards the door.

"That's gone too," I say.

"We need everyone out immediately so the firemen can assess the building," the male voice shouts again.

"Suzy, there's no other option. We'll find your clothes later," Miss Lewis says. "Wrap your towel around you, it'll be fine, and here's my cardigan, let's go, now!"

"But, but, no…"

Miss Lewis isn't listening. And now she's herding me outside. I'm shuffling along, holding onto my towel so tightly my knuckles are white.

Waiting in the corridor are several large firemen, who do their best not to laugh when they see me.

"Outside, straight away," says one of them. "We're pretty sure it's a false alarm, but we need to complete our checks of the building."

"Can't I wait over by the doors?" I plead.

"Afraid not. We need everyone off the premises," the

fireman says. "You might want to get dressed a bit more quickly next time."

Heaving the heaviest of sighs, I push open the doors and walk out, holding onto my towel for dear life and praying that Miss Lewis's cardigan covers up more than I think it does.

Everyone's gathered together on the tennis courts, trying not to look impressed by the firemen or the fire engines, and probably already gossiping about who it was that set off the alarm. I certainly can't see any smoke.

And then there's the horrible moment when I'm spotted.

One person points me out to their neighbour and the news spreads until the whole playground is cracking up. I can't see Millie, Jamie or Danny anywhere, but at the front of the crowd are Jade and Kara.

They're killing themselves laughing and then Jade tugs the waistband of her trousers slightly down. Underneath is another pair of trousers. *My* trousers. And then Kara pulls the neckline of her shirt aside to reveal she's wearing another shirt underneath. *My* shirt.

They're wearing my clothes.

There are not enough words in the world to describe how much I hate them both right now.

Rounders couldn't do it, but it seems the afternoon

has finally provided a common goal for everyone to bond over: laughing at me wrapped in a towel and the PE teacher's cardigan.

Mrs Cooper, the headteacher, rushes over. "Miss Lewis, what are you thinking, letting Suzy outside dressed like that?"

"She couldn't find her clothes and the firemen said we had to evacuate. I thought there could be a fire..."

Mrs Cooper shakes her head slightly. "There's no fire. We think it's a false alarm. Suzy, back inside, quickly."

As Miss Lewis ushers me indoors, I can hear Mrs Cooper shouting at the assembled crowd, "Anyone taking photographs or making videos of what happened here had better delete them immediately. If any find their way online, it will result in an immediate suspension from school, do you understand?"

I suppose at least that's something. But that's little comfort to me right now. I'm abso-flipping-lutely *mortified*.

I've said it before, and I'm sure with my luck I'll end up saying it again, but *how* do these things always end up happening to me?

CHAPTER TWO

"**HOW WAS** the rounders match?" Mum asks, struggling into the kitchen with bags of shopping. "That was today, wasn't it?"

"Don't ask," I say, turning a page of Amber's gossip magazine and trying not to shudder at the memory.

Me.

A towel.

Half-naked in front of the whole school... argh, stop it, brain! Stop!

I suppose at least I got my clothes back. Found hanging neatly in the corner of the changing room not long after we'd all gone back inside, like they'd been there all along. Convenient, no? I didn't see them do it, but they must have put them back when I was hanging around outside the staff room, waiting for Miss Lewis to find some spare clothes for me. At least I was saved the embarrassment of wearing the dregs of the lost property box.

So there was no point telling a teacher about it. Jade and Kara would only deny everything, anyway.

"Can you give me a hand unpacking these?" Mum asks, unloading packets and tins onto the worktop.

"Yeah, in a minute…"

I've been reading a piece about how Dylan Waters, half of the TV duo Dylan and Jake, has been secretly photographed playing strip poker, but I'm distracted by a picture underneath of my fave band, The Drifting. And the article seems to suggest… Oh. My. God. It says there are rumours the band's about to split. Apparently they've all fallen out while touring and are travelling across America on four separate tour buses.

No, no, no! This can't be true. The Drifting can *never* break up! My life would be over without them. I need to tell Millie. Immediately.

"Help, please," Mum says more insistently.

"I'm a bit busy, Mum. I need to speak to Mills…"

"You can do that after. And there's something I want to talk to you about."

Huffing, I grab a carrier bag, shoving some milk and economy cheese into the fridge. Mum's not going to give up. She's extremely persistent.

On the counter, Mum's unpacking tins of value beans. Ever since Amber's blow-out wedding earlier in the year, money's been kind of tight around here. Once the final bills came in, and Dad realised just how much his wife and eldest daughter had spent, he immediately implemented the Puttock Emergency Budget. Things are better than they used to be – but still not great. It's not helped by the fact that there's so many of us squished into our house: Mum, Dad, me, my utterly irritating younger sister Harry, Amber and her husband Mark *and* the two babies. As Dad keeps pointing out, it's a lot of mouths to feed, because even the formula milk the babies have costs a bomb. Mum started doing competitions to try and help win our way out of poverty, but since the caravan she won in the summer – now on loan to Dad's brother, who's off touring Europe – she's not had even a sniff of success, so it's not looking like our diet will be upgraded any time soon.

Mum looks around, spy-stylee, and says under her breath, "Your father's not here, is he?"

"Nope. Think he went to get some petrol or something."

"Good. There's something *very important* I want to discuss with you," she says in the same low tones.

I have no idea what's up with her; my mother's idea of very important never matches mine. There's nothing

Mum loves more than a drama, so who knows what her cloak-and-dagger act's about.

"What's up?" I ask. "Is it something to do with Dad?"

"Shhhh!" she says, her eyes wide and frantic. "I'm hosting an urgent family meeting. I'll tell you everything then. Wait for me in the utility room once all this is put away. I'll tell the others."

"The utility room? Why?"

"Don't ask daft questions," Mum says. "Just go to the utility room. I'll explain when we're there."

Um, harsh, much? I actually don't think it's *that* daft to ask why we're having a family meeting in the utility room, which is about one metre square, when we could go to, say, the lounge. Where there's ample space. And sofas. And windows.

We finish unpacking the shopping, Mum dashes off to round up everyone else, and I perch myself on the chest freezer.

I'm joined moments later by Harry, who's holding Amber's old phone. Harry's pet rat, Hagrid, is sitting on her shoulder, nose twitching. Over the past year Harry has become obsessed with several things – practical jokes, magic, Harry Potter – and now she's recording everything that goes on in this house, using the phone. She's decided she wants to be a world-famous film director. I duck my head and reach my hand towards the lens. Make-up-free and crazy-haired, I am SO not ready for my close-up.

"Turn that thing off," I tell her.

"Nope," says Harry. "I don't want to miss anything good. What's this all about, anyway?"

"No idea," I say, shrugging, as Mum opens the door and squeezes in.

"We're waiting for the others," she says.

"What's going on?" I ask.

"I'll tell you when the others arrive," Mum says.

"Why are we in here?" Harry says.

Mum ignores her and opens the door. "Amber!" she bellows. "Hurry up!"

"Why are we in here?" Harry repeats.

"Because I don't want your father to see us."

"But Dad's gone out, hasn't he?" I ask.

"That's not the point," Mum says.

"But if Dad's out, why are we having a family meeting without him?"

"Because Dad's what I want to talk to you about," Mum says.

An icy trickle runs through my veins. Uh oh. What does that mean? Maybe something's wrong with Dad, like he's ill or something. Or they're getting a divorce.

Millie's parents had real problems a few months ago, and even now they're still having counselling, trying to sort themselves out. Mum and Dad had that stupid row last night about who ate the last custard cream (it was me, although I didn't 'fess up), but surely that can't mean they're splitting... can it? Maybe I should have admitted to being the biscuit thief.

"But if it's about Dad and he's out, we're in here because...?" Harry asks.

Mum sighs like we're the most stupid people in the entire world. "Would you two stop all the questions? It's because I don't want him to come back and see us."

"Is everything okay?" I ask apprehensively.

"Where *are* the others?" Mum says, ignoring me. She sticks her head out of the door again. "Amber! Mark!"

"We're here," Amber says. We shuffle up as Amber and her husband Mark squeeze in, carrying Chichi and Uni, their twins. The girls are actually called Violet-Chihuahua and Lily-Unicorn — only my bonkers big sister and her husband could name their kids after their favourite flowers and animals. We tried using their full names for a while, but they were way too much of a mouthful. Especially when there's two of them. So we started calling them Violet and Lily, but Amber got all kinds of upset, saying the names were too 'normal'. She's obsessed with celebrities, especially a vacuous airhead called Conni G, who called her first-born Pashmina. Despite us trying to explain that normal names were a good thing, Amber was having none of it, as it's not what Conni would do. Which meant we had go with Chihuahua and Unicorn... and now these have been shortened to Chichi and Uni.

"What's happening?" Mark asks. He looks exhausted. There are huge dark circles under his eyes. Amber, however, looks fantastic. She's got a full face of make-up and you'd never know she'd had babies recently.

Part of me suspects the reason Amber always looks so good is because she's got Mum eager to do everything for her. Mum loves babies, and has been doing *a lot* since the twins arrived, giving Amber plenty of time to chill out and catch up on her sleep.

"Keep that rat away from the girls, please, Harry," Amber says. "Rats carry the plague and these two haven't had their vaccinations yet. Ooh, what's the matter, Chichibooboo?" Amber asks as the baby crumples up its face. "This is Chichi, right?" Amber looks anxiously at Mark for confirmation. The main problem Amber seems to have with her twins is remembering which is which. They're not even identical.

"I'll take her," Mum says eagerly, practically snatching

the baby out of her arms. Chichi's always crying. Uni's slightly better, but Chichi's permanent state of being seems to be scrunched, purple and furious.

Pfff. I don't know what she's making such a fuss about. It's not like *she* appeared half-naked in front of her school or anything. Then she'd really have something to complain about.

Argh, stop it, brain! You're doing it again!

"Did you get my honey and chilli flakes from the supermarket, Mum?" Amber asks.

"Yes, they're in the cupboard," Mum says.

"Honey and chilli?" I ask.

"Yeah, it's for my new diet. I can't wait to lose the rest of this baby weight," Amber sighs. "I look like a hippo."

"You don't," Mum says.

"You really don't, Ambypamby," Mark agrees.

"Look at me," Amber says, pinching a non-existent fat roll. "I'm huge! But Conni G was talking about this diet she did after she'd had Pashmina, where she ate honey and put chilli on all her food, and it really worked, so I want to try it too."

"Well, you don't need to," Mark says loyally. "You look more beautiful than ever to me."

"Aw, you're so sweet," Amber says, leaning in to give him a snog. Uni, squished between her mum's boobs, gives a cross squawk and Harry makes puking noises.

"Sorry, baby-bun," Amber says, dropping a kiss onto Uni's head.

"Um, when you two have finished," Mum says, "I wanted to talk to you all about Dad."

Chichi starts to grizzle and Amber eyes her. "Oh gosh, she's going to kick off again, isn't she? Quick, what do we think she needs? You just changed her, didn't you, Mark? Do you need feeding, Chichipops? Do you want Daddy to get you some yummy scrummy milk to fill up your tum-tum? Mum, can we do this in a minute? I think she needs a bottle."

"No, we can't," Mum says.

Harry and I exchange a glance.

Oh God. This *is* about something serious. Mum's usually falling over herself to make sure the twins have everything they need. Maybe Dad's dying? He did look a bit pale earlier, but I thought that was because one of the twins was having a particularly loud screaming fit.

"It's about his birthday," Mum continues, and Harry and I both sag with relief. I don't think Amber and Mark are really listening – Uni's started grumbling now too and both the babies are being jiggled up and down.

"Ow!" I glare at Mark as he elbows me accidentally in the shoulder.

"Sorry," he says, yawning.

"Don't, Mark, you'll set me off," Amber says, yawning prettily. "I'm so tired. I miss sleep so much."

"Wasn't Mum up with the babies last night while you went to sleep on the sofa?" Harry asks.

"Yes," Amber says. "But I still had to wake up to go downstairs, didn't I? I haven't had ten straight hours in months, and Conni G says that's the minimum you need for your beauty sleep."

"Can we focus on Dad's birthday for a minute?" Mum says, raising her voice.

"What about it?" Harry asks. "Dad hates birthdays."

"Which is precisely why we should try to give him one he'll like," Mum says. "He's forty-five this year, it's an important landmark. I want to throw him a surprise party."

I stare at her in horror. Here, in no particular order, are things Dad especially hates: his birthday, parties, any kind of fuss, surprises.

"Um, are you sure that's a good idea?" I ask, tentatively.

"Yes," Mum says firmly. "I know he's a bit grumpy about the whole birthday thing, but that's why we've got to make it really good. Becoming a grandfather has thrown him a bit, you know…"

Amber starts to get upset and Mum hastily explains, "Not that he doesn't love being a Grampy. You know he does. But I'm worried it's making him feel... old. And he's been acting ever so strangely lately. He keeps getting these peculiar ideas in his head. I think a party will help him feel young again. Now, I'm going to need you all to help me organise it, okay?"

"Um, okay," we mutter, although we probably couldn't sound less enthusiastic if we tried.

"Fantastic," Mum says, smiling happily. "That's all I need at this point. I'll let you know when the next secret meeting is then we can start planning things properly. It's so exciting! Give nothing away to your father, do you hear? Nothing! Oooh, Chichi, you're a bit stinky, aren't you? Have you done a poo? Does Granny need to change your bottom?"

The front door opens at the same time as we're all emerging from the utility room. Dad curses as he falls over the huge double buggy that's parked in the hallway. "This damn thing! Takes up so much space." He stares as we all appear in front of him, red-faced and slightly sweaty. Turns out it's mighty steamy squeezing seven people into such a minute space. Even if two of them are babies.

Amber's dog, Crystal Fairybelle – the other Chihuahua in the house – runs to greet him and jumps around Dad's legs. Dad shakes him off. He hates the dog, and avoids it whenever possible.

"Get away, you stupid thing! What are you lot up to?" Dad asks suspiciously.

"Nothing!" Mum says, her voice shrill and unfamiliar as she clutches Uni to her chest. "Nothing at all!"

"What were you all doing in there?"

"Er…" Mum says, with this scary fake smile on her face. She's going to give the game away for sure.

"Problem with the tumble dryer," Harry says.

"Oh for goodness sake, don't tell me something else has broken," Dad sighs. "Did it really need all of you in there to look at it?"

"I was seeing if it was possible for us all to fit in such a small space. I wanted to film it. Kind of like elephants in a Mini. Only with people in a utility room," says Harry.

Dad shakes his head. He's lived in this house long enough to believe any old nonsense by this point. "Fine. Whatever. Is the tumble dryer working now?"

"Yep," Mum says, with the scary fixed smile still on her face.

"Well, that's a relief. We can't afford to replace anything else at the moment. Are you all right?" Dad asks Mum.

"Of course I am," Mum says.

"If you say so. You look like you've had a stroke."

"Charming!"

"You're welcome. Now, I'm off to watch the monster truck marathon. Harry, want to watch it with me?"

Harry shakes her head. "Can't. I'm going to Skype with Ant."

"Wooooooo," I tease.

"Shut up," Harry says defensively.

Ant's this boy Harry met on our summer holiday and although she'd never admit it, they were totally crushing on each other. They bonded over Harry Potter and have kept in touch ever since.

"Are you sure?" Dad wheedles. "It's going to be a good one."

I can tell Dad's trying not to look disappointed his youngest daughter has abandoned him.

"Sorry," Harry says.

"What's that?" Mum says, spotting Dad holding a bag from the chemist. "I thought you were going to the garage."

"I did," Dad says, immediately hiding the bag behind his back. "This is nothing."

"Then why are you hiding it?" Harry asks.

"No reason," Dad says, looking decidedly shifty.

"Is it something embarrassing?" Harry asks. "Like

those nappies for grown-ups?"

"I didn't buy incontinence pants," Dad says crossly.

"So why won't you tell us?" Mum says.

"There's nothing to tell."

"But there's something in there."

"Oh all right," Dad says in defeat. "It's hair dye."

"Hair dye?" we all chorus together in disbelief.

"Is it... for you?" I ask.

"Yes. Is there something wrong with that?"

"No," I say. "It's just, you haven't really got that much hair, so..."

Dad looks genuinely hurt, so I rush to explain myself. "I didn't mean that, but I didn't know you cared about that kind of thing..."

"I'm going too grey," Dad mutters. "Makes me look old. Wondered if this dye might help."

"We love you exactly the way you are and you're dyeing your hair over my dead body," Mum says, confiscating the bag and steering Dad into the kitchen. She flaps her hand at us behind his back, code for 'leave us alone'. "Now, would you like a nice cuppa? I'll put the kettle on before I go and get a new nappy for this one."

CHAPTER THREE

"**Does anyone** know what this assembly's about?" I ask as we weave our way outside and towards the main hall. There's major building work going on at the moment, so half of the walkways in school are barricaded behind gridded barriers. I can see a huge JCB scooping up earth while the builders stand around shouting at each other. They've already had several warnings from the teachers as their language has a tendency to get a little 18-rated. We all think it's hilarious.

Someone stands on my foot and I wince. Because we're all being squished into such a small space along these paths, it's seriously claustrophobic when you're trying to get anywhere. I've been bashed by a tennis racket and several bags so far, and narrowly avoided concussion from a passing cello. This place should come with a health warning. And hard hats.

Millie shakes her head and raises her voice to be heard

over the sound of drilling. "Nope. It could be another lecture about how much time and money it wastes when the fire brigade gets false calls."

"Didn't they deal with all that yesterday?" Jamie says. "Guaranteed it wasn't one of us, anyway. I'd put money on it being someone from St Edward's."

"Can we not keep mentioning the fire alarm, please?" I ask.

Every time someone brings it up, it makes me feel all shaky and sick again. Ugh, the humiliation. It's even worse than the time I fell over and accidentally pulled down Ryan Henderson's shorts in the middle of a school football match. I thought nothing was ever going to top that. How wrong can a girl be?

How *could* Jade and Kara steal my clothes? Evil. Pure, pure evil.

Then a horrible thought strikes.

What if the assembly's about me?

No. It can't be. Can it? But what if there's photographic evidence that's got out somewhere? Everyone was made to delete any photos or videos they'd taken, and were told if any went online there would be suspensions, but even so… my stomach flips over and I feel a bit queasy.

"I don't think it's about the fire alarm," Jamie says.

"I heard Mr Patterson's been fired after getting caught in a cupboard with a Year Twelve."

"No way!" Millie and I exclaim together.

"Stevo told me that some Year Nine's pregnant and we're getting a safe sex lecture," Danny says, hoiking his backpack higher onto his shoulder.

"No way!" Millie and I chorus again.

"That can't be true, can it?" I ask incredulously.

Rumours are flying like wildfire and get increasingly more outrageous the closer we get to the assembly hall. Nobody seems to know for definite what's behind the summons we've received, but everyone's got an opinion on what it might be. We hear a married science teacher's eloped to Australia with one of the dinner ladies (which would be quick work, since they were in school only yesterday). Then that the deputy head, Mr Groves, was killed in a car accident last night. Some of the younger kids start crying. Then someone says it wasn't him, it was the school secretary. Then someone else says it was actually the librarian and she was poisoned.

Surely with this many rumours going around *somebody* must have died?

As we file into the assembly hall, the room's buzzing, hissed whispers passing from seat to seat. The excitement is growing by the second. I mean, nobody actually *wants* someone to be dead, that would be bad, but everyone loves a bit of drama, especially first thing in the morning. Plus the intrigue is loads more interesting than double history, which is what I should be having right now.

We find four seats together and collapse into them, eager to know what's going on.

"I heard a rumour this assembly was to tell us you'd been expelled for indecent exposure," says a voice near my ear.

Jade and Kara are sitting right behind us, smirking. My heart sinks into my shoes.

"No you didn't, shut up," says Millie.

"Shall we move?" I say under my breath.

"We're not going anywhere," Millie says firmly. "Don't give them the satisfaction."

Jade sits back in her chair, entertaining herself by kicking the back of my seat repeatedly as I try not to think about what she said. Gah! She's *so* annoying!

She can't really have heard that rumour... can she?

Our headteacher, Mrs Cooper, steps onto the stage and everyone shuts up, pronto. Jade even stops with her incessant kicking. As one, the whole school leans forward to listen to what Mrs C's got to say. You could hear a pin drop. Usually nobody cares about assembly, everyone's sitting there with headphones in, chewing gum, texting their mates, passing notes… but we don't usually get called out of lessons for a special assembly. Something's going on. Something big.

Mrs Cooper's been here forever, like nearly thirty years or something bonkers like that. There are photos of her with classes in the late eighties where she's got this huge perm and massive shoulder pads. Hilarious. I know it's not normal to like your teachers, but Cooper's actually okay. I like her even more since she rescued me from the whole fire alarm thing. That was the first time I'd seen her for ages, she doesn't seem to have been around much lately.

"Good morning, Collinsbrooke," Mrs Cooper says, and we all chorus back, "Good morning, Mrs Cooper," like automated robots.

She gives a few notices and then gets down to the good stuff. "Well. Now, you've all been gathered here this morning because we have some big news," Mrs Cooper says. "It affects each and every one of you, and the school as a whole. I'm afraid I… I…"

Whoa. Is she *crying*? Mrs Cooper, who's always über-composed, apparently even after the stink-bomb attack of '94 that's passed into school legend, looks like she's wiping away a tear. Maybe the death rumours are actually true.

"I'm very sorry to have to tell you that…" She takes a big breath.

Who is it? Everyone's peering around, trying to see which staff member isn't here.

"… I'm retiring, effective immediately."

The whole school slumps with an 'uhh' as one, in disappointment.

Which probably makes us a smidge evil. But we were hoping for some big news, explosive news, news that would keep us entertained for the rest of the day. This, well, yeah, it's sad, but it's not exactly dramatic, is it? No big deal.

"Some of you might be wondering why I'm retiring a few weeks into a new term," Mrs Cooper says. "I've been in the hospital recently, having various tests. While I'm not going to go into details of what's wrong, I've been advised to avoid stressful situations and, as lovely as most of you are, some of you push my blood pressure in the wrong direction. So, I'm taking early retirement. I'll miss you all – well, most of you – very much."

At this point, Mr Groves walks onto the stage. "I'm sure we'd all like to offer Mrs Cooper a huge round of applause for everything she's done for us during her time here."

"Mr Groves will be taking over as your new head,"

Mrs Cooper says after the clapping dies down, "although I'll still be consulting on various matters, and will be in school every Monday morning for a few weeks during this handover period. Now. Before I go, I've got one more piece of news, rather more exciting, I think. Having been at this school as long as I have, and being required to leave in the way I am, I'm rather keen to leave behind a, well, a tribute, if you will. I won't call it a memorial, as I'm hoping I've got many years left in me yet. As many of you know, I'm a passionate musician..."

There are groans from around the hall as everyone remembers being made to sing along to her guitar, piano and, over more recent years, trumpet. She's not exactly the most talented musician in the world. Mrs Cooper's the one responsible for the tuneless school orchestra (attendance means immediate social death) and the never-ending trips to classical music recitals.

"All right, simmer down," Mrs Cooper says. "Listen to what I've got to say. What I'd like to leave the school with as a tribute is a music recording studio."

Now everyone's paying full attention. A recording studio? For *us*? That would be all kinds of amazing!

"Now, obviously, a recording studio is going to cost a lot of money, so we're going to need to start fundraising," Mrs Cooper continues. "As you know, we've been having extensive building work to improve the school facilities, and we can incorporate the studio into these current plans. But it's still going to be expensive. So this is where it's going to be interesting for you. We're going to hold a farewell fundraiser party in November, so I can say goodbye to you all properly, but you're going to organise it, with a bit of help from the teachers and the PTA, of course. I want you to go away and think about what could raise the most money, and then you'll vote on which you think is the best idea. A committee will then be formed to organise everything. Mr Barnes is waiting by the double doors, he'll be handing out information sheets with all the details as you leave."

The room is now frantic with excitement. This sounds amazing! Whatever issues people have had with Mrs Cooper before now, they've all been forgotten. A recording studio! A party! This is way, way exciting. There are loads of muso types here, and who hasn't fantasised about becoming a totally famous pop star at least once?

"There's just one more thing," Mrs Cooper says. "I'm sorry about this, as I know it won't be popular, but only those in Year Ten and below are allowed to pitch. The rest of you need to be focusing on your exams."

There's a deafening groan of disappointment.

"We are so doing this," says Millie. "We'll come up with a fantastic idea."

There's a snort from behind us. "Yeah, right, as if you losers could come up with anything good," Jade says.

"Shut up, Jade," Millie says, not even turning round.

Up on the stage, Mr Groves is trying to give out some announcements, but it's hopeless – nobody's listening to a word he's saying – so in the end he dismisses us before the bell rings for break.

"We need to think about this," Millie says, grabbing my hand and pushing at Jamie's back with the other. "Go, go!"

Millie's enthusiasm for everything means she gets an idea in her head and she's off running with it at speed. Usually it's sugar-fuelled, but if she's still on her sugar-free diet, this must be the natural Millie energy force we're witnessing.

"Nothing you can come up with will be better than what we're going to suggest," Jade says.

"You may as well give up now," Kara adds. "Nobody's going to vote for you."

"Yeah, well, we'll see," Jamie says.

"Won't hold my breath," Jade sneers, then she and Kara shove their way through the crowds.

44

"Now we have to come up with something amazing in order to beat them," I say.

"And we will," Millie says. "Let's go and find somewhere to sit down."

Behind us, the JCB roars into life. They've knocked down some of the buildings to create a new humanities block, and there's an arts centre that's due to be started after Christmas. We knew there was going to be a suite of music rooms in it, but a recording studio as well – suddenly the arts centre is sounding *much* more interesting.

We find a space on the wall outside, and within about five seconds have turned blue with cold. Millie passes around some sugar-free jelly bears and then leaps to her feet, bouncing with excitement as she scans the information sheet Barnes gave us.

"Sugar-free sweets? Really?" Danny says sceptically.

"They're better than you'd think," Millie says. "Mum got them for me."

I take an orange bear and put it into gingerly into my mouth. Actually, they're not too bad. Not as good as the real thing, but edible.

"See? They're all right, aren't they?" Millie says. "I needed to find a sugar-free sweet substitute, cutting them out altogether was killing me."

"Um, you know these are laxative if you eat too many?" Jamie says, scanning the packet and spitting out his jelly bear.

Danny and I immediately do the same.

"What?" Millie says, grabbing the bag to check. "Shut up, you're lying. Oh God, you're not. What am I going to do? I ate loads in maths."

We all fall about laughing at Millie's stricken face.

"You ate poo bears," Jamie snorts.

Danny howls. I can't stop laughing either.

"Seriously, you guys, what am I going to do?" Millie asks. "Stop it! You have to help me!"

"Mills, I don't think there is anything you can do," I say. "Hope for the best, and make sure you're not too far away from the toilet for the rest of the day."

"Yikes," Millie says. "Oh well, I feel okay at the moment. And Mum's at home, she'll have to come and pick me up if I need her to." She takes the bag of jelly bears and throws them in the nearest bin. "I never knew sweets could be so evil. So, let's talk about the fundraising party. It's so cool we get to choose what happens at it. I still can't believe we're going to get a recording studio, either. Amazing. Just amazing."

"It is pretty fantastic," Danny agrees.

"This says that we need to present our ideas at a

special assembly being held next week," Millie says, scanning the piece of paper in her hand. "It's supposed to help inspire confidence and public speaking or something, but who cares about that? What ideas have you had, guys?"

"I've had a good one," Danny says.

"Great, what is it?"

"*Star Wars* party," Danny says proudly. "What?" he asks, genuinely perplexed as he sees three cynical faces staring at him.

My heart sinks. Don't get me wrong, I love my cute, funny boyfriend. But his *Star Wars* obsession? Not so much.

"*Star Wars*, mate?" Jamie says. "For real?"

"Yeah!" Danny says. "It'll be great. We can dress the whole gym up in black sheets with these fibre-optic lights so they look like stars, and hire people to dress up as Stormtroopers and give everyone a lightsaber and there could be Ewoks and Yoda and *Star Wars* themed food. It would be epic."

"I'm not sure everyone would go for it," I say, trying to be kind. Danny's *Star Wars* obsession is, well, kind of dorky. And his pitch sounds a smidge like a party for a six-year-old, not that I'd tell him that.

"No, come on, give it a chance, it'd be great," Danny

says, warming to his theme. "Picture it... the gym as a solar system, all dark, with the stars shining, and then in walks Darth Vader..."

"Yeah, but how's that going to make any money?" Jamie asks. "People aren't going to pay much to come and see that, are they? A tenner, max."

"There could be a DJ," Danny continues weakly. I think he knows he's fighting a losing battle.

"I'll write it down, but it sounds more like a theme party than a way to make money," Millie says kindly. "Anyone else got any suggestions?"

"What about an all-you-can-eat competition, like you see in America?" says Jamie.

Millie rolls her eyes. "Who's going to pay to see you throw up?"

"We need someone cool to come, like a band or someone famous," Jamie says.

"It would be amazing if we could get The Drifting," I say wistfully.

"As if," Danny says. I think he's still narked nobody liked his idea.

"I know we never could," I say. "But it would be so super amazing. And people would pay loads of money for tickets."

"Yeah, but it's never going to happen. We need to

think of an idea that could actually work," Millie says. I can tell she's getting frustrated. "C'mon, guys, we need to think of something better than whatever Jade and Kara are going to come up with. We can talk about famous people coming but unless anyone's got any contacts, it ain't gonna happen."

"Well, what do you suggest then?" Jamie asks.

"There's got to be loads we could do! Like a... a... urgh, I don't know! Why can't I think of anything?"

"A raffle?" I suggest.

"It's a bit church fete, isn't it?" Jamie says.

"Not if there were really incredible prizes," I say, warming to my theme. "Like a car or something."

"A car?!" Danny scoffs. "My *Star Wars* idea's better than that. Only the sixth formers and teachers can drive and where are you going to get a car from?"

"All right," I mumble. "A car wasn't the best suggestion, although I bet parents would buy tickets. Mum and Dad would love to replace our old Volvo. But maybe you could get people to donate prizes. Like clothes from the local shops in town, cinema vouchers, tablets, that kind of thing."

"That's not bad," Millie muses. "It'd take some work to get people to donate stuff, but I bet we could do it. But we can't only have the raffle. We need something to go along with it. A theme. And stuff to make it a fun party. Crikey. This is hard. Loads harder than I thought it would be. I thought we'd have tons of good ideas."

"We've had loads," Jade says, walking past with Kara. "You might as well give up now — it's obvious our suggestion's going to be the best."

"You don't know that," Millie says.

Kara snorts. "So do! You're all so lame there's no way you're going to come up with anything worth listening to."

"Shows how much you know," Jamie says.

Jade raises one eyebrow at him and crosses her arms. "I do know. Nobody's going to care about anything you lot come up with. As if. Come on, Ka, let's stop wasting time and go and find someone interesting to talk to."

As Jade and Kara stalk off, we stare after them.

Are they right? With the only idea we've got being a raffle for which we have no prizes, and a *Star Wars* theme we're trying to ignore, I wonder if maybe they have a point, much as I hate to admit that those two witches could be right about anything.

But then my stubbornness kicks in.

We are *not* going to let Jade and Kara dictate what happens at this party. We can do this! We just need a little bit more time.

CHAPTER FOUR

"**What is** the matter with this dog?" Dad says as I pass the lounge en route to the kitchen. I need some toast. I'm always starving after school.

Crystal Fairybelle is sitting by Dad's feet, staring up at him and whining. His enormous bug eyes seem bulgier than ever.

"He won't flipping leave me alone. Shut up, you stupid mutt," Dad mutters. "Go away."

"He's been acting all kinds of weird since Amber had the babies," I say.

"Hmm. Does he look sad to you?" Dad asks, poking Crystal with his toe.

"Sad?"

"He seems a bit depressed."

"Er, it's a dog. I'm not sure they get depression." Since when has Dad cared about anything to do with Crystal, anyway?

Crystal whines again, louder this time, and starts pawing at Dad's chair.

"Perhaps he's jealous of the twins," I say.

"You just told me dogs couldn't get depressed," Dad says. "Is it likely they'd get jealous?"

He does have a point. Not that he needs to know that.

"Maybe you should try stroking him," I say. "Maybe he wants some attention."

"It's not my dog. What's it want attention from me for? I'm trying to watch the footie."

I shrug. "Only a suggestion."

Crystal's whining increases another notch.

"Oh for goodness sake." Dad reaches down and gives Crystal's head a little scratch.

Crystal immediately starts to pant happily, and rolls over to have his tummy rubbed.

Dad obliges, looking a bit bemused. "Do you like that? Seems you were right, Suzy."

"Told ya."

"I'm only doing this to shut you up, right?" Dad tells Crystal. "Um, Suzy, while you're here, is, er, is everything all right with your mum?" He continues scratching Crystal, but sounds oddly subdued and isn't meeting my eye.

"Yeah, I think so, why?" I say.

"No reason. She seems to be a bit distracted lately, that's all."

I knew Mum was acting too weird! She's going to give away the surprise if she keeps behaving the way she's been doing – Dad will guess for sure. I'll have to tell her to tone it down a bit.

"She seems fine to me," I say, then my phone buzzes with a text from Millie.

I've finalE L d toilet ☹. On R way c U s%n. X

Poor Millie, she's really been suffering the effects of those evil jelly bears. She texted earlier that no amount of iPads in the world were worth the trauma, and is back on proper sugar. And now my friends are on their way over to meet me before we go off to Bojangles café. Bojangles is our favourite place to hang out, and we couldn't think of anywhere better to go to figure out an idea for the party.

The fact we can stuff our faces with cake and drink the best hot chocolate while we're there helps, too.

"Gotta go, Dad. See ya laters."

"Hi, Suze. Finished your homework?" Mum asks as I wander into the kitchen.

I nod.

I'm lying, but Mum doesn't need to know that. What does she think registration's for? Catching up with homework that didn't get done the night before, of course.

"In that case, maybe you could give me a hand getting the tea ready?" Mum says, washing some potatoes and putting them onto a chopping board.

"I'm not staying for tea," I say. "I thought I'd eat at Bojangles, if that's okay?"

Mum frowns. "On a school night?"

"Oh c'mon, Mum, everyone else is going," I say. "We're working on a project for school."

"I don't know. We're still trying to save money and," she lowers her voice to a barely audible hiss, "I'd hoped to start planning Dad's party tonight. I'd like you there for it."

"Yeah, about that, Dad's getting suspicious. You need to dial it down."

With excellent timing, Dad appears, checking his phone.

Mum puts her finger on her lips.

"Just had a text from Andy," Dad says. "He's cancelled tonight, so we're not going out now."

I look at Mum. "Does that mean I can go?"

"Oh, I suppose so," Mum sighs, still chopping away.

"Why couldn't Suzy go out if I was going out?" Dad asks.

"Um... I want enough hands on deck to help with the babies," Mum lies quickly.

"Then maybe I should go out after all," Dad says, looking panicked.

"Too late. Although..." She looks thoughtful. "Actually, isn't there anyone else you could go out with? Any of your other friends free?"

"Don't think so."

"Do you want to text around and ask?"

Dad pulls a face. "It sounds like you're trying to get rid of me."

Mum laughs, shrill and fake-sounding. "No, no, not at all."

So much for dialling things down. She's hopeless.

Dad walks over to the fridge and scans the food inside. "I've been meaning to talk to you. I'm thinking about starting a project in the garden," he says, trying to sound like it's not a big deal, but Mum's ears prick right up.

"A project? What sort of project? Are you putting in that gazebo I asked for a couple of years ago? Or building a pond? It'd be lovely to have a water feature... although with small children around maybe it's not such a good idea."

"Er, no, none of those," Dad says. "It's something I've been thinking about for a while. Don't worry," Dad says, as he clocks Mum's face. "It's fine. Not a big deal at all.

Just a little treat to myself. An early birthday present, if you like."

Mum frowns. "But why won't you tell me what it is?"

"Because you'll stop me doing it," Dad says. There's clearly nothing in the fridge that takes his fancy, because he shuts it again.

"I —" Mum starts to protest, but Dad's not listening. He's staring at the collage of photographs stuck to the door, and at one snap in particular, of him and Mum on a boat. I took it when we were on holiday in Scotland, about five years ago.

"I've aged so much," he mutters, pulling away the picture. "Look at me," he says, thrusting the photo into Mum's face. "Look! No grey hairs. No belly. It wasn't even that long ago. Andy's not going grey *and* he's still got a flat stomach. Do you think he's more attractive than me?"

"Andy's a good-looking man," Mum replies, pushing the photo away. She's engrossed in the spuds and I suspect she isn't really listening.

"I knew it! I knew you thought he was better looking than I am. You should have let me dye my hair."

"What?" Mum drops the knife and turns round. "What are you talking about?"

"You. And Andy."

"I'm confused," Mum says, absolutely baffled. "What about me and Andy?"

There's a knock at the door, and I rush to answer it. My mates have arrived quicker than I thought they would, and thank goodness for that. The parentals' conversation is getting all kinds of awkward.

But when I open the door, it's Mrs Green, our neighbour. She seems very upset, and is tightly holding her cat, Pickles, who looks very wet and exceptionally cross.

"Oh, Suzy, thank goodness you're home. Are your parents in? One of my pipes is leaking and there's water everywhere. Look at Pickles, he's got into a terrible state, poor thing, he's ever so distressed..."

"Come in," I say, holding open the door. "Mum, Dad! Mrs Green's here!"

I head back into the kitchen as Mrs Green starts to explain her trauma. A moment later, Mum calls from the hall, "We're popping next door, Suzy. Won't be long!"

"So can I go to Bojangles?" I call back.

"What? Oh, yes, okay, I suppose so," Mum says. "But don't be late back. You've got school in the morning."

"Fab. Thanks, Mum. See you later."

I mooch into the lounge, and turn on the TV. Might as well watch something while I wait for my friends. I hear Amber and Mark clatter down the stairs. Chichi has been crying for hours this evening, and is busy howling in Amber's arms.

"At least one of them's asleep," Mark says, glancing down at where Uni is slumbering on his chest.

"This one's a proper pickle, aren't you, Chichiboo?" Amber says, tickling her daughter under the chin. Chichi screams louder.

"Aw, it'll be so much easier once you can tell Mummy what's wrong, won't it, babyboop?" Amber says. "Where's Mum?" she asks me.

"She popped next door."

Amber crinkles her nose. "But I need her! She's the only one Chichi settles for."

"She probably won't be long. Mrs Green sprung a leak and needs her cat drying off, or something."

"But I need her *now*," Amber says. The next thing I know, she's thrusting a baby into my arms. "Here, take her for a bit, would you? I need to go to the toilet."

"Erm, okay," I say. I still get a bit freaked out around the babies. They're just so small, with their heads wobbling around all over the place. Chichi's large, teary eyes blink while her cries get louder. The girls remind me a bit of baby monkeys, not that I'd ever say so to Amber. She'd go nuts, big-time.

"Actually, a toilet break sounds good," Mark says.

"Can you keep an eye on Uni, too? I'll lie her down here. She'll be fine, she's fast asleep."

As Mark and Amber dash from the room at the speed of Olympic sprinters, Chichi ups the volume of her screaming. Uni jumps at the increased volume of her sister's voice, wakes up, finds herself on the floor, then begins to bawl too.

Aaaah! Now what am I supposed to do?

"Please stop crying," I say to Chichi, jiggling her up and down and trying to stroke Uni with my toe. She's clearly way unimpressed, and starts to shriek even louder.

Good grief, these girls are loud, considering how small they are. Nothing wrong with their lungs, that's for sure.

"Suzy? Your friends are here," Harry shouts. I turn to see Millie, Jamie and Danny standing in the doorway, Harry hovering behind them, videoing. The babies have been so deafening I didn't hear the doorbell ring.

"Harry! Come and take one of the girls," I say. "I need to go out."

"Hah! No chance," Harry says, darting away.

"Where are Amber and Mark?" Jamie asks.

"Toilet," I shout. "Someone help, would you?"

My friends all look at each other.

"I'm not doing it," Jamie says, making a face.

"You know I can't hold babies," Danny says. "I've got no idea what to do."

"Oh for goodness sake, you two," Millie says, striding over. "It's easy. Which one's this?"

"Uni," I say.

As she takes Uni, Millie sniffs and a look of disgust crosses her face. "I can smell something... oh, gross."

There's a brown stain on the carpet underneath where Uni has been lying. And the back of her babygro is all brown too.

"Urrrrggghhhh!" we all chorus in horror. Millie holds Uni out in front of her at a distance, like she's a bomb. Which I suppose she is. A poo bomb.

"I'm sorry but I'm not sorting that out," Millie says. "There are limits. Cuddling babies is one thing but sorting out stinky nappies? I don't think so."

"Maybe you can take off the babygro? That might be why she's crying."

"Nuh-uh," Millie says. "Here, pass Chichi over and you can sort out this one."

We swap babies and I lie Uni back down on the floor. Amber usually uses a mat, but I don't know where it is. The carpet's already covered in poo, a bit more won't hurt, will it? I peel off the babygro, doing my best not to gag.

This is disgusting. And it's going to be a seriously long

time before I ever eat korma again. Where's my flipping sister? Or my parents? They should be sorting this out, not me!

"It's a good job I love you," I mutter to the baby, who doesn't hear a word I've said, she's crying so loud. Argh, this bawling's so stressful! Does that mean there's something seriously wrong? What if something happens to her while I'm in charge? That would be awful. My poor niece looks so *miserable*.

"Please stop crying, please stop crying," I beg, as I do my best to remove the clothes without getting covered in poo myself. It's easier said than done, because the poo is *everywhere*. Up Uni's back, all down her legs… don't even get me started on how hard it is to get a dirty vest over a baby's head without smearing poop all over their face. No wonder Uni's so cross.

"It stinks worse than one of yours, mate," Jamie says, punching Danny on the arm.

"Ha ha," Danny says.

"Now what do I do?" I say. I've got a naked poo-covered baby lying on the floor, screaming her head off. And her parents are nowhere to be found.

"I'm sure Amber and Mark won't be long," I say, admitting defeat. "They'll sort them out in a minute."

So we wait. And we wait. But they don't come back.

And still the babies are crying.

"Surely there's only so long you can spend in the loo?" Millie asks. "My arms are getting tired..."

"That's it. I'm going to find out what's going on," I say, pushing myself up from my hands and knees.

The downstairs toilet door is open. No sign of Mark. Upstairs, the bathroom's empty too. Where've they gone?

"Ambs?" I call. I knock on her closed bedroom door. There's no answer. I knock again... then turn the handle.

My sister and her husband are comatose on the bed, sprawled like starfish and snoring their heads off.

Now what?

Downstairs I hear Mum and Dad's voices by the back door. Thank goodness. They're back. I sprint down and grab my friends, stopping only to help Millie lie Chichi next to her sister on the floor. On the way out I stick my head into the kitchen.

"The babies are in the lounge," I say, brightly. "They might need changing. We're going out, okay? See you later. Go, go," I mutter, shoving at Danny's back and hurrying my friends outside.

No way do I want my parents discovering the poo-stained carpet and nappy-less, naked baby before I'm well out of the way.

CHAPTER FIVE

Compared to the screamy, poo-filled nightmare that is currently my house, Bojangles café is a peaceful haven of tranquillity. It had a bit of revamp in the summer holidays after a burst pipe flooded everywhere, and it's looking great in here, with new tables, settees and chairs, different-coloured paints on the walls, and fairy lights that twinkle invitingly. Danny and Jamie actually helped with the decorating, and despite never having done it before, I think they did a pretty amazing job.

I sink into our favourite squishy sofa by the window and sigh happily.

"Hi, guys," calls Hannah, the café owner, from the counter. "We're a bit short-staffed today, so come up with your order when you're ready, okay?"

"Okay," Danny calls, shooting her a broad smile.

Hannah's got a real soft spot for Danny and Jamie

since they helped her out with all the renovation stuff. She didn't have to close for as long as she thought she'd have to, which saved her a ton of money.

"So. The fundraiser. Let's make a list of ideas," Millie says. "I brought my notebook along. Let's write down everything we've come up with so far. Even the rubbish ideas."

"Make sure *Star Wars* is on that list," Danny says. "Which was not a rubbish idea, no matter what you lot say. And it's one of the best we've come up with, you have to admit. None of you have suggested anything even half as good."

"It would go down really well at a *Star Wars* convention," I say, trying to be as kind as possible. "I just don't think there are enough *Star Wars* fans at school to make it work."

"But this could get people into the movies," Danny pleads. "I've been thinking about it, and we could have a cinema room, showing the films..."

"I'm really not sure, mate," Jamie says.

"Other ideas I've got include the raffle and, er, that's it," Millie says.

Danny leans back in his chair and crosses his arms smugly, with a told-you-so look on his face.

"We could have a talent show," I suggest. Then I

remember the talent show that we were forced to enter while we were camping, back in the summer. Dad ended up playing trombone wearing nothing but tiny gold hot-pants. It was a fortnight before I stopped seeing that particular image every time I closed my eyes. Shuddersome.

Millie writes it down.

"Maybe a sports event? Like a school Olympics or something?" Jamie suggests.

"Not everyone loves sport as much as you do," Millie points out, although she notes it on her list. "You're not going to convince the couch potatoes to participate, or even vote for that."

"Yeah. You're right," Jamie says. "Let's face it, none of these ideas are strong enough. None of them are going to raise enough money."

"We need to come up with something really original, something that hasn't been done a million times already, and that will appeal to the largest possible group of people," I say.

"You're right," Millie replies. "But what?"

Cue more blank faces.

Gnargh. Why is this so flipping difficult?

"Do you think Jade and Kara have really come up with an amazing idea?" I wonder.

"Wouldn't be surprised," Millie says gloomily.

"Let's order some food," Jamie says after we've sat in silence for a while. "I can't think on an empty stomach."

We scan the menu, check out the specials, then settle on what we always have — pizza.

"This really shouldn't be so hard," Millie says, when Jamie returns from placing our order.

"Okay. Let's think about this properly. It needs to be something spectacular. Something that people will spend money to come to, otherwise we're onto a complete non-starter," Danny says.

"What do people like?" I ask. "Let's start with that and see if that sparks anything. What do the people we know spend their money on?"

"Apps and video games, films, clothes, music, concerts, books, magazines, gadgets..." Danny reels off.

"Sports events, trainers," Jamie adds.

"Bags and jewellery?" Millie offers. She's frantically writing all this down.

"Food should be on there as well. We should've thought of that one first, given where we are," Jamie adds. "I hope Hannah hurries up — I'm starving."

"Anything else?" Millie asks.

"What about what people our age like to do?" I ask. "We should make a list of those things too, then hopefully we'll have enough to start getting some ideas."

"Cinema, watching movies at home, playing and watching sports – just because you lot aren't fussed, some people enjoy them," Jamie says when he sees the look I shoot him.

"Hanging out in cafés, going shopping," Millie writes.

"Eating," Jamie adds.

"It always comes back to food with you, doesn't it?" Millie says.

"What? I'm hungry!"

"That's enough for now, I guess," Millie says, sitting back to look at the enormous list of frantic scribbles on the paper in front of her.

"Food's ready," Hannah says. None of us noticed her coming; we've all been too busy staring at Millie's notebook, hoping to get some inspiration.

"Ooh yum, thanks," I say, as the plates of pizza land in front of us. "I think Jamie's about ready to eat your table."

"How about I offer you some free cakes and you leave my table alone?" Hannah says, her eyes twinkling. "I've got some that'll have gone off by the end of the day, would you like them?" She knows there's not a chance we'll say no.

"Yes, please!" we all chorus.

"You're the best," Jamie says through a mouthful of pizza, as Hannah returns with our selection of cakes and puts the plate in the middle of the table.

"Don't tell any of my other customers, or they'll all be wanting free pudding too," Hannah says.

Jamie scoops up a huge amount of lemon icing and pops it into his mouth. Cake and pizza together. The boy really is a human dustbin.

"What are you guys up to?" Hannah asks, peering over Millie's shoulder to try and see what she's written. "A school project or something?"

"Kind of," Danny says. "We're trying to come up with ideas."

"Ideas?"

"There's a fundraising party happening at school," Jamie explains. "The students get to choose what kind of party it gets to be, but it obviously needs to raise money. A lot of money."

"What are you fundraising for?"

"A new recording studio," I tell her.

Hannah's eyes widen. "Wow. That's pretty amazing. What a fantastic thing to have at your school."

"We really want to come up with the best idea," Millie explains. "Then we get to organise it all. Plus it means these totally vile girls in our year, who think they're going to get to plan the party, don't get to boss everyone around."

Hannah looks thoughtful. "Well, as it's a recording studio you're raising money for, why not do something musical?"

We all look at each other. That sounds good and everyone likes music...

"Have you ever heard of the programme *Stars in Their Eyes*?" Hannah continues. "It used to be on TV when I was a kid. People went on and dressed up as their favourite band or singer, then performed one of their songs. You could do something like that."

"That's a really good idea," I say. "We could mix it up with what they do on the *X Factor*, and have judges, buzzers, that kind of thing."

"Ooh, yeah!" Millie says. "And we could call it 'The Star Factor'!"

"Wouldn't it be like glorified karaoke?" Danny asks.

"Kind of," Hannah says. "But it's actually a lot more fun than that."

"Yeah," I say. "If we had a load of costumes, wigs and make-up, and people were dressing up as the musicians they were pretending to be, it would be hilarious."

"And there could be lots of things to help boost the profits," adds Millie. "As well as the raffle, people could also bid money to be a judge, and the highest amount offered would win. Plus we'd have to sell tickets for people to come, of course, which would raise even *more* money..." I can tell she's really excited.

"Actually, that all sounds pretty great," Jamie says. "We could make a ton of cash."

"Sorry, I've got to go and serve that customer," Hannah says, seeing someone waiting over by the counter. "Let me know how you get on."

"Thanks, Hannah!" we call after her.

"This could work, you know," Millie says.

"It really could," I say, starting to feel excited. "This is an idea that could blow anything Jade and Kara have come up with out of the water."

CHAPTER SIX

I can hardly keep my eyes open at school. In fact, I actually do fall asleep in history, and only wake up at the end of the lesson. I'm pretty sure the teacher hadn't noticed until I jumped so hard when the bell went that I nearly fell off my chair.

Awkward.

Fortunately I managed to escape from the classroom before anything was said.

It's not even like it's my fault I'm so tired. It's not as if I was out late or anything, oh no. It was Chichi. She was up pretty much every hour, screaming her head off. And as Amber's bedroom is next to mine, I woke up every time she did.

She's proper loud.

I read somewhere that a crying baby is noisier than a pneumatic drill. Chichi's certainly doing her best to try and prove that theory.

Mum and Dad were up too, trying to stop the baby yelling – Amber's still convinced that Chichi settles best for Mum – but nothing was doing the trick. Eventually Mum convinced Dad to take Chichi for a drive until she went to sleep.

That was at 4 a.m.

He didn't get back until 5.30 a.m. Chichi was sleeping soundly by this point, but for the rest of us it really wasn't that long until it was time to get up.

Breakfast this morning was interesting. I've never seen everyone so grumpy. Mum practically threw a piece of toast at Harry's head and Dad was getting very aggressive with his spoon. Both of them were hardly speaking to me. I've not exactly been their favourite daughter since they discovered the half-naked pooey twins abandoned on the lounge floor, and lack of sleep hasn't helped their mood any.

It's a huge relief when school's done and I can finally go home. I want something to eat and then I'm going to go and lie on my bed and ponder what I can fashion earplugs from. I mean, I love my nieces, I really do. But they're so flipping *loud*.

For once, I'm greeted with silence when I arrive home. Which is unusual. With so many of us living here now, that never happens.

I head upstairs. Out of my window, which overlooks the back garden, I can see Dad's left work early and is outside, working on his secret project. There's a cement square covering what used to be the vegetable patch. Mum had this idea that we'd grow all of our vegetables and save money by living off the land, but the birds and slugs ate half of the seedlings, then Mrs Green's cat adopted it as a litter tray, so Mum admitted defeat.

I collapse down onto my bed for a while then wander downstairs to see what's going on. Mum's back from work, and dumps her handbag and keys on the side before yawning widely.

"Gosh, I'm tired," she says. "How did you get on today? Manage to stay awake?"

"Had a quick power nap in history, but the teacher didn't notice," I say.

Mum nods wearily. "I don't know what we're going to have for tea tonight. I haven't got the energy to cook. Maybe beans on toast. That's nice and easy."

I shrug. I don't really care. I think I've got to the point where I'm so tired I don't want to eat. And I never thought that would happen.

The back door slams and in comes Dad.

"Hiya, Jen," he says, coming over to give Mum a kiss hello.

I pull a face. Gagfest. Who wants to see their parents snogging? Can't they be more respectful when their kids are around? They should shake hands or something if they want to greet each other. That would be way more appropriate.

"What are you doing back already?" Mum asks.

"Couldn't concentrate," Dad says. "I was too tired. So I came back and I've been doing some work in the garden." He glances over at me. "Suzy, could you give me and your mum a minute, please? We need a chat."

"Sure," I say. But once I'm out of sight, I loiter in the hall so I can hear what they're talking about. I don't want to miss anything interesting.

There's a pause, where presumably they're waiting for me to get upstairs, then Dad starts speaking.

"Jen, we can't go on like this. It's ridiculous."

"I know," Mum sighs. "But I don't know what to suggest."

"We need to do something," Dad says. "There are too many of us being disturbed at night. You and I have jobs to do – I could scarcely function all day. And the babies are waking up Suzy and Harry. Harry's teacher apparently found her asleep on a bench at lunchtime after she didn't go back in to her lessons. She didn't even want to come out and help me, she just went straight to her room she was so tired. You don't know how much I'm starting to wish we'd kept that caravan instead of lending it to Neil. I could have slept in there."

Mum sighs. "I know it's hard. But what are we supposed to do? New babies are difficult, and Amber needs us. Maybe we should be doing more to help out..."

"More!" Dad snorts. "We do far too much already. I notice Amber left and went to sleep on the sofa during the worst of the crying. I saw her there when I took Chichi out for that drive."

"Would you really want Amber driving the girls around?" Mum asks. Amber's driving skills are notorious. And not in a good way.

Dad rolls his eyes, but agrees. "I suppose not. None of them would come back in one piece."

"And we can't kick them out on the street. You know they're saving up for their house deposit, but babies are expensive."

"I know, I know," Dad sighs, giving a heavy yawn. "But I need some proper sleep. I'm too old for all this..."

"You're not old," Mum interjects.

"I *feel* old. Especially with all this getting-up-in-the-middle-of-the-night malarkey. I thought that was well behind me. And this house isn't big enough for all of us. There's nowhere for anyone to escape. There's not even room for me to put my cup of tea down on the side because of that enormous bottle steriliser. And I've got bruises all down my leg because I bash myself on their pram every time I come through the front door."

"But you love spending time with the babies," Mum protests.

Dad grunts. He'd never admit that in a million years. "*Small* amounts of time," he concedes. "Not *all* of my time. I also love sleep. And non-bruised limbs."

"So what do you suggest we do about it?" Mum asks.

"I don't know," Dad says. I hear someone shut a cupboard door and footsteps across the floor. I duck back in case anyone's coming out; I don't want to get busted. But then I hear a chair being scraped across the floor, and guess Dad's sat down.

"I'll talk to them both at dinner tonight," Dad says. "They can't have failed to notice this isn't really working for any of us."

"This is Amber and Mark we're talking about here."

"Good point," Dad says. "But even they can't be that away with the fairies, can they?"

Mum doesn't answer.

Later that evening we're all sitting round the table, eating chicken casserole. Harry's picking the green beans out of hers and whenever Mum and Dad aren't looking she's pretending to stick them up her nose so they look like bogeys (grossness overload), while I'm waiting with interest to see how this is going to go. Amber's blathering on about what she and the girls have been up to all day. Sleeping, mainly. Because it seems that while Chichi objects to sleeping at night like a normal person, she wholeheartedly embraces napping during daylight hours.

She's clearly as tricksy as her Aunty Harry.

"I seriously need to catch up on my beauty sleep," Amber's saying, not realising that actually, she's not the only one. "I'm so tired these days. Nobody told me babies would be so exhausting. I thought it'd be like having a doll to look after, but it's really not, is it?" She pops a sweet into her mouth.

Amber's not eating the same as the rest of us. She's currently on the red foods diet. This means she can eat whatever she likes as long as it's red, so my sister is sitting at the table with huge bowls of strawberry jelly and red Skittles in front of her. I'm not quite sure that's how the diet is supposed to work, but there's no telling her.

"I was a bit worried about one of the poos Uni did today," Amber says. "It was really weird, like mustard with bits of green in and this kind of stringy gunk I've never seen before. Do you think she needs to go to the doctor's?"

Gagarama.

Amber doesn't notice the rest of us look down at our plates and put down our cutlery. Nobody fancies chicken casserole any more.

"It's perfectly normal," Mum says reassuringly.

"Really?" Amber says. "I'm not sure. Maybe I'll speak to the health visitor about it in the morning."

"If that would make you feel better, love," Mum says.

Amber turns to Mark. "Ooh, Markymoo, did you see the new outfits that arrived today? Aren't they the cutest?"

"Super cute," Mark agrees.

Since the babies were born, Amber's been buying new outfits online on a pretty much daily basis. And we're not talking cheap supermarket baby clothes here, either. Her packages arrive wrapped up in tissue paper, tied with pretty ribbons. Properly expensive.

Dad clears his throat. "I –"

"I saw these adorable pink shoes with ribbons on the front on one of the websites today, what do you think?" Amber asks Mark.

"But they're only a few months old!" Dad says.

"They're not walking yet. In fact it's doubtful they even know they have feet. What do they need shoes for?"

"Silly Daddy," Amber laughs. "Of course they need shoes. They're not properly dressed without them."

"Do they really care?" Dad asks, genuinely baffled. "They spend most of their life pooing or puking on themselves."

Amber laughs harder. "You're funny."

Dad shakes his head in bewilderment. "Anyway. I wanted to ask you both something. I was, um, wondering, how's the saving for a house deposit going?"

Mark, who's jiggling Chichi in a bouncer with his foot while he eats, shakes his head and smiles apologetically.

"Not that great, I'm afraid, Chris. All our house deposit money is being ploughed into buying nappies and stuff for these two."

I suspect Dad already knew what their answer was going to be, but there's no mistaking the expression on his face.

"Do you want us to move out?" Mark says.

"Don't be daft, Markymoo, Mum and Dad love having us around, don't you?" Amber says.

"Well —" Dad begins, but Mum leaps in.

"No, no, of course we don't want you to move out. Stay as long as you need," she says, glowering at Dad.

"We know this isn't ideal, and we're really grateful to you for letting us stay here, and for all the help you're giving us," Mark says. "Last night was awful."

"For all of us," Dad emphasises.

"We really appreciate you doing all that you are," Mark says. "We love our girls, and hope they'll start sleeping soon. We're finding it tough, all of us in one room, aren't we, Ambypamby?"

"Four in that room is a lot," Mum says.

"It's actually five if you count Crystal Fairybelle," Amber says. "Not that he's been in there for the past few nights. I don't know where he's sleeping at the moment."

"Down my side of the bed," Dad mutters darkly. "I nearly trod on him this morning."

"You're so lucky, having a room all to yourself," Amber says enviously, looking at me.

"I loved sharing a room with my brother when I was younger. Maybe Harry could move into Suzy's room and the twins could go into Harry's?" Mark suggests. "That would give us all some more space."

Er, no it flipping wouldn't!

Amber gasps and claps her hands. "That's perfect! Markymoo, what a great idea! And it would be so nice for you two. What do you think?" she says to us.

Harry and I are horrified. I can't think of anything worse than having to share a room with my sister. She'd have every opportunity to do all sorts of evil things to me while I was sleeping, and I'd be only metres away from her rat.

No. Freaking. Way.

I adore my nieces, but this is happening over my dead body. I'd rather sleep in the garden.

"Mum," I say pointedly, but Mum's looking thoughtful.

"You know, girls, that could work," she says.

"No!" Harry says in alarm. She seems as freaked out as me by the whole idea.

"Come on, you two," Amber says excitedly. "It would solve all our problems."

"Solve all your problems, but give me a whole heap of new ones," I say.

"Suzy snores," Harry says. "No way am I sleeping in a room with her. I'll run away!"

"It's all right, girls," Dad says. "Look, it's not fair to ask these two to give up their space, I'm sorry."

Wow. Dad's actually talking sense for once.

"We'll have to come up with another solution," Dad says, sitting back in his chair and folding his arms.

Unfortunately, nobody's got any suggestions.

CHAPTER SEVEN

At school, all of the tutor groups have had a notice saying that if anybody wants to pitch an idea for the fundraising party, they need to meet at break with Mr Groves who'll talk us through what we need to know.

Millie's herded me, Danny and Jamie towards the arts block, and now we're gathered in one of the English classrooms, waiting for Mr Groves. Jade and Kara strut in after us. We're on opposite sides of the room so I'm studiously avoiding all eye contact with them when... oh God, Zach's walked in.

At the beginning of this year, things weren't going too great with Danny and me, and we split up for a while. I started seeing Zach, but it turned out he was only going out with me for a bet. No prizes for working out Jade and Kara were involved. Major ouch. Along with the whole appearing-half-naked-in-front-of-the-school disaster, it's one of the most upsetting and humiliating things that's ever happened to me.

Zach's still as gorgeous as ever, but his good looks don't do anything to help make up for his dirtbag personality. I avoid him wherever possible, but every now and then I bump into him and it's like I can't breathe and want to disappear all at once.

As Zach starts talking loudly to his mates, I feel Danny's body stiffen next to me. He's clocked Zach as well. It wouldn't be too much of an exaggeration to say Zach's probably top of his Most Hated list.

This is all kinds of awkward.

Luckily Zach sits down with his back to us before he seems to notice we're there. Millie gives us an encouraging smile. Jade and Kara are pointing at people and whispering, heads bent close together. At a guess, they're eyeing up their competition and dismissing each of us in turn.

I look around to see who else we're going to be up against. Jade and Kara; Zach and his mates; April the Goth; Sophie and her friend Eve. I can't wait to hear what ideas everyone else has come up with. I'm also surprised there aren't more people here, the school has been buzzing about this for days, and I whisper so to Millie.

"Jade and Kara were telling people not to come," Millie whispers back.

My eyes widen in alarm. "What? Why didn't you say anything?"

Millie laughs. "Because I knew you'd freak. Nobody in this room cares about their stupid threats or they wouldn't be here. You shouldn't either. Chill."

There were *threats*?

I open my mouth to ask for more details, when Mr Groves walks in.

"Okay, troops, take a seat," he says, sounding bored. He doesn't look overly impressed at having to give up his break to start organising this fundraiser. "I'd like to get this over with as soon as possible. Thought there'd be more of you here, to be honest."

Jade and Kara smile smugly at each other.

"I asked you to come so I know how many of you are pitching ideas at the assembly tomorrow. Even though there's not as many as I'd expected, there are still quite a few of you, so I think the best thing to do is get everyone to vote. We'll organise it like a proper election," Mr Groves says, clearly warming to his theme. "You can pitch your ideas, we'll give everyone pieces of paper to vote on, we'll count the votes during break, and then come back to see who wins. Excellent

PSHE. When we've chosen the winning idea, you lot will be in charge of making it happen."

"Don't you want to hear our ideas now?" Jade asks, looking disappointed.

"Not really," Mr Groves says, checking his watch. "Now, I need to give you a few guidelines about what your ideas should feature. Nothing illegal, nothing that's not age appropriate, nothing dangerous. The objective is to make as much money as possible, remember? Right, I'll make a list of your names, to help get an idea of how much time we'll need... Okay, done. Now, I need a coffee. Thanks for coming, see you tomorrow."

We all stand up to leave, slightly taken aback. Is that it? That took all of about three minutes.

"Oh, one more thing," Mr Groves says, stopping in the doorway and glancing back at us. "Anyone who pitches has to be on the final organising committee, regardless of whether or not their idea gets chosen. So that means each and every one of you in this room will be on the committee. We need plenty of people to make this party happen, do you understand?"

"But, sir —" Jade starts to protest.

"If you've got a problem with it, don't pitch your idea," Mr Groves says. And then he's gone.

"So does that mean..." I say, my brain slowly starting to tick over.

"That if we pitch and Jade pitches we'll all end up working together?" Jamie says. "Looks that way."

"And Zach," Danny says. "Don't forget him."

I honestly can't think of anything worse.

"Millie, maybe we need to rethink this," I say. The thought of being on a committee with those three is freaking me out, big-time.

"Oh, come on, you guys," Millie says, as we make our way down the stairs to the ground floor. "We can't let them win. We've got a great idea, remember? And do you really want them organising this party? They'd never let us come, for one thing."

Nobody says anything.

"We've finally got a chance to put Jade and Kara in their place," Millie says. "They're using intimidation to get their own way. Please don't bail on me now. I really want us to do this, and I really think we have a good chance of winning with The Star Factor. People don't like those guys that much, you know. They might not get voted for. And then they'll have to do what we tell them. Imagine bossing them around for months."

It does sound appealing, the idea of having the upper hand for a change. Although I'm trying not to think about how miserable they'd make our lives in the process.

"We have to do this," Millie continues. "We can't let them scare us into giving up. That's what they want!"

Danny shrugs. "She's right."

She is?

"We can't not do things because we're worried about what Jade and Kara might do," Danny says.

"I guess," I say. *It'd just be easier if Jade and Kara weren't quite so scary,* I add silently.

"Yay!" cheers Millie, as we burst out of the double doors into the sunshine. "We're doing this. And we're going to win!"

It's impossible not be caught up in her excitement. And who knows, maybe she's actually right.

The next day I've forgotten every ounce of that excitement. We're standing at the side of the stage at the front of the assembly hall, watching everyone file inside. The butterflies in my stomach are tap-dancing at speed. Yikes. There's so many people in here. I'm trying not to vomit onto my shoes and am secretly wanting to maim Millie for ever getting us into this.

Are we really going to talk in front of all these people? *Really?*

Ooooh, this is horrible!

"I'd kill for some jelly babies," Millie mutters.

Yep, even she's feeling the strain.

I feel someone reach for my hand, and then Danny's fingers are clasped round mine. He gives them a quick squeeze, and gives me a reassuring grin.

Breathe, Suze. Deep breaths. Think calm thoughts.

Mr Groves climbs up the stairs onto the stage and gives a brief introduction to why we're here, how it's an important tribute to Mrs C and how it's all going to work, then he smiles broadly and says, "Without further ado, let me bring on the people with the ideas they want you to hear."

To cheers and whoops, we file onto the stage. Ooooh, I'm so nervous. There are loads of people staring at us. This is usually the point where something embarrassing happens, like I trip over or my trousers fall down.

That couldn't actually happen, could it? Why on earth would I think such a stupid thing? It's not like I need anything else to stress about, for goodness sake. I subtly try to hold up my trousers with one hand. Although they've never randomly fallen down before, it would be just my luck for it to happen right here, right now. And it's not like the school needs another glimpse of half-naked me.

"I see you remembered to put on your clothes today,"

Jade says, poking me hard between the shoulder blades.

"Oh ha ha," I say, while trying not to freak over the possibility that Jade can actually read my mind.

I swallow, hard. The last time this many people were staring at me I was wearing only a towel and a cardigan. Thanks so much for that reminder, Jade.

"Ignore her," Millie says. "She's trying to psyche you out."

"No need to psyche anyone out," Jade says, smugly. "Our idea's fantastic. We know we're going to win."

"We'll see," Millie mutters.

"Right then," Mr Groves says. "I know you're all really excited to hear about your possible parties. We've got several groups ready to pitch their ideas to you, so without further ado, first up, we have…" Mr Groves consults a piece of paper. "Zach, Max and Ryan."

The three boys step forward, shoving at each other and laughing. I shrink back, trying to seem inconspicuous. My mouth's gone all dry and I'm not sure I'm going to be able to speak ever again.

"You go," Max says.

"Nah, you go, man."

"I'll do it if neither of you have got the balls to," Zach says.

"Language," says Mr Groves, frowning.

"Sorry." Zach shoves his hands into his pockets and stares out at the audience. "So, you know how in America they have those huge homecoming football games? With, like, the cheerleaders and marching bands and stuff? And then there's a huge party afterwards?"

I can see people's heads nodding and some people are smiling. Hmm. A homecoming party would be pretty cool, and some of those cheerleading routines are amazing. I'd never give Zach the satisfaction of thinking I liked his idea, though.

"So are you proposing an American football match with cheerleaders and a band, and then a homecoming dance afterwards?" Mr Groves says.

"Uh, no," Zach says, shaking his head. "We thought we could give it a British twist. So it would be a soccer match, and then a party afterwards."

Oh. Well, that doesn't sound nearly as good.

"What kind of party?" Mr Groves says. "What would you have there?"

"I dunno, it'd be, like, a normal party," Zach says. "With a football theme, maybe. Football plates and napkins, that kind of thing."

"Hmmm," Mr Groves says. "Maybe we could develop your idea a bit. Thanks for that, lads. Let's hear from Sophie and Eve."

The girls bounce forward on the stage, holding hands and giggling. "We thought it would be fantastic to have a school sleepover," Sophie says. "Where we all dress in our pyjamas and hang out and watch movies and eat popcorn."

Several of the boys in the audience start nudging each other and laughing.

"Er, I don't think that's appropriate, girls," Mr Groves says. "I'm not sure many of the parents would go for that idea. And it's rather a lot to expect the teachers to sleep overnight to chaperone you all."

"We wouldn't need chaperoning," Eve says innocently.

"I beg to differ," Mr Groves says. "I'm sorry, you two, but that idea's not going to work. We can't put it forward."

Sophie and Eve slink off, looking disappointed.

Mr Groves gives himself a little shake, then consults his piece of paper again. "April, you're up."

April, dressed in her trademark all-black outfit, walks to the front of the stage.

"I want to put on a Fright Night festival," April says. "We could have different things going on in different spaces, like clairvoyants and mediums, and we could hold a séance…"

"Um, I'm not sure —" Mr Groves starts, but April's on a roll.

"There could be a dance, and maybe a ghost train, and a TV room showing scary films and TV shows... everything that would frighten the pants off us," April says.

I shiver. I hate all that kind of stuff. My imagination is way too wild.

"My Dad said he'll donate an iPad from his shop to have as a prize for the best costume," April the Goth continues.

Hmm. Well that sounds pretty good. Even if the rest of the party is kind of... *freaky*.

"Right, well, thank you, April," Mr Groves says. He's now clearly wishing he'd taken the time to listen to our ideas before we pitched them to the entire school, especially as a lot of the other teachers seem to be frowning. He consults his clipboard. "Jade and Kara, you're next."

Jade and Kara step forward, smile at each other and then Jade starts speaking. "We thought we'd hold a Hollywood-themed awards ceremony that people would buy tickets to attend," she says, her voice steady and strong.

Gnargh. She's so annoying. Where does she get all that flipping confidence?

"We thought we'd create award categories for people to vote in beforehand, like they do in those American yearbooks, such as 'Most sporty' or 'Most likely to succeed' and then have a ceremony to present them all. It would be all-American glamour, people dressed in black tie, a red carpet outside the school, arriving in limousines..."

Oh God. Their idea is really good. As much as I hate myself for admitting it, I'd like to go to that party. It sounds *amazing*.

Now people are leaning forward in their seats, eager to hear more.

"And then afterwards," Kara says, clearly keen to grab some of the glory for herself, "we'd have the after-show party. So there'd be a DJ, and you can pay him to play your favourite songs..."

Pfff. A DJ. That's not so amazing. Anyone can come up with that.

"My mum knows one of the technicians at Illusion and she might be able to get one of their DJs to come," Kara went on.

Now the buzzing in the hall increases. Illusion is our local radio station. That would mean an actual radio DJ would be here!

"We also thought we could set up a fairground in

the playground and in the playing field," Kara continues. "With a Big Wheel and dodgems and games that could raise even more money."

Mr Groves is nodding his head thoughtfully. "Well, it all sounds good, girls, but how are you going to pay for all this? A fairground sounds very expensive."

"My parents know someone who runs a company supplying this stuff, and they should be able to give us a discount," Jade says. "Plus we thought we could get local businesses to sponsor us, or sponsor each of the awards. We'd need to talk it through properly to figure out the exact details."

There's a growing buzz of chatter in the room. Everyone thinks Jade's idea sounds good. Curse her and her loaded parents. Surely that's not fair.

Mr Groves smiles. "That all sounds great," he says. "You seem to have thought it all through very thoroughly. Very impressive."

"That's not quite all," Jade says. "There's a possibility that we might be able to get someone famous to present the awards."

There's an audible gasp around the room. Kara looks at her in shock.

"What? Who? You didn't tell me!"

"It was all very last-minute," Jade says. "I didn't really

have time. Didn't want to say anything until it was definite."

Ooh, she's such a liar! It's obvious to everyone she's enjoying getting one over on her so-called mate. I really don't understand their friendship at all. Is there nothing these two won't compete over?

"Shall we let Jade finish?" Mr Groves asks.

"*My* mum used to go to school with Dylan Waters, and she spoke to him about what we're up to. He said he'd need to check his schedule, but should be able to come along. He wouldn't charge anything, because it's for such a good cause."

And with that, Jade smiles smugly and waits for the impact of her announcement to reverberate around the room.

It does have quite the impact.

Dylan Waters! He and Jake are never off the TV, they present loads of those reality talent shows. He's proper famous!

Oh, it all sounds fantastic. And if I didn't loathe Jade and Kara so much, I'd be voting for them.

Someone starts clapping, and then everyone's whooping and cheering as Jade and Kara stand there, huge grins plastered all over their stupid faces.

"Told you we'd win," Jade says to us out of the corner of her mouth. "Nobody will care about your lame idea now. We may as well skip it all together."

"Shut up, Jade, our idea's even better than yours," Millie says, but I can tell she's rattled. Because although our idea is good, it doesn't involve any famous people. Nobody's going to vote for us, and we're going to be stuck on the stupid committee, pandering to Jade and Kara's whims.

"Listen to the clapping," Jade says. "Do you really think you're going to beat us? Really? Might as well give up now."

"You wish," Millie says.

She smiles encouragingly at me, and I do my best to grin back, but the thought of having Jade and Kara lord it over us, making us do their bidding, is beyond awful.

"Let's hear what you've got," Jade whispers in our direction.

"Bring it on," Kara adds. "I don't think we've got anything to worry about."

The most annoying thing is that I know they're right. We can never compete with what Jade and Kara are offering. Who could? Nobody else has got parents prepared to go to such crazy lengths for a bunch of kids. It sucks. Properly, properly sucks.

"And now, finally, we have Suzy, Millie, Jamie and Danny," Mr Groves says.

Oh God. We're up.

"Who's going to do the talking?" Jamie asks.

"I'll do it," Millie says, bouncing forward to the front of the stage. She's refusing to let Jade and Kara squash her enthusiasm. "Actually, Danny, do you want to do your bit first?"

Despite us trying to talk Danny out of pitching his idea, he's not having any of it. It's testament to how much he loves *Star Wars* that he's doing this, because right now, he looks like he wants to disappear. He's actually pretty shy, and the thought of talking in front of the whole school must be killing him. My heart flips as he chews his thumb nervously.

"So, I want to do a *Star Wars* party," Danny says.

"Speak up!" someone shouts. Danny pauses, looks unsure, then repeats himself.

Behind us there's a snort. "How lame?" Jade says, loud enough for Danny to hear.

"Jade," Mr Groves warns.

Danny stumbles over his next words, but bravely ploughs on. "There'd be Stormtroopers and stuff. You can hire them to come and walk around and fight and things, it'd be great..."

"Worst. Idea. Ever," Jade says loudly, and Danny falters. The tips of his ears turn red, and then the blush spreads. He shoves his hands into his pockets and stands there, shuffling awkwardly.

"Go on, mate," Jamie says, punching his shoulder encouragingly. "Ignore them."

"So, um, yeah, we could also have —" Danny's voice cracks with nerves, and people start to laugh.

"Problem, Danny?" Jade asks. "Actually, let me help you out. I think the biggest problem here is that you're the only person in this room that likes the sound of this."

"*Star Wars* is for kids," Kara adds.

"That's *enough*, you two," Mr Groves says sharply.

Oh. My. God. Why do these two have to be so nasty all the time? How dare they talk to Danny that way? It's just so cruel. My hands clench into fists.

Danny takes a deep breath but he's lost all his confidence. He mumbles and rushes through the rest of his pitch as quickly as he can, talking to the floor the whole time.

There's a smattering of applause once Danny's done, but anyone can tell they're sympathy claps.

I wish I could give him a huge hug to make him feel better, but a public display of affection like that in front of the whole school would make things a zillion times worse. Danny's weird about that kind of thing, and anyway something tells me the teachers definitely wouldn't approve.

"Thank you, Danny. And now we've got our last pitch from the others," says Mr Groves.

As Jamie, Millie and I step forward, I give Danny's arm a comforting rub and Millie smiles as she passes him. It's obvious he feels pretty awful, his shoulders are slumped and his face is downcast.

"Last seen semi-naked, we give you... Suzy Puttock!" I hear Jade say, and Kara cracks up laughing.

"Jade and Kara, I said that's enough," Mr Groves tells them. "Don't make me give you detention."

Honestly, the man is useless. Talk about a wet lettuce. Just give them detention already!

Millie makes like she hasn't heard anything as she gives a beaming smile to everyone and begins her speech.

"We thought that because it was to raise money for a music studio, we could give the party a music theme. We're proposing a talent competition called 'The Star Factor'. We'd have people pay to dress up as their favourite singers or bands, and perform songs as them, then other people would judge them and vote them off until we were left with a winner."

"So you're suggesting a karaoke party?" Jade says scornfully.

"No," Millie says quickly. "It's different. It's a singing and impersonation competition. And there'd be lots of costumes there for people to put on, and wigs and stuff. There'd also be a raffle, so people could buy tickets, and we'd have prizes donated by local businesses."

"Told you we had it in the bag," Jade says to Kara.

She's right. There's no way we're going to win. But there's something about the way Kara and Jade sound so self-satisfied, and have been so horrible to us all — they're not even giving anyone a *chance* to respond to our idea and say what they think. I'm getting crosser and crosser… and then something inside me snaps. My mouth opens before I've had a chance to really think things through.

"Yeah, well, that's not the best part. After the singing competition, The Drifting will play," I say.

Even as the words are coming out of my mouth, my inner voice is screaming, *Shut up, Suzy! Shut up, shut up, shut up!*

There's an audible gasp around the hall, and then everyone's talking excitedly all at once.

"What?" Jade shouts, trying to be heard over everyone's chatter. "You're lying!"

"That's quite a claim," Mr Groves says, raising an eyebrow quizzically.

"It's true," I insist over the noise. "We'd need to do

100

some final checks on the details, but we're pretty sure they'd come…"

I can hear what I'm saying, and yet I don't seem to be able to stop talking. I'm telling all these lies, in front of my teachers, in front of the whole school. It's like my mouth has been hijacked by an alien force, and won't stop blabbering.

One of the Year Sevens screams in excitement.

"Shut up already," Kara says. "You're such a liar "

"I'm not, it's true!"

Why can't I stop?! It's the rage, I think. I'm taken over by a crossness that's been boiling up inside me; it's brought to a head now by the way Jade and Kara are treating me and my friends.

"All right, all right, simmer down," Mr Groves says, trying to get some semblance of order back in the room.

He fails. Dismally.

Everyone is way too hyped about the idea of The Drifting coming to our school. And to be honest, if I was them, I'd be pretty chuffed, too.

As I stare triumphantly at Jade and Kara, glad that they've finally been put in their place, the realisation of what's happened starts to sink in.

An icy sensation, which starts at my toes and spreads upwards, floods my whole body.

Oh no. Oh no, oh no!

What have I done? What have I *said*? My friends are staring at me in horror.

Backtrack! I have to make this better!

"I mean, it's not definite yet..." I say, weakly, trying to rescue myself from the damage I've caused.

But nobody hears me. Nobody's listening.

"Attention! Attention!" Mr Groves shouts. It's ages before everyone's even vaguely focused and looking in his direction again.

"Okay, you've heard all the suggestions, now you need to cast your votes. I'd like you to write down on your pieces of paper your top two ideas, and number them clearly so we know which is your top choice. We'll count up during break and let you know afterwards who's won."

I can't get out of the assembly hall fast enough. I push through the crowds of people all trying to talk to me, stopping for nobody, and race out into a quiet corridor, where I lean my head back against the wall, and wait for my friends, trying to calm down.

What have I *done*? And more importantly, how am I going to fix it?

102

CHAPTER EIGHT

"Oh, Suze," Millie says. "What have you done?"

I'm still standing in the quiet corridor, where my friends are now huddled around me.

"I'm sorry," I say miserably. "I don't know what came over me. It was like I got possessed or something. They were being so nasty, and so flipping smug, and it just came out."

"Maybe we won't win," Jamie says. "Jade and Kara's idea was really good, as much as I hate to say it."

"Jamie, this is The *Drifting* we're talking about," Millie says. "If people think there's even the tiniest chance of them actually coming they're going to vote for us."

"Look, we'll have to go back in and tell people that we made a mistake," Jamie says rationally.

"But we'll look really stupid. And people will hate us," I protest. "Well, mainly me. Jade and Kara will be vile."

"Like they need any extra ammunition," Millie says.

She pulls open a bag of jelly babies and starts chewing them thoughtfully. "But then, they hate us already. This won't change anything."

"Here, let me have some of those," I say, grabbing a handful of sweets.

"You hate jelly babies," Millie says.

"Yeah, well, desperate times and all that," I say. "I feel sick, anyway. I'm hoping they might calm me down."

"We might not even win," Danny says. "People did love Jade and Kara's pitch."

"Yeah, you're right. I think all we can do is wait and see what happens," Jamie says. "If we don't win, then we're stressing about nothing. If we do... well, then we've got no choice. We're going to have to 'fess up, say The Drifting can't come, and take the flack. Jade and Kara will take over with their idea, they'll be vile about it, but everyone will get over it and will have forgotten about it all by next week. I don't think we've got any other choice, do you?"

As we all shake our heads, the bell rings.

My heart zooms into overdrive.

"Right then," Danny says, grabbing my hand and giving it a squeeze. "Let's go and see what's been decided."

I don't think people have ever come back from break

quite so quickly. Usually people are killing as much time as they possibly can, but not today. Today they're desperate to hear what kind of party they'll be getting.

"So, we have the results of the vote," says Mr Groves.

My stomach is squirming like crazy. Please don't let us have won. Please, please don't let us have won.

Mr Groves reads out the list in reverse order. Zach and his mates and April the Goth only get a small number of votes. The sleepover idea was disqualified, and Danny's *Star Wars* party gets one vote, which I suspect was from Danny himself. I'm now trying my hardest to ignore the fact I'm so nervous I desperately need to pee.

Then there are two results left. Us, and Jade and Kara.

Come on, Jade and Kara have got to win, haven't they? People won't really think we can get The Drifting to play here, will they?

Please, please, please don't let us win, I pray silently in my head, crossing my fingers behind my back. I don't even care that it means getting beaten by Jade and Kara. We can't win. We just can't...

Jade and Kara are casting evils in our direction as Mr Groves pauses for the longest possible time.

He really has been watching too many reality TV shows. Come on, already. This is killing me.

"Jade and Kara's Hollywood idea… gets eighty votes," Mr Groves says. "But Suzy's group, with the promise of The Drifting, is the winner with a hundred and twenty-six votes!"

The roar that fills the hall when it's announced that we've won is so loud my ears start ringing.

"Well done to our winners," Mr Groves says. "We'll keep you posted on how the party plans are going. Now, you lot can be dismissed, but those of you who pitched ideas I'd like a quick word before you disappear off the stage." He turns his attention to us. "Now, I look forward to seeing all of you at our first committee meeting —"

"Er, yeah, Mr Groves, about that —" Jade begins, but Mr Groves shakes his head.

"No trying to wriggle out of it," he says, raising his voice over the noise of everyone leaving. "That was the deal. If you pitched an idea, you ended up on the organising committee, whether your idea won or not. I'm sure the others will find your help invaluable, won't you?"

We stare at him dumbly. Earlier it sounded appealing, having the upper hand and bossing Jade and Kara around. Now I think about it properly, I can't imagine anything worse than having to work alongside them, giving orders and expecting them to do what we say.

Actually, yes, I can. I've remembered Zach's going to be there, too.

Oh God. This isn't going to end well, is it?

There's no way they'll do anything we ask them to. No way in the world.

"Suzy! So excited!" someone shouts as they leave, which sets off a new wave of whooping and cheering.

They are SO hyped.

And it's then I realise that I can't tell them it's not happening. The whole school will hate us. We'll be lynched. I stare helplessly at the others, who've clearly come to the same conclusion I have.

We can't say anything. Not yet. We need to give everyone a chance to calm down first.

Oh God. This is horrible.

I can't pee all over this parade now, not if I want to walk through the school corridors safely ever again. A knot of anxiety forms in the pit of my stomach as the realisation of what I've done, what we've promised, sinks in.

We're going to have to bring The Drifting to the school.

And how the flipping flip are we going to do that?!

CHAPTER NINE

It's Saturday morning and I've hardly slept. It's not even because of the twins this time. It's because I'm so completely stressed about what I've done.

I've promised The Drifting are going to come to our school.

The Drifting.

This isn't some tiny local group we're talking about here, this is a world-famous, majorly-in-demand, crowds-riot-when-they-see-them band.

I've got no idea how I'm going to make this happen.

But if I don't, my life is over.

I wonder if Mum will let me transfer to a different school? Although the only school nearby is St Edward's, and somehow I suspect that might be even worse. If only boarding didn't cost so much...

Ooooooooooh, my life *is* over.

O.V.E.R.

Why do I have such a big mouth?

It's about 8 a.m. when I get a text from Millie. I would think she's been up worrying about things too, but she's often up this early, the freakoid. She thinks mornings are the best part of the day.

Her text tells me that we're all getting together for a crisis meeting at Bojangles later on. The four of us were texting and messaging and speaking for most of yesterday trying to come up with a solution. Nobody had any genius ideas, so maybe a face-to-face meeting is what we need. Surely *someone* will have come up with a solution overnight?

I flipping hope so, anyway.

I type "OK" before flopping back onto my pillow.

I'm lying there, still racking my brains to try and think of an answer as to what on earth I should do about things, when from outside there's a huge crash. Followed by another.

And then I hear someone shouting some extremely rude words.

What's going on?

Opening the curtains and peering outside, I see Dad and his mate Jon are hefting huge panels of wood around the garden. The high winds really aren't helping matters.

Harry charges into my bedroom. "What's happening?"

"Hey, get out. You're supposed to knock."

"Yeah, yeah," Harry says, ignoring me as she starts to film out of the window. Another gust of wind threatens to grab the wood from Dad and Jon's hands. "What are they doing?"

"No idea," I say, as Jon lets rip with another round of decidedly dodgy language. "Would you get out of my room?"

"I'll have to bleep those words out," Harry says, totally ignoring me. Gnargh. She is *so* annoying.

"What's all that noise?" Mum rushes up behind us, still in her pyjamas.

"A lot of swearing and hefting of wood," I tell her. "What's Dad up to now? What's he building?"

"I haven't the foggiest," Mum says. "But they need to keep the noise down. I've only just got Chichi off to sleep, I don't want her being woken up again. Harry, turn that off, would you?"

"But, Mum..."

"No buts. Let's go and get some breakfast. I'll tell your dad and Jon to keep it down."

We all troop downstairs to the kitchen, and I do my best to ignore Harry while Mum busies herself making us some food. After we've finished our tea and toast, Dad's still hard at work.

"Do you know, while your Dad's distracted, this might be the perfect moment to start planning his party," Mum says.

"What? Do we have to?" I ask. I'd been intending to veg out in front of the TV for a bit.

"We need to get organised, time's ticking on," Mum says. "I'll go and get Amber and Mark – they must be up, I think I can hear one of the babies."

"Bet it's Chichi."

"Probably," Mum agrees. "I'll grab some supplies and we'll meet in your room."

A few moments later, we're all standing around assessing the Party Plan, which Mum has written in big letters on a piece of A3 paper stuck on my wall. As if I'm not stressed enough with the school party I'm trying to organise. This is the last thing I need. More party stress.

"So, where are we going to start?" Mum asks. "Amber, can you do something about the dog, please?"

Crystal Fairybelle is lying on the floor, trying to chew my rug.

"Crystal!" I shout indignantly.

Amber, who's trying to give Chichi a bottle, gently prods at the dog with her toe. "Stop it."

Crystal Fairybelle yelps, eyeballs Amber with a wounded expression, then returns to chewing. I pull him away and deposit him outside in the hall, closing the door firmly. There's some frantic whining and then everything's quiet.

Amber makes a sad face. "I don't know what to do with him. He's been so naughty since the girls were born."

"And he's peeing everywhere," I say. The memory of last night's wet foot after I stood in a puddle on the way back from the bathroom in the middle of the night is still traumatic. Wee toe – gross.

"He's probably unsettled," Harry says, from behind her phone. She's videoing the planning meeting.

"Maybe you're right," Amber says. "I remember Conni G writing that her dog, Princess Tallulah, got all kinds of stressed after she had Pashmina. Maybe Crystal needs to see a therapist, what do you think, Mark?"

Mark doesn't answer. He's rocking Uni in his arms and she's almost dropping off. Instead he just nods his head.

"Or perhaps I should look into getting a dog whisperer to come and see us," Amber muses. "That's what Conni G did…"

"Sounds like a good idea," says Mum. "Can we get back to the party, please? We don't have long."

"Sure," Amber says, hoiking Chichi up onto her shoulder and starting to wind her.

"So where do we start?" Mum says. For the woman who helped Amber plan an all-singing, all-dancing wedding, she seems surprisingly clueless about what to do.

"The basics?" I say. I suppose I can use this as a practice run for what we're going to need to sort at school.

"Good thinking," Mum says. "So date, time, venue, theme, guest list..." She writes all of these things on the paper in big letters. "Excellent."

"Isn't the date kind of obvious?" Harry says. "We all know when his birthday is."

"I was thinking about having the party the day before his birthday," Mum says.

"How does that make any sense?" I ask.

"Well, it would be more of a surprise that way," Mum says. "Dad's birthday's on a Sunday, so he'd be expecting to celebrate then."

When she puts it like that, I guess, yeah, that's kind of logical. But there's one little detail I can't helping thinking that my mother's forgotten...

"Aren't we forgetting that Dad hates surprises?" I say. "And I don't mean hates, I mean loathes. He's not a big fan of parties, either. I'm still not sure a surprise birthday party is a good idea."

"I think he'll love it," Harry says. "*I'd* love it. And there'll be cake. Dad likes cake."

"You're right," Mum says, nodding. "Stop being such a party pooper, Suzy. And I definitely think it'll be more of a surprise the day before his birthday. So we'll have it then."

As she writes the date on the piece of paper, I stare at it... it's ringing a bell for some reason. Why does that date look so familiar?

Then I realise.

Oh no. Oh no!

"Uh, Mum, that's the date of the school party," I say nervously.

"Sorry, but your dad's more important than a party with your friends."

"But it's kind of a big deal..." I'm now regretting not telling her anything about how I'm one of the people heading up the planning committee. "I sort of have to be there."

"Family comes first," Mum says firmly. "We're keeping the date."

I slump further down onto the bed. I'll add 'date clash' onto the list of problems I'll be sorting later, then.

"Right, let's move on to time," Mum says. "I think evening would be good."

And it's then I have a brainwave. "What about a lunch party?"

Please say she'll go for it. Please, please, please. This is my only chance, if she's set on this date, of going to both parties. The school one is in the evening, but if Dad's is at lunchtime, I can probably do both.

Mum frowns. "I'm not sure that's going to work."

"He's never going to suspect a party at lunchtime," I say persuasively. "It'll be a total surprise."

"He would be pretty surprised at a full-on party in the middle of the day," Harry says, and Amber nods in agreement.

"I suppose you're right," Mum says.

"And it might be cheaper to hire somewhere in the afternoon," I say.

"Okay," Mum says. "Let's do it. Good idea, Suzy."

I breathe a huge sigh of relief. Phew. That should buy me a bit of time.

"Oh, Mum," Amber suddenly says.

"Have you got a suggestion for the party?" Mum asks.

"Nooo... Chichi's sicked up her feed. My leg's soaking. Can you take her for a minute while I get changed and grab her some clean clothes?"

"Sure thing. Right, we need a guest list," Mum says, holding Chichi at a distance.

"Are friends allowed to come?" Harry asks, hopefully.

"We'll see how we do for numbers," Mum says.

"Now, family members. His family, obviously, there's loads of them... and Great Aunt Lou from my side..."

"Aunt Loon?" I say. "He's not going to be pleased about that."

"Well, we can't not invite her. Besides, she's practically the only family I have. And let's not forget a few of my friends..." She continues scribbling names on a list. "Gosh, we've already got quite a lot of people."

"Er, don't you want to think about inviting some of Dad's mates," I point out. "Seeing as how it's his party?"

"Oh. Yes. I suppose you're right," Mum says, starting to laugh. She writes some more names on the pad and then quickly counts them up. "Fifty-two. That's about right for a birthday party, isn't it? Sorry, girls, that means none of your friends will be able to come."

"I'm sure they'll survive. Although fifty-two seems an awful lot..." I say. "Didn't Dad say he didn't want too much of a fuss for his birthday? That he wanted it keeping quiet?"

"Well, yes, but he didn't mean it," Mum says dismissively. "Now. We're going to need to find a venue, and work out what we're going to do about costumes..."

"Costumes?"

"Of course," Mum says. "It's going to be a fancy-dress party. We can't not dress up."

"But Dad hates fancy-dress parties."

"Suzy, would you stop being so negative," Mum says, crossly.

Hurrmph. I was only trying to help. How is she not seeing that it's highly likely Dad's going to hate everything about this party and leave early in a strop? If a surprise fancy-dress party doesn't break him, the sight of Aunt Loon probably will.

"Now what do we think Dad should dress up as? I was wondering about an eighties theme..." Mum's carrying on.

"What did he like in the eighties?" Harry asks.

"Rubik's Cubes. *Ghostbusters*. Michael Jackson," Mum says, making yet more notes on her piece of paper, struggling to hold both Chichi and her pen. "I'll Google and we can decide something a bit later. What else do we need? Food? Games? I'll go and have a think about eighties-themed foods. We can have a Rubik's Cube cake perhaps, or maybe a Pac-Man."

"What's Pac-Man?" Harry says, confused. I'm glad she's asked the question, because I've got no idea.

"An arcade game," Mark says, smiling at Amber as she walks back into the room.

"Now what do we think about party games?" Mum says.

"We can't have a party without games. Maybe a quiz?"

Harry wrinkles her nose. "What about karaoke?"

"Karaoke! I love it!" Mum says excitedly. She's frantically writing more notes. "We can sing eighties songs. And we definitely need a band. Actually, that's given me a brilliant idea..."

Mum starts to laugh to herself, which is never a good sign. I'm about to ask what she's plotting, when Amber starts talking.

"I don't know what I'm going to dress up as," she says. "I'm still so fat."

"You're not fat," Mark says. "Ambypamby, you're beautiful. As beautiful as you've always been."

"But I've still got so much baby weight," Amber says. "Conni G was back in her skinny jeans a fortnight after she gave birth."

"Yeah, well, she had a tummy tuck at the same time as her C-section," I say.

Amber gasps in horror. "How could you say that?"

"Because I read it in a magazine," I tell her.

Amber's eyes widen in disbelief. "I don't believe it. Conni said in her magazine column her weight loss was a combination of healthy eating and exercise."

"Okay, sure, if you want to believe that," I say.

"I just need to stay on my red Thai curry paste and

anchovies diet," Amber says determinedly. "Then I'll be back in my skinny jeans by the party. We'll have to start thinking about what we want to go as, Markymoo. We could theme our costumes. Like, maybe Mario and Luigi, those Nintendo characters."

"Er, weren't they both boys?" I ask.

"Really?" Amber looks surprised. "I thought Luigi was a girl's name. Oh well. We'll keep thinking."

Downstairs, a door slams.

"That's your father! Nobody say a word," Mum hisses, grabbing the paper and flapping it around wildly. "What am I going to do with this?"

"Stick it under the bed," I say.

Mum tries, but there's heaps of stuff under there — clothes, boxes of books I read yonks ago but can't bring myself to chuck, hairdryers, hair straighteners and goodness knows what else.

"There's no room!"

"Then chuck it in the bed," I say, throwing back the duvet. There's a pair of pants underneath, which I grab, quickly, and throw into my laundry basket before Mark can see, ignoring Mum shaking her head at me.

As Dad's footsteps come up the stairs, I throw the duvet over the paper, and we all try to look casual.

"What's going on?" Dad says suspiciously.

"Just talking about… um… women's things," Mum says.

Nothing makes Dad leave a room quicker than Women's Things.

"With Mark here?" Dad looks at Mark oddly. "Actually, I don't want to know. Came in for a bathroom break," Dad says. "And I'm hungry. Is there anything I can make for lunch? Jon's headed off for a while."

"Sandwiches and crisps," Mum says. "Or there's pizza in the freezer, if you'd rather."

"Great. I'll sort something when I go back down," Dad calls, disappearing down the corridor. "We've finished outside if you want to come and see. No peeping before you come down!"

"Phew," Mum says. "I don't think he suspected anything. Shall we go and see what they've been up to?"

The toilet flushes and Dad joins us as we all troop downstairs. Dad leads us out of the back door, where he stops in front of a very large shed, smiling proudly.

"You've built a shed," Mum says, looking confused. "Right next to our old one."

"Yup," Dad says proudly.

"And this is your birthday present to yourself?" Mum asks. "You wanted another shed?"

"I did."

"But we already have a shed," Harry says.

"Not a shed like this one, young Harry."

"Oh well, whatever makes you happy," Mum says, shrugging. "I suppose it'll be useful storage, the other is full to bursting. Do you want me to help you to move some of the things across? Maybe the lawnmower could go in it. And those sun loungers..."

"Uh-uh," Dad says, grabbing Mum's wrist gently. "None of that is going in my shed. This is a special shed. A shed just for me."

Mum frowns. "I don't understand. What are you going to do in it?"

"Enjoy the peace," Dad says.

Harry crosses the lawn and flings open the shed door. Inside, it's empty apart from a comfy reclining chair and a radio on a shelf.

"Heaven," Dad says, smiling proudly. He walks inside and spins around with his arms outstretched. "The house is getting too much. There are too many people in there. Can't hear myself think a lot of the time. This is going to be my place for restful contemplation. So if you'll excuse me, I'll be in my shed until lunch is ready."

And with that, he shuts the door in our faces.

"Are you looking forward to your birthday?" Harry

says a little later, after Dad's been convinced to return inside. She takes a huge bite of her sandwich, and ignores Mum's 'shut up now' face.

Dad rolls his eyes. "Not particularly. I'm trying to pretend it's not happening."

"Oh, don't be such a grump," Mum says. "It's forty-five! It's an important landmark."

"It's a sign I'm heading towards fifty at a rate of knots," Dad says. "How did that happen?"

"You've still got five years before you get there," Mum says. "Let's get forty-five out of the way first, eh?"

"I love birthdays," Harry says.

"I don't," Dad says. "And I don't want any celebrations, or any of that nonsense, okay?"

Mum laughs nervously. "What makes you think there'll be a celebration?"

"Just making sure," Dad says. "You know I hate fuss. Get me steak and a cake and let me go to the pub for the evening, and I'll be grand."

"You can't celebrate by yourself," Mum says.

"Oh yes I can," Dad says. "Best present you could give me. The gift of peace."

"More crisps, anyone?" Mum says, ignoring him.

"I've been wondering about getting a new car to replace the Volvo," Dad says, as he helps himself to a handful of potato hoops. "Perhaps a convertible."

Mum nearly spits out her water. She chokes for a moment, before composing herself. "What? Why? You know we can't afford it. And convertibles aren't exactly spacious. How are we supposed to get everyone around? I know we were talking about getting a new car when we've got a bit more money, but I was thinking more along the lines of an MPV."

"MPVs are for old, boring people," Dad says.

"MPVs are for people with families," Mum retaliates.

"I want to feel the wind in my hair," Dad says wistfully.

"You hardly have any hair," I say.

"I just want a car that's not filled with crisp packets, and that you don't have to hit to get started," Dad says. "That's not too unreasonable, is it? It's not too much to ask?"

"Chris, we can't get a convertible," Mum says. "It's not going to be practical. There are too many of us now."

"Mark has a car for Amber and the babies," Dad says.

"But there's still Suzy and Harry to think about. What about getting them about the place?"

"There's always the bus. And we're always hearing how kids these days don't walk enough. More exercise would do them good."

"Yeah, cheers, Dad," I say.

"What about a convertible with a backseat?" Dad negotiates.

"Those seats are tiny. There'd be no room for the girls. We're not getting a convertible," Mum says.

"I'll talk to you about it later," he mutters.

"You can try," Mum says. "But I won't change my mind."

Dad looks gutted. He really has been acting so strangely lately. Like wanting to dye his hair, and freaking over that photo where he thought he looked old, and now this whole convertible malarkey… he's totally having one of those mid-life crisis things. How does Mum not realise? And oh lordy, if he is, there's no way he's going to want a party to celebrate the fact he's one year nearer to the grave, is he? He'll go nuts! What if he breaks down and cries in front of everyone? That would be awful…

I'm distracted from my thoughts as my phone bleeps with a text. It's Danny.

On r way c U n 10 D X

Finally! A chance to escape.

"I've finished, Mum," I mutter, shoving the rest of my sandwich in my mouth. "I'm going out with my friends to Bojangles, is that okay?"

Without waiting for a proper reply, I run upstairs to change out of my slobby joggers and sweatshirt and wait for my friends to get here.

CHAPTER TEN

My mates and I file into Bojangles and queue by the till, waiting to be served. It's busy today. It's always packed on the weekends, but luckily Jamie texted Hannah to say that we were coming and she put one of her reserved signs onto a table for us. She's the best.

"Ugh, I'm so sorry for saying what I did about The Drifting," I say for the zillionth time. I feel awful that I've dragged my poor mates into this with me.

"Stop apologising," Millie says. "Kara and Jade were winding all of us up and someone had to do something."

Danny puts his arm around me.

"It was such a stupid thing to do," I say.

"Admittedly it wasn't the best, but it's done now. We just have to figure out a way to fix things," Danny tells me. "And we will. We'll think of something."

"I bet people don't really think we're going to bring the band to the school," Jamie says.

"Because we can't!" I screech.

"Maybe we can fob them off with a new release video or something to play," Danny says, ignoring my dramatics.

"We could still just tell them the truth," Jamie says.

"Oh yeah, great plan, and then watch everyone kill me," I mutter.

"What's up?" Hannah asks as we reach the front of the queue and she sees our downcast faces. "Are you guys okay?"

"Long story," Millie says gloomily.

"We're fine," Jamie says. "Just got a bit of a situation."

Hannah raises a quizzical eyebrow. "Okay, then I won't ask. Hey, how did your fundraiser idea go down?"

We all wince.

"Oh. Like that, is it? Definitely won't ask any more then. Food and drink I can do, though. What can I get you?"

"Hot chocolate with cream and marshmallows for me, please," I say.

"Yeah, and me," Millie says. "I'll have a slice of that lemon cake, too."

"I'll take a smoothie, a couple of rounds of toast with Marmite and a chocolate brownie," Jamie says. "What?" he asks, when he sees our incredulous faces. "I'm hungry!"

"How you're not the size of a house is beyond me," Millie mutters. "It's so unfair."

"I burn it all off," Jamie says. "I played football at lunch, remember?"

"Danny? What would you like?" Hannah asks, making notes on her pad.

"Uh, I'll take a chocolate shake and one of those brownies," Danny says.

Hannah plates up the cakes and passes them across the counter. "I'll bring the rest over in a minute," she says. "Hope you get yourselves sorted. I couldn't get you guys your sofa, but that table over there's for you."

"Thanks, Hannah," we chorus and head over to a table for four in the corner, flinging down our bags and wriggling out of our coats.

"The Drifting are never going to actually come to our school," I say despondently.

"Don't be so pessimistic," Millie says. "I've been doing some Googling. They did a surprise appearance at a school in Scotland last year."

"Oh yeah. I read about that," Danny says. "Wasn't it because the parents of one of the students won a visit on a TV show or something?"

"Well, yeah," Millie says. "But it shows they do personal appearances. At schools. We've just got to figure out how to get them to come to ours."

"It's impossible," I say. "Let's face it, I've majorly, majorly stuffed up and the chances of The Drifting coming are tiny. I'm so stupid."

I collapse with my head on the table dramatically.

The bell over the door rings and I sit up to see my friends' faces fall.

Jade and Kara have walked in.

What are they doing here? They *never* come here. This is one of the places we're usually safe. They're normally hanging around the older boys at Tastee Burga or in the shopping centre.

"Well, look who it is," Kara says to Jade, nodding in our direction. They bypass the queue and head towards us.

"I see a liar and her lying friends," Jade says. "And the liar should know she's in a whole heap of trouble."

I swallow as my tummy convulses.

"You'd better bring The Drifting to that party," Jade says, leaning so close I can smell her minty chewing gum. "You made us look stupid in front of everyone. And you know how much I hate looking stupid."

"And there are a lot of people we've told about the band coming that you wouldn't want to annoy," Kara adds.

My mouth is dry and my heart's thumping. I hate

confrontation. Thank goodness my friends are here.

"You'd better see this through," Jade says. "Our party would have been brilliant, and you know it. At the moment, yours is a sucky glammed-up karaoke show with a band that won't turn up. The only way you're going to save yourselves is if The Drifting actually come. And don't think we're going to help on your committee, either."

"Yeah, well, we'll see what Mr Groves has to say about that," Jamie says. "And actually, we didn't invite you to join us, so why don't you leave? We don't care what you think, or what you've got to say."

Jade does a weird snorty huff down her nose and glares at Jamie coldly. He holds her gaze until she finally looks away.

"Want to get something?" Kara says, and the girls wander over to the counter. As they place their order and wait, I realise the only free table is the one behind us.

"You all right, Suze?" Jamie asks.

"I'm so finished," I mutter under my breath.

"We'll think of some way to figure this out, don't worry," Millie says reassuringly.

Jade and Kara sit down right behind us, and none of us are feeling exactly comfortable. They're having a loud, staged conversation about how sucky the party's going to be, and how their idea was loads better.

"Shall we go?" Danny asks.

"We shouldn't have to leave because of them," Millie says crossly. "We haven't had our drinks yet."

"Yeah, I know, but this is a bit full-on, isn't it?" Jamie says. "And there's no way we can talk about what we need to with them here," he adds quietly. "Let's go round to mine."

"Sorry to be a pain, but could we get our drinks and that toast to go, please?" Millie asks Hannah. Hannah hands them over and smiles at us sympathetically. She can tell what's going on without us having to say anything.

A short walk later and we're trooping up the drive to Jamie's house, which takes my breath away every time. It's one of the most amazing houses I've ever seen in real life. It's just like something out of a magazine. It's on an estate, but not a normal housing estate, an enormous fancy one with massive detached houses. His parents are both designers, and they had the place redone over the summer. Their whole house is white and glass, contemporary and mind-blowing. It puts ours to shame. I'm kind of scared to touch anything when I'm there, in case I leave fingerprints or smudges, or in case I break anything. They've got Bang & Olufsen media centres everywhere and huge vintage film and band posters hanging on the walls.

We grab crisps, dips and popcorn from the kitchen – Jamie's house always has the best snacks – then go and collapse into the world's comfiest sofas in the lounge.

"Anyone want to watch anything?" Jamie offers, waving the remote at a screen that's almost the same size as my bedroom.

"Can't concentrate. Too stressed," I say. "We're going to have to let Jade and Kara have their party instead, aren't we?"

"No way do I want them in charge," Danny says, shaking his head.

"We'll figure something out," Jamie says. "The rest of the party is epic. We've just got to make it all as good as possible, then maybe everyone will have such a great time they won't mind about The Drifting not being there."

We all look sceptical.

"Well, nobody else has got any other suggestions," Jamie says. "And no matter what, we're going to have to make sure we give them a party they'll never forget. They won't forgive us otherwise. Our only other option, like I said in the café, is to come clean and tell the truth."

"This is a nightmare," I moan, rolling onto the floor and staring up at the ceiling. "We're never going to be able to sort it out and I'll have to change schools or something and my life is *over*!"

"Hi, Mum," Jamie says, as Lia walks in.

"Hi, guys. Wondering if you'd all like to stay for tea? I can get some pizza delivered if you like?"

Jamie goes to give his mum a big hug. A lot of boys are dead embarrassed to be seen showing affection to their mums, but Jamie and his parents have always been tight. His mum and dad are workaholics, so Jamie has a lot of independence and money, and that's a pretty winning combination. Parentals can't annoy you if they're never there, and when you do see them they give you cash.

"Cheers, that sounds great," he says.

"I'll get those ordered in a minute. So, what's going on with you lot?" Lia says. "Suzy, why is your life over?"

"Because I promised the school The Drifting would turn up at our fundraiser in November," I say. "I'm so completely stupid. I've got such a big mouth."

Lia makes a surprised face. "You promised the school The Drifting would come?"

"Yeah, yeah, I know," I say.

"It's certainly quite a claim. Why did you say that?"

"Long story," I mutter. "I was trying to prove a point."

"We're kind of stuffed," Danny says. "Suzy's going to be public enemy number one if we don't think of some way round the problem."

"Yikes," Lia says. "Hope you manage to figure something out. Give us a shout if we can help, won't you, Jamie?"

"Thanks," Jamie says.

"I, um, also wanted to remind you that your dad and I will be in London tomorrow," Lia says, fiddling with her phone. "We've got a client meeting, and won't be back until late. Trying to win some big business."

"Okay," Jamie says, completely disinterested.

"Come and hang out at mine after school tomorrow if you like, mate," Danny offers. "We can tackle that chem homework together."

"Great," Lia says. "Right then, I'll get those pizzas ordered. What do you guys want?"

"Thinking about it, it's obvious what we do about the whole The Drifting situation," Danny says, after we've given our order and Lia's gone.

"Is it?" I turn to him hopefully. Has he come up with a genius brainwave to get us out of this?

"I don't think we've got any choice. We're going to have to do what Jamie said and tell the truth," Danny says.

Oh.

"But I'm going to get slaughtered if we do that," I protest.

"You're going to get slaughtered if they don't turn up on the night, too," Danny says.

I huff as he continues, "Look, we'll go in on Monday, talk to Mrs Cooper – she's more reasonable than Groves is – and say we're sorry but there was a mistake, The Drifting have got, I dunno, a gig, or a TV appearance or something that night and they won't be able to come after all."

"What do you guys think?" I ask Millie and Jamie.

"As much as I hate to say it, I don't think there's any other way round it," Millie says.

There's the sound of the doorbell and then, "Pizza!" calls Lia.

As I trail after the others, I can hear the intro to my favourite new song from The Drifting, 'Fly High'. Jamie's dad, Phil, is sitting on a bar stool at the kitchen island staring at his iPad, watching the video on his screen. He hits the stop button as we walk in.

"Ham and pineapple, grim," Jamie says, grimacing as he opens the box. "Who thought fruit on pizza was a good idea?" He opens up another lid and helps himself to a slice of chicken supreme.

"I like it," Phil, says, reaching for a piece of pineapple.

Jamie shoves his hand away.

"Oi!" Phil protests, laughing.

"Mum got the pizzas for us," Jamie says.

"Well, I paid for them," Phil replies.

"Yeah, whatever," Jamie says, although he's barely

understandable through his mouthful of food.

"There's plenty, I ordered extra," Lia says, bringing over some glasses and pouring from the bottle of orangeade.

As Phil gets up to leave, he knocks the iPad and it begins to play again.

Jamie makes a face. "What are you doing sitting down here, watching The Drifting?"

"I thought they were one of your favourite bands?" Phil asks, switching it off quickly.

"They are," Jamie says. "But you're way old to be listening to their stuff."

"Hey, less of the old, thanks. I'm trying to keep up with you lot," Phil says.

"Well, don't," Jamie says. "Leave our bands to us, yeah?"

"Fine," Phil says, laughing. "C'mon, Lia, let's leave them to it. We've got a pitch to perfect."

"See you later," Lia says as they leave.

I stare at the pizza gloomily. Usually I'd be jamming it in my face faster than you can say 'stuffed crust', but today I'm far too busy freaking out to even contemplate food.

Are we really going to confess I told a total lie?

My tummy's churning so much I don't think I'm going to be able to eat anything ever again.

CHAPTER ELEVEN

"Okay, are we ready?" Jamie says, as we meet outside the school gates.

"No," I say gloomily.

"You guys are amazing!" A couple of Year Nines stop in front of us as we're about to go through the gates. "We've loved The Drifting since forever. I still can't believe they're actually coming to Collinsbrooke!"

"And that we might get to touch Nate Devlin," the other says, shivering with delight.

"Or talk to him!"

"Oh stop!" squeals her friend. "It's too exciting! When do the tickets go on sale?"

"Um, in a few weeks," I mumble. "We're still ironing out the details. We'll let everyone know, don't worry."

"I'd pay any amount to go and see them."

"Me too."

"Eeeeee!" the girls squeal again, before linking arms and dashing off.

"Oh God," I say. "Everyone's so hyped."

We walk through the reception area round to where Mrs Cooper's secretary is sitting. She rings through and then Mrs Cooper's door opens.

I'm so nervous I can hardly walk straight.

"Ah, it's my star pupils," Mrs Cooper says. "Come in."

Inside Mrs Cooper's office it's looking really empty, with half-filled cardboard boxes everywhere. There are usually photographs from all the years that she's been teaching on the giant pinboard by the computer, but they've gone too.

"What can I do for you all?" Mrs Cooper asks. We look at each other, then I open my mouth to spill the beans. I figure I should be the one to do it, seeing as how I got us into this mess in the first place.

"Actually, before you start, there's something I'd like to say," Mrs Cooper says, sitting down. She puts a hand to her chest and breathes in deeply. "Excuse me a moment. It's this ridiculous heart problem. Although I wasn't supposed to say anything... Not that I suppose it matters now I'm leaving at the end of the week. Anyway, I wanted to say to you all how thrilled I am you've got such a wonderful fundraising party planned."

"Er, yeah, that's actually what we wanted to talk to you about," Jamie starts, but Mrs Cooper holds up her hand.

"Let me finish, please, Jamie. Working at this school has meant a lot to me, and I didn't want to leave so suddenly. I still feel like I've got years left in me, but having this fundraising project is making it so much easier to go. We were really worrying about how we could raise enough money to afford a recording studio, because it's not going to be cheap, you know, but with The Drifting coming…" Mrs Cooper shakes her head in astonishment. "I don't know how you've managed it, it's incredible, but I'm so pleased you have. Delighted. It's been the highlight in a month of bad news, to be honest. I'm so pleased with you all. I'll never forget this."

There's a crashing silence. Nobody wants to make eye contact with her, or each other after that, we're all staring intently at different parts of the room.

How on earth are we supposed to say anything now?

"So, what did you want to say?" she asks.

"Yep, um, wanted to say thank you for the opportunity to plan your fundraiser," Millie improvises quickly.

"It's a pleasure. I can't wait to see what you come up with – it sounds fantastic. That's the bell," Mrs Cooper says. "You'd better get moving otherwise you're going to be late for class. Tell your teachers you were with me. Your first committee meeting is soon, isn't it?"

"Yeah, tomorrow," Danny says.

"Well, good luck! Nice to see you all. I'm very excited about the party."

"Millie, what happened?" I hiss once we're back out in the corridor. "We were supposed to tell her The Drifting weren't coming."

"She has a *heart problem*," Millie says. "We couldn't deliver her the worst news in the world after everything she said, it would be awful. Imagine how stressed she'd have been! We could have given her a heart attack, or anything. We could have *killed* her!"

"She'd have been more likely to kill us, you mean," Jamie says.

"Well, it looks like we're back at square one," Danny says.

"So we're going to have to figure out a way to bring The Drifting here," Millie says confidently.

"Yeah, cos that's going to be a complete doddle," I say.

"We won't know until we try, right?" Millie says, flinging her arm around my shoulders.

I wish I had her optimism.

"I guess the first thing is to try and contact the band," Danny says. "It can't hurt, can it?"

"Yeah, I'll just get Nate's number out of my contacts," Jamie says.

Danny punches his arm. "There are other ways we can get in touch, smartarse. Like, via their Facebook group. We can't Tweet, because that's too public. But we can try emailing their record company."

"Danny's right," Millie says, nodding frantically. "Nothing's impossible. Let's meet in the IT room at lunch, and we'll start sending emails and stuff. Even if The Drifting can't come, they might be able to do something else, like send us some freebies. We could tell everyone they cancelled last-minute but sent us some complimentary goodies."

Millie smiles at me encouragingly, and although I'm still not convinced this is going to work out, I can't help getting caught up in her optimism. Maybe things aren't as bad as I think. Maybe there is still a tiny bit of hope.

"See you in there later," I say, as my friends and I split off into different directions.

I pull my bag's strap up onto my shoulder, and head off towards class.

CHAPTER TWELVE

IT's the day of the first committee meeting and I'm pretty nervous.

Taking charge isn't really my thing, and I've already got tons to sort out because Mum's given me loads of jobs to do for Dad's party. Hopefully if I keep quiet I'll be able to take a back seat, and nobody will notice.

Although that's unlikely. Because even though signing up for this was Millie's idea, The Drifting disaster is nobody's fault but my own. And now the only thing I can think of is that I'm going to have to make the party the best ever, which is the only thing that might stop the whole school from wanting me killed.

Get The Drifting in or die. I've had anonymous messages online telling me exactly that. Along with billions of messages from excited people who think the group's actually coming, and thanking me for making it happen.

I think it's pretty safe to say I'm done for.

There have been no responses from The Drifting to our Facebook messages or emails yet. I sent a couple more before I left for school to make sure.

"You ready?" Millie says, as I join her by the lockers.

"Yup," I nod, trying to sound more confident than I feel. "Where are the boys?"

"Here," Danny says, joining us with Jamie. "Let's go. It's in the drama studio, right?"

"Yup. Mrs Morgan's lair," I say darkly.

"So, how do we think this is going to go down?" Jamie asks, tearing open a packet of crisps as we start to walk.

"Who knows?" I shrug. "It'll be interesting to see who shows. That detention thing won't have made people happy."

"Eh?" says Danny. "What you talking about, detention?"

"Anyone not coming to the meetings is getting detention. I think Groves looked at the committee and saw problems ahead. So he figures the only way to get us all there is to threaten us."

"He's probably right, to be fair," says Jamie.

Outside the studio, I push the door open apprchensively. I always find the drama studio a bit freaky. It's a large black room with no windows. I never feel likc I can breathe properly in here. I guess other people feel the same way, because a new drama studio – complete with windows – is being built as part of the school refurb.

"Where is everyone?" Millie asks.

"Maybe they've forgotten," Danny says.

"Maybe," I say doubtfully, but then the door swings open. Mrs Morgan strides in, carrying a mug of coffee and a clipboard. She's dressed in black leggings with a fluoro pink jumper over the top, accessorised with way OTT chunky plastic jewellery.

Mrs Morgan glances around and then raises her eyebrows. "Is this it?"

"Um, yeah, so far," I say. "I'm not sure where everyone else is."

"Aren't you in charge? It's your idea we're doing, yes?" says Mrs Morgan.

"Yes," I say.

"Hmm. Well, this isn't a terribly good start then, is it?"

Ugh. Cantankerous old bat. Mrs Morgan's never really made a secret out of the fact that she doesn't like me much. It goes back to our first drama lesson, where we all had to pretend to be trees. When I thought she wasn't looking, I acted out being a dog peeing on Millie. Of course Mrs Morgan saw, and she's never quite forgiven me.

"I'm sure they'll be here soon," I say, and then in comes Zach and a few other people. Soon everyone's arrived except Jade and Kara.

The door opens again, this time Mr Groves strides in, followed by Jade and Kara, who look like they'd rather be anywhere else. They scowl fiercely in my direction.

"Hello, Mrs Morgan. Have we got everyone?" Mr Groves asks. He consults his checklist and nods his head. "Yep. Right, now, I know I've been coordinating things so far with you all, but I'm the acting head now Mrs Cooper has left."

He pauses proudly for a moment, adjusting his tie and looking around the room. I don't know what he expects, a round of applause or something?

As nobody looks particularly bothered, Groves clears his throat and continues. "As I said, I'm acting headmaster, so I've got a heavy workload. Unfortunately I don't really have time to coordinate the fundraiser as well, as much as I'd love to. So I'm leaving you in the trusty hands of Mrs Morgan, who will be taking over from me. She's had a lot of experience in organising events, she puts on our fantastic Christmas shows every year and coordinates all our school productions –"

"Directs," Mrs Morgan interrupts.

"Pardon?"

"You said organising and coordinating," Mrs Morgan says, smiling broadly. She's got raspberry-pink lipstick on her front teeth. "The correct term is directing, when one is talking about the theatre."

"Ah, okay. My apologies," Mr Groves says. "As I was saying, Mrs Morgan has *directed* our Christmas shows and school productions –"

"And I'm RADA-trained," Mrs Morgan interrupts.

"And she's RADA-trained," Mr Groves says. "Taking all that into consideration we thought she was the perfect person on the staff to take over."

You know, just when I think things can't get any worse, somehow the universe still manages to poop on me from a great height.

"So I'm going to leave you in her capable hands," Mr Groves says. You can practically see him doing a little jig of joy at having got rid of us. "Thank you, Mrs Morgan."

And with that, he's gone.

"Right then," Mrs Morgan says, looking around. "Let's get started. As you know, everyone voted for Millie, Jamie and Suzy's 'Star Factor' theme, so they'll be coordinating everything. The PTA will, of course, be helping out too, managing finances, budgets, all that kind of thing. But you'll be choosing what you want to happen at the party – it's a great test of your organisational skills and will be a wonderful learning experience for you. You'll gain so much from this. I'll be sitting back here if you need anything."

And with that Mrs Morgan plonks herself in a chair, pulls some marking out of her bag and gets to work.

Which leaves me and Millie staring at each other helplessly. Yes, it was our idea, but we thought we'd be getting more help than this! I thought that's what Mrs Morgan was for. We've never done anything like this before, we've got no idea what we're doing!

"Aren't you going to help?" I say.

Mrs Morgan looks up. "With the insurance and the technical bits. But the fundraiser itself, well, that's down to you." She smiles at me falsely. "Of course, I think I could have directed a wonderful play and sold tickets to raise money for this, but I was pooh-poohed by certain staff members. Away you go, girls."

Right. That explains why she's not helping out then.

Nobody really looks like they're paying much attention. A couple of the boys are swinging on their chairs. Some of the others are texting.

"Um, I guess the first thing we need to do is appoint a committee leader," I say.

"That should be you, shouldn't it?" Jade says. She fake-smiles across the table.

"Definitely," says Kara. "It really should be, seeing as how you're the one with The Drifting contacts, right?"

"It means you'll be in charge of all the meetings," Jade points out helpfully.

"And keep us up to date with where we are with things. Like The Drifting," Kara adds.

Gah. I hate them both so much. They totally know I've backed myself into a corner. And aren't they loving rubbing it in?

It's clear from the expression on Mrs Morgan's face she doesn't want me in charge of this party. No way, José.

"Are we sure we're all happy with Suzy?" she asks.

"I am," Jade says.

"Me too," Kara adds.

A couple of the others shrug. I look at my friends in desperation, but they just make helpless faces at me.

"We'll back you up, don't worry," Millie whispers, giving my shoulder a squeeze.

"Well, then, I guess you're in," Mrs Morgan says, barely disguising a sigh. "Are you up to the task?"

I grit my teeth and say casually, "Course. Not a problem. So, um, let's get this meeting going." I think quickly, remembering how Mum started planning Dad's party. "I guess the next thing to do is write down a list of the things we're going to need to sort out. Mills, have you got some paper you can lend me?"

Millie pulls a notebook from her bag and slides it across the table.

"Okay. Great. So, I, er..." *C'mon, Suzy, wake up!* Show everyone that you're confident and in charge and totally the kind of person The Drifting would be happy to talk to.

"Food!" I blurt, as I see Jamie pull a sandwich out of his bag and start tucking in. "We need to think about catering. And... costumes."

"Decorations," contributes Millie.

"Yep," I say, nodding as I continue to write. Finally, someone else is helping!

"Venue," she adds.

"Don't we already have a venue?" Jamie says. "Aren't we having it at the school?"

"We don't have to," Millie says. "It could be amazing if we could find somewhere else to host it —"

"The PTA want it in the school, to save money," interrupts Mrs Morgan.

"Okay," Millie says. "We'll just have to think of a way to decorate it to make it look amazing."

"Budget is something else we need to think about," Danny says. "Working out prices and how much the tickets and stuff are going to cost. We need to get enough money to pay for everything and make enough money on top of that to put towards the recording studio at the end of it all. The recording studio's going to be seriously expensive."

Danny's right. Gulp. This could turn out to be harder than we'd thought.

"The PTA will sort all that and let you know how much you've got to spend," Mrs Morgan says. "They're meeting soon; I'll get the figures to you after that. Just concentrate on what you need to get organised for now."

"Okay, venue's done, so catering, decorations, entertainment," Millie lists. "Then we'll need to do all the admin, ticket sales, posters. And sorting out sound-systems for the singers. People will need mikes, and all that kind of thing. And costumes. Also, if anyone knows anybody who'd be able to help us out, shout. We're going to have to talk to businesses about donating raffle prizes, too."

Wow. I take a deep breath and lean back in my seat. There's SO much to do.

"And, of course, there's The Drifting," Jade says snarkily. She raises one eyebrow. "I assume they *are* still coming?"

"Course," Millie says confidently. "Suzy and I are handling that, aren't we?"

I nod my head weakly.

"Let's start divvying up some of these jobs," Millie says. "Anyone here into art and can put some poster and tickets designs together?"

"You're good at designing stuff, aren't you, Zach?" Sophie says. "I'm in his art class. He's really talented."

"Um..."

It's obvious Zach is torn between wanting to agree because he's flattered by what Sophie's said, and not wanting to participate in this whole fiasco.

"You two are helping," Zach mutters to Max and Ryan. "I'm not doing it by myself."

"I —" I don't know how to say I don't trust them to do anything like that. I guess I'll just have to hope it'll be okay.

"Great, thanks," Millie makes a note. "Why don't you mock up some designs before the next meeting and we'll choose which one we like best."

"Anyone else want to volunteer for anything?" I ask, doing my best to sound like I'm totally in control. "We'll give out specific jobs next time, but is there anything anyone really wants to do?"

Silence.

Funnily enough, Jade and Kara, who had all the people in the world willing to help out when it was their idea, don't say a word. Nobody else wants to meet my eyes either.

"We'll help with whatever you need," Danny says.

Thank goodness my friends are here.

"What do you two think about coordinating the stage?" I ask. "You could paint the set?"

Jamie shrugs. "Sure."

"Great. So, um, what next?" I look at Millie for help.

"Decorations? We need to have a chat about how the room's going to look."

"We can do that," Jade says, looking at Kara with a sly smile.

"Um…" I'm trying to think of a way to say 'No way in hell are we leaving YOU in charge of something so important' politely.

"Are you sure?" Millie says, clearly having the same doubts as me.

"Yeah," Kara says, nodding in a totally false way that makes me instantly suspicious. "We'll get it sorted."

"You'll need to let us know what kind of thing you're planning," Millie says.

"Why?" Jade says. "Don't you trust us?"

Nobody dares say no.

CHAPTER THIRTEEN

I've now sent five emails to The Drifting Facebook account, and seven to the record company contact details I found online. Not that I'm becoming obsessive or anything.

But why haven't they replied? Why? Why? Don't they know this is an emergency? Aargh, what if it's because they're splitting up, like that magazine said?

I hit the F5 key to see if anything's come in, but nope. The last email I have is one from Millie, sending around the minutes from the committee meeting.

I sit back in the chair and spin round aimlessly. I've got loads of emails and things I need to be sending to get stuff sorted for Dad's birthday party. My brain wants to explode at the moment with the amount I've got on. I've just opened up the internet browser when, from upstairs, I hear a huge crash followed by a scream and then the sound of babies crying.

Oh lordy. What was that?

I race upstairs, knock on Amber and Mark's bedroom door and when I throw it open, inside it's chaos. There's an enormous heap of clothes on the floor, and it seems that Mark's tripped over, he's sitting on the floor rubbing his forehead, which now has an enormous purple lump on it. He's whacked it on the chest of drawers on the way down, I think. Amber's crying her eyes out, as are Uni and Chichi. In the corner, hiding under a chair, is Crystal Fairybelle, whimpering and trembling.

"Are you all right, Markymoo?" Amber says between sobs. "Please say something."

"What happened?" I ask.

"Crystal Fairybelle got under my feet, I tripped over him and this pile of clothes, went down and whacked my head," Mark says. He blinks in a confused fashion.

Mum comes rushing in. "What's going on, what was that noise?"

Amber starts crying all over again. "Mark fell over the dog and hit his head and the babies are crying and the dog's upset and... and... and..."

Mum picks up Uni and passes her to me before picking up Chichi. I juggle Uni up and down awkwardly and soon she starts to calm down. Huh. Maybe I'm getting better at this baby stuff.

"Are you okay, Mark?" Mum says. "Sit down, let's have a look at you. It's quite a lump you've got there, you might need it checked."

"I think I'll be all right, but I should probably try to get the swelling to go down. Is there a bag of peas in the freezer?"

Mum nods, while Amber looks confused. "How is eating peas going to help your head?"

Mark laughs. "I'm going to use the bag to help the lump go down."

Amber dashes off down the stairs and soon returns with the open bag, shedding peas all over the place.

"Thanks," Mark says. He presses the bag against his forehead, wincing slightly as he does so. "We really need some more room."

"I know," Amber wails. "But where are we supposed to go?"

"Nowhere," Mum says. "You're not going anywhere. We'll find a way to make this work. I don't want you thinking you have to move out."

"It's not that we feel we have to," Mark says. "But four of us, plus a dog, in here... it's not working, this kind of proves it. And we'll have to think of something else when the babies get bigger, anyway. We'll never fit two cots in."

"I'll talk to your dad and see what we can do," Mum says, putting her arm around Amber.

"Thanks, Mum," Amber says, smiling weakly.

It's strange to see her like this. Amber's usually so happy and fluffy, drifting around on her own private planet.

"Shall I take Uni down and put her under the play gym?" I ask.

"That would be great, thanks," Amber says.

Mum and I head downstairs with the babies.

The next day, when Mark gets home from work, he and Amber disappear into their bedroom for a really long time. I can hear them talking, although I can't make out what they're saying. Turns out that glass-against-the-wall thing doesn't work nearly as well as the movies would have you believe.

It all goes quiet, then there's a knock at the door. I leap away from the wall guiltily.

"Can you come downstairs?" Amber asks. "I've got something I want to talk to everyone about."

I follow her downstairs to the kitchen, where everyone else is already waiting. My mind's whirring about what they could be about to say. It's not necessarily something big. Amber has been known to make a huge drama out of tiny things on regular occasions. She probably wants to dye her hair and is canvassing opinions.

"What's this about?" Dad asks.

"Mark and I have got something to tell you –" Amber begins.

"Oh good grief, you're not pregnant again, are you?" Dad interrupts.

"No way!" Amber looks appalled. In her arms, Chichi starts to grumble. "You can't be hungry again. You're like an eating machine. Mum, could you grab the milk, please?"

"Course," Mum says, grabbing a sterilised bottle and a small carton of milk. She makes the bottle up, and then gently takes the baby from Amber. "I'll do it, love."

"Great, thanks. Is she still asleep?" Amber asks Mark, who's got Uni snuggled up on his chest.

"They're growing every day, aren't they?" Mum says, as Chichi's big blue eyes stare up at her while she sucks hard on the bottle's teat. "It's so lovely to see how much they're changing."

"So what did you want to talk to us about?" I ask impatiently. Jeez, these two are easily distracted.

"Harry, can you turn that off, please?" Amber says, as she spots Harry zooming in on her face. "I look terrible."

"Just filming family moments," Harry says. "There, I've turned it off, see?"

She's so lying. The red light is still flashing.

"So. Um, we've had some good news, haven't we, Mark?" Amber says.

"You're moving out?" Dad says hopefully, taking a big gulp of tea.

"Actually... yes."

Dad starts to choke. "You are?"

All the colour drains from Mum's face. "You're moving out?"

Mark nods. "You know my friend Josh? He's got a placement out in Australia for a year so he's been asking at work if anyone was available to housesit. I spoke to him about it today. It's been short notice and he's been struggling to find someone, so he agreed to give us a really cheap rent. By the time he gets back we might have saved up enough to put down a deposit on our own place."

"Well, this is fantastic," Dad says.

"Daddy!" Amber says crossly. "You don't have to seem quite so pleased. I know you've dropped a billion hints, but I thought you'd be a little bit sad to see us go."

"Hah, no chance," Dad says. He's practically dancing a jig in the corner of the room.

158

"*I'm* sad," Mum says. She stares down at Chichi nestled in her arms. "I'm going to miss you all."

"You won't miss being woken up in the middle of the night," Dad mutters.

Mum ignores him. "The thought of not having you around... are you going to be all right, love?"

"She'll be fine," Mark says, putting his arm around his wife. "You've seen how amazing she is with the girls."

Mum doesn't look too sure, and I know why. I don't think Amber realises how much Mum does to help out... cooking their meals, washing their clothes, doing some of the night feeds... she could be in for serious trouble when Mum's not on hand any more.

"And does this mean the dog's going, too?" Dad says. "This gets better and better."

"Um, well, actually Dad, Crystal's a bit of a problem," Amber says. She glances over at Crystal Fairybelle, tucked up in his basket, head between his paws. "One of the conditions of us staying there so cheaply is that we look after Josh's cat. But the cat hates dogs, so we're not going to be able to take Crystal. I was wondering if we could leave him with you." Amber's eyes brim with tears. "The thought of leaving him behind is killing me."

"I'm not sure," Dad says, frowning. "Who's going to look after him?"

"Not me," Harry says. "I've got my hands full with Hagrid. I'm trying to teach him to do a forward roll."

"We'll only be there a year, and as soon as we get our own place Crystal can live with us again," Amber says. "I can't bear the thought of getting him rehomed."

"That won't happen," Mum says. "Of course Crystal can stay. I'll look after him."

"Oh, thank you, thank you, thank you!" Amber says.

"I can't believe you're actually going," Mum says. "When are you moving?"

"Josh leaves in a fortnight, so pretty soon."

Mum squeezes Chichi tightly. "And where's his house? Is it far?"

"The other side of Collinsbrooke," Mark says reassuringly. "Not far at all. Just a fifteen-minute bus ride."

"Does that mean I can move into their bedroom?" Harry asks. "It's bigger than mine."

"Hey, I'm older, I should get it," I protest.

"Neither of you are getting it, I've got big plans for that room," Dad says. "I can turn it into a games room... or a workshop... it's going to be brilliant."

"We haven't even left yet!" Amber says.

"Nobody's having that bedroom," Mum says. "I'm going to keep it as a nursery for the twins, so they'll have somewhere to sleep and play when they come to stay.

Which they'll be doing a lot. Won't they?" She looks at Amber and Mark for reassurance.

"Of course," Mark says. "I'm sure my gorgeous girls will be here all the time. You'll hardly even know we've gone. You've been so generous letting us stay, but it's time to move on, and this is the only way we're going to get our own house."

"You're not going to be coming back in a year's time, are you?" Dad says.

Mark laughs. "Hopefully not. We'll cross that bridge when we come to it, shall we?"

A tear drips down Mum's nose and Amber gasps. "Mum, don't cry!"

"I'm sorry, love, it's just, I've so enjoyed having you all here... you're absolutely right, you do need your own space, but I'll be sad to see you go."

Amber's eyes also fill with tears. "Now you're setting me off. Please don't. We aren't going far. And you'll come and visit, won't you?"

"Course I will," Mum says.

"You promise?"

"I promise," Mum replies, but it's hard to make out, because 'promise' has turned into a snuffly-snort as both she and Amber are bawling their eyes out. I grab Chichi before they're clinging onto each other, crying like

Amber's the one moving to Australia, not Josh.

"I'm going to miss you so much," Mum cries.

"I'm going to miss you more," Amber wails.

"Just another day in the Puttock household," narrates Harry, zooming in for her close-up.

CHAPTER FOURTEEN

I never knew party planning could be so totally stressful.

One party would be bad enough, but two together? On the same day? Argh. It's enough to make a person want to run away to New Zealand or something. Which I would, in a heartbeat, right now. Okay, I've never been there, but I've seen it on TV loads. It's sunny, and has nice beaches, and whales. I bet whales wouldn't be freaking over how to get an internationally famous band to play at their school party or bugging me about whether or not we should have Frazzles or Wotsits at an eighties party.

When Mum's not hassling me about crisps or cakes or music or decorations I'm sure something's going on with her. She's playing this old Madonna song over and over again on repeat, and acts really sheepish and embarrassed whenever I walk into the room. I'd ask her about it, but I've got enough other things going on to wonder what she's up to.

Even school isn't an escape, what with trying to keep on top of all the fundraiser stuff.

"Committee meeting time?" Danny says, walking up with Millie.

"Committee meeting time," I agree, trying not to sound like I'm being led to the electric chair. Which, quite frankly, is what these committee meetings are starting to feel like.

"What else do you think we can do to contact The Drifting?" I ask as we wait outside the drama studio. "It's been ages and we've not heard from them."

Danny looks thoughtful. "We've tried emailing them. You've tried Facebooking them –"

"And they've not replied to any of the messages," I say. "What if it is because they're splitting up, like that magazine article said?"

"You shouldn't believe what you read in those dumb magazines," Jamie says. "They print lies all the time."

"Yeah, but what if it's true? That might be why they're not getting back to us."

"Shhh," Millie says. "Morgan's coming."

The meeting gets going. We go over lots of bits and pieces, while everyone else sits around looking awkward, because basically the four of us are doing *everything*. Millie's been telling me I should delegate, but what if things don't get done? Besides, it's not like people are falling over themselves to volunteer to help. I thought at least Sophie, Eve and April might want to do more.

The meetings so far have all followed pretty much the same formula. Mrs Morgan ignores us, Jade and Kara make snide comments, everyone else looks bored and Millie and I end up doing most of the work while lying our butts off about how things are going with The Drifting.

And today doesn't seem to be much different. We get through most of the agenda, running through the various jobs and what still needs doing. Thank goodness Mrs Morgan's turned up to this meeting – she missed the last one, and just left a list pinned to the drama studio door with instructions of what she wanted us to do.

At least Max, Zach and Ryan have designed the tickets and posters (mainly because Mrs Morgan forced them to), and they actually look fantastic. The tickets went on sale last week and there were queues all round the field to get hold of them. We raised a ton of money, although I feel seriously guilty about selling tickets under false pretences.

"So, we have some exciting news," Jade says.

My heart sinks. What's she up to now?

"We contacted the local paper to let them know what was happening, and they're sending a photographer over to cover the event. Isn't that great?" Jade continues, smiling snidely in my direction.

My heart sinks into my shoes. Every time I think things can't possibly get any worse, they do. I can't believe they've done this! Well, I can, because that's exactly the kind of thing they would do, but now the whole town is going to hear about my humiliation. Everyone, and I mean *everyone*, will know.

If an immediate self-destruct button was available, I'd be pressing it around about now.

"Girls, that's wonderful," Mrs Morgan is saying. "That will really help get sponsors interested and increase the amount of money we're going to make. Well done, both of you. Now, how are things going with the decorations? You're organising that, aren't you?"

"Yep, everything's fine," Jade and Kara say.

"Um, could we get a more thorough report than that, please?" Mrs Morgan says, making notes. "The PTA are keen to know where we're up to with things."

Jade sighs heavily. "Fine. We're getting lights and stuff organised. There'll be a red carpet outside for people to walk up."

"I was doing some research and thought it might be a good idea to go to Party Props to get some things to dress the room with," Millie says. "Have you heard of them? They're a huge warehouse on the outskirts of Collinsbrooke, maybe you should go and check it out."

"I don't think so," Kara says. "We're very busy."

"Okay, it's fine, if you'll do all the other bits, Millie and I can get the props sorted," I say quickly. "We'll head over to the warehouse after school tomorrow."

I ignore the look Millie's shooting me. At least if we're doing things ourselves we know they're getting done.

"Right, that's nearly everything. We still need to get some costumes for the karaoke, and how's it going with the band?" Mrs Morgan asks. "The PTA are keen to see some kind of formal acknowledgement they're coming, girls. Is there someone we could talk to at the record company? Maybe their manager?"

"We got an email from them, if that helps," Millie says, sliding a piece of paper across the table.

I turn and stare at her, wide-eyed. We've got a *what* now? But that's amazing! Why didn't she say anything before?

Mrs Morgan scans the piece of paper, puts it down and smiles. "Well, that looks good to me. Excellent. See you at the next meeting, everyone."

As soon as everyone's gone, I start demanding answers from Millie. "You got an email from the band? That's flipping brilliant news! Why didn't you say something?"

"Because it wasn't real," Millie says sheepishly. "Sorry. I set up a pretend account and faked an email to get everyone off our backs."

Oh. Gutted doesn't even begin to cover it.

"But Mrs Morgan did give me an idea," Millie continues hurriedly, seeing my disappointed face. "I don't know why we didn't think of it sooner. Why don't we just ring The Drifting's manager at the record company and ask to speak to them?"

Everyone's silent. It can't be that easy... can it?

"We'll meet at lunch behind the science block," Millie says. Nobody ever goes there because it's so close to where the JCB dug through the sewer pipe so it still stinks.

"I've just found the number for Firefly Records," Danny says, glancing up from his phone.

"Brilliant," says Millie. "We'll call the manager at lunch. This is how we're going to get The Drifting to come to our school, Suze!"

At lunchtime, we all gather together. It's still way whiffy round here. It's hard not to gag.

"Who's going to do it then?" Jamie asks.

"Not you, Jamie," Millie says. "You mumble on the phone. Do you want to do it, Suzy?"

No. No, I don't. I'm worried I'm going to make a complete idiot of myself and ruin our only chance.

"I'll do it if you want me to?" Millie says.

It's tempting. Really tempting. But I'm the one that got us into all this.

I shake my head. "I should do it. Read us the number, will you, Mills?"

My heart's pounding as I key in the numbers. There's a short pause and then the phone starts to ring.

"Hello, Firefly Records."

"Er, hello," I attempt, but my voice cracks and stutters.

"Hello?"

I try again. "Hello. I, um, I was wondering, I need to speak to The Drifting and –"

"Are you a fan?"

"Well, yes, but –"

"Then you need to contact the fan club. You'll find the details online. Thanks for calling, bye."

"Whoa," I say, holding the now dead phone away from my ear.

"That was quick," Danny says.

"Yeah, they didn't really give me a chance to say anything," I say.

"Try again," urges Millie.

I press the redial button.

"Hello, Firefly Records."

This time I'm more prepared. "Hi, I was wanting to get in touch with The Drifting. It's about... um..." My gaze falls on a magazine sticking out of Millie's bag. "Um, an interview," I say, suddenly inspired. My friends nod, impressed, while Millie gives me a thumbs up.

"You need their press office, they operate out of a different building," the voice says. "I'll give you the number, got a pen?" He reels off a telephone number and then hangs up.

Hmmm. Getting through to their manager is proving harder than you'd think.

Nothing works.

Not pretending to be a hotel trying to get unpaid bills sorted (they directed us to an accountancy firm), or saying we need to talk to them about acoustics in their concert venues (we'd need to speak to stage management about that). Danny came up with that last one, he was dead proud of himself.

"Guys, I'm all out of ideas," I say.

"One more try," Millie says. "Here, let me have a go."

I throw the phone over.

"What are you going to do?"

"Wait and see," Millie says. "Hello?" she says a moment later. "I'm Coco, from MTV. I was wondering if you could put me through to the person who manages The Drifting, please? I've spoken to the publicity team already, they said you'd be able to help." There's a pause and then...

"I'm on hold!" she gasps. It feels like an eternity passes before she starts talking again:

"Hello, yes, are you the person that manages The Drifting? You're not? Well, can I speak to them please? Oh. Okay. Then could you give them my details and tell them I need to talk to them? It's urgent. Thank you." And she leaves her fake name and phone number.

"How did you know to say that?" I gasp in awe when she's off the phone.

"Cos I'm a genius. That was the manager's assistant," Millie says. "I've left a message, but who knows if they'll actually call back. We'll have to wait and see. I've changed my answerphone message ready, though. From now on, just call me Coco."

CHAPTER FIFTEEN

"**Are you sure** you know where we're getting off?" I ask Millie, as the bus pulls into an area of town I've never been to before. We've been on the bus nearly an hour, heading for a trading estate on the other side of Collinsbrooke where the Party Props warehouse is situated.

"I don't think it's much further," Millie said. "I'll go and ask."

Mr Bus Driver doesn't appreciate Millie's appearance by his left elbow, as he doesn't seem to have heard her coming and jumps about a foot in the air, then shouts at her to sit down.

Despite her protestations, Millie doesn't get the answer she needs.

"Grumpy old goat," she mutters, flopping down into the seat next to me. "Let's get off at the next stop."

She reaches out to press the bell, and the bus jerks to a halt.

"Thank you!" I say as we climb off.

The bus driver practically slams the doors on us, such is his haste to get away.

Millie was right. He *is* a grumpy old goat.

But we don't have time to worry about him right now. We've got a warehouse to locate. I look around us. All I can see are rows and rows of warehouses. This industrial estate is enormous.

"You do know how to find this place, right?" I say. "You looked up the directions before we left?"

Millie looks sheepish. "Um, I kind of figured it'd be easier to find than this. I thought it would be simple to spot a huge warehouse. I didn't realise there'd be *loads* of huge warehouses. It won't be far though, c'mon."

It takes an hour before we finally find the place we're after. As we walk towards it, the Party Props logo looms large above the entrance, complete with a picture of a large banana wearing shades, grinning broadly and holding a bunch of balloons.

Inside, there's a bored-looking guy, about university age, sitting behind the desk. He's got a tufty beard and greasy hair, and is fiddling with his phone. He doesn't acknowledge us as we walk up to the desk and hover awkwardly.

Millie clears her throat.

Still no response.

"Um, hello?" she tries again.

The man raises an eyebrow, although we can hardly see it under the strands of clumped-together hair.

Ew. He's grimmola.

"Hi," Millie says. "We're here from Collinsbrooke School? We've come to have a look at some props."

Greasy leans forward and runs his finger down a piece of paper.

"Suzy and Millie?" Millie adds.

Greasy is starting to freak me out. What's the deal with him? Why isn't he speaking?

The guy eventually finds what he's searching for and then he points at the double doors.

"Um, okay," Millie says, her voice starting to waver.

What if this is how he lures people to their unsuspecting deaths? The thought pops into my head from nowhere and once it's there I can't get rid of it. There could be who knows what waiting on the other side of the door. Aaagh! Stupid thoughts like this are the reason I don't watch horror movies any more.

"How does all this work?" Millie asks.

The man pushes a piece of paper in her direction. "Go in there," he mutters. "Find what you want. Write down the corresponding number. Then come back here and fill in the details of your event. You can then hire whatever it is you want for that night."

"Okay."

The man returns to his phone. We've clearly been dismissed.

"Shall we?" Millie says, tilting her head towards the double doors.

"Let's do it," I reply, trying to push all thoughts of murderers and axes out of my head.

We both gasp when we push the double doors open. This place is something else! The warehouse is huge, and it's crammed with everything under the sun.

There are trees, Egyptian mummies, fake cows, cannons, phone boxes, a vintage blue car, a giraffe wearing a Stetson, pink flamingos and a whole variety of other weird and wonderful items, all with individual numbers on. There's even an enormous Statue of Liberty tucked into one corner. It's like I'm having the world's craziest cheese dream.

"Whoa!" Millie says, staring around in delight. "This place is *epic*!"

"How are we going to know where to start?" I ask in awe. "We could be here hours."

"Pfff, who cares?" Millie says. "I want to see *everything*, don't you?" She runs over to a red-velvet chaise longue, and sprawls out, draping her hand onto her forehead dramatically as if she's swooning.

"I wish we'd gone for a Western theme, then we could have had one of those," Millie says, jumping up and pointing to a bucking bronco. "We could have put Jade and Kara on it at full speed. Serve the pair of them right when they got thrown off."

"We're not that lucky," I point out. "Jade would probably hang on looking all sexy, boobs bouncing around all over the place, and half the boys in the school would be watching with their tongues hanging out."

"Good point," Millie says. "I was having delightful visions of them being flung out of the window. Your version is probably more realistic."

Near me there's an eighties section, which I know Mum would go nuts over if she could see it. Although the way she's spending money lately, I'm not sure I should tell her. I hope she manages to hide the bills better than she did the ones for Amber's wedding.

Some of this stuff does look amazing, though. There are glowing silhouette pictures of some of the big stars of the time – Madonna, Michael Jackson and Harrison Ford – as well as some weird poster for something called 'Space Invaders'. No idea if Space Invaders are a band or something. I'll have to ask Danny; guaranteed he'd know. There are also huge brightly coloured beanbags that look super cosy, and giant Rubik's Cubes.

"Millie, look at these!"

Millie gasps when she sees what I'm pointing at. "They're perfect! Just what we need!"

I've spotted giant microphones, jukeboxes and, off to one side, some purple and gold thrones that would be ideal judges' chairs.

I take a couple of pictures of some of the items and am about to tuck my phone into my pocket when a text comes in. It's from Danny.

How r u getin on?

My eyes widen as I see a Stormtrooper statue not far away. I run over, drape my arm around its neck, then grin as I take a selfie of the pair of us. Hah! Danny's going to freak when he sees this...

I smile to myself as I send the pic over. Sure enough, there's an instant reply.

U hv 2 gt it!

Then another text comes in:

Dat pic iz my nu screensaver ☺!

I can't help but laugh. Danny really does love *Star Wars*. But there's no way I'm ordering a Stormtrooper. He'll have to be happy with the photo.

As I look around, I realise I can't see Millie any more. Where's she gone?

"Millie?"

No answer.

"Mills?" I call again, starting to walk towards the place I last saw her.

"Hello, Suzy, how are you?" A hand appears from behind an enormous green dragon moving its mouth up and down as if it's talking.

Despite my thumping heart, I crack up laughing.

"This place is the best," Millie says, laughing too as she emerges from behind the dragon. "I could stay here forever!"

"Look at all those statues," I say, pointing to a row of enormous Oscar statuettes. They're even taller than me.

"Ooh, I want this polar bear," Millie says. The bear is bigger than she is, holding its paws in front of him as he stands on his two back legs. "He seems kind of friendly, don't you think? I'd keep him in my bedroom."

"Murphy wouldn't approve. He'd eat it," I point out, thinking of how crazy Millie's enormous dog is.

"Hmm. Yeah. You're probably right. He is utterly amazing, though."

"Look at these!" I pull out some fabulous feather

headdresses, with plumes of purple and silver, along with some amazing enormous feathery fans.

"Oooh, gimme!" Millie snatches one of each and puts hers on. I join her and fan myself, batting my eyelashes.

"Now all we need is sequin leotards and we'll be well away," Millie says.

I snort. "No chance."

Millie starts to dance and twirl about.

Ah well, if you can't beat 'em...

I start leaping around, flinging my fan to the left, then to the right. Then we do a kind of routine, swishing our fans above our heads.

Millie starts to twirl again, and I copy her, spinning, spinning, until – whoa. Now I'm feeling all kinds of dizzy. I stop, trying to get my bearings, but everything's still moving. Completely unable to stop myself, I stagger towards the line of enormous Oscar statuettes, and put a hand out to steady myself.

Unfortunately the statuettes are nowhere near as heavy as they look.

One falls... and knocks over the one behind it... which knocks over the one behind that... and on, and on, until they've all gone down like dominoes.

Millie and I are paralysed with fear as we watch them. There's absolutely nothing we can do to stop it.

By the end of the line there's an enormous crash as the last one knocks into the polar bear.

The polar bear wobbles and then topples over onto the floor...

And its head falls off.

Millie and I stare at each other in horror. "What did you do?" Millie whispers.

"I don't know," I whisper back, and then I start to laugh. I can't help it. The polar bear looks so daft lying headless underneath a pile of statuettes.

Millie starts to laugh too. Soon we're howling in the middle of the shop, with one of those shaking giggling fits where you can't stop. The double doors across the room fly open, and Greasy rushes in.

"What's going on?"

We stop laughing in an instant.

He skids to a stop when he sees the broken bear. "Oh my God, did you do that? My bosses aren't going to be happy."

"I'm so sorry. It was a complete accident," I say.

"You're going to have to pay for it," he says, pointing to a sign on the wall. "All breakages must be paid for."

"But... but... that's not fair!" I protest.

"Rules are rules," Greasy says. "I'll check the paperwork and tell you how much you owe."

I stare at Millie in dismay. "We haven't got much budget. Now what are we going to do?"

"Let's see how much it's going to cost first," Millie says.

"Mills, we decapitated a giant polar bear. Do you really think it's going to be cheap?"

A few minutes later Greasy strides back over. "You owe £150. We've got insurance, but you need to pay towards the costs."

"£150!" I'm horrified. That's all of the budget the PTA gave us, and we were working on a shoestring anyway. How are we going to be able to get all the props and stuff we need now?

"This is a nightmare," I mutter.

"Is there really no way round this?" Millie pleads. "Please? Pretty please?"

Greasy shakes his head. "'Fraid not. You've got fourteen days to pay."

I sigh. "Mrs Morgan's going to love this."

We leave as Greasy's trying to fix the head onto the polar bear. I take one last longing look at the giant microphone and the jukebox and the judges' thrones before the doors swing shut. All the stuff that would have looked so amazing, but now we're not going to be able to get.

"That went well," I say.

"Aw, Suze, don't stress, we'll figure something out," Millie says, giving me a big squeeze.

But I don't know what we're going to do. I don't know what we're going to be able to figure out. How are we supposed to come up with the props for the party now? It's going to look rubbish.

I could cry, I really could.

CHAPTER SIXTEEN

We're hanging out at Jamie's. His parents are in London again, and this feels like the best place for us right now. Shut away from the rest of the world, trying to figure out the mess that we're in.

Although my friends are obviously concerned about the way things are going, I'm definitely the most stressed. After all, I promised that The Drifting were coming. And I was the one that decapitated the polar bear. I got into a ton of trouble with the PTA over that, and they've said we can't have any more cash, the budget doesn't allow for it. We're going to have to figure out a way to get free props now. Mrs Morgan was seriously unimpressed. I swivel miserably on one of the bar stools.

"Why are your parents spending all this time in London?" Millie asks Jamie. "They've been there loads lately."

Jamie doesn't answer, instead he grabs a loaf of bread and starts hacking slices off it.

"J?" Millie asks. "What's up?"

When Jamie turns round, his face looks glum. "They started off working up there, but now I think it might be more than that."

"What do you mean?" Millie asks.

Jamie sighs. "I have a horrible feeling they're thinking of moving."

"What?" shrieks Millie. "Are you kidding? You can't move to London!"

Jamie shrugs.

"Why do you think that, mate?" Danny asks. "Have they said anything?"

Jamie shakes his head. "I found some London property details in the study. They've been looking at houses there."

All the colour has drained out of Millie's cheeks. "No. You can't go. You can't leave us behind."

"It's not like I *want* to," Jamie says, making everyone doorstep cheese and pickle sandwiches.

"Have you asked them?" I say.

Jamie pulls a face. "Course. And they said they weren't. But I dunno, they looked all weird and secretive. I'm not sure they were telling the truth. And it's not like I see

184

the parentals much at the moment, anyway. Since they won this huge business pitch they've been working on some hush-hush project that's taking up all of their time. I'm not allowed to know what it is. They've had to sign disclaimers and all sorts."

"Aren't you curious?" I ask. I'd be dying to know what was going on if it was my parents.

"Nah," Jamie says, sliding the plates of food across the worktop. "They've done this kind of thing before. The last one was for a new design for a bleach bottle. Majorly unexciting."

"But it could be something exciting this time," Danny says.

"Unlikely," Jamie says. "Although if it's for food, we sometimes get loads of freebies, which is cool. You guys want to go through to the lounge and hang there?"

I can tell he wants to chat to Millie and make sure she's okay, so Danny and I head to the lounge where we flop on one of the ginormous sofas.

"You all right?" Danny asks. His hand briefly rubs over my back. "It sucks about Jamie."

"It does. As if enough didn't suck already," I say self-pityingly.

"We'll figure something out," Danny says. "I'm kind of worried about you. You're getting so stressed."

"I know, I'm sorry," I say, and then it all comes tumbling out. "I just feel like everything's my fault. I'm the one who opened my stupid big mouth. I'm the one who lost all the props budget after what happened in the warehouse. I'm the one leading this committee in what's building up to be the worst party in the history of parties. And I'm the one who's going to be in major trouble with all the teachers when they find out I told a big fat lie!"

My eyes are brimming with tears.

Danny leans forward to give me a big hug. "Oh, Suze. It'll be okay..."

I don't have a chance to answer him because my phone rings. It's Mum.

"Where are you?" she asks.

"At Jamie's. Why?"

"Have you forgotten that Amber and Mark are moving out tonight? You were supposed to come straight home after school."

Flip. That had completely slipped my mind.

"Um, I was only picking up a textbook for homework," I lie. "I'm leaving now, see you soon."

"Okay," Mum says. "See you in a bit."

"I've got to go," I say, as I end the call. "Amber's moving out today; I'm supposed to be there."

"No prob," Danny says. "Want me to come with you?"

I shake my head. "Nah. I'm okay. Thanks, though."

"I'll talk to you later, yeah?"

"Later," I say, as I stuff the last of my sandwich into my mouth and grab a handful of crisps for the walk home.

Back at the house, it's chaos. There's stuff everywhere, mainly shoved into black bin liners; they've obviously run out of boxes. Mum, Dad and Mark are doing most of the lifting and packing of things into the cars, while Amber seems to be wafting around in more of a supervisory capacity, not doing very much that's actually useful.

Wow. I can't believe moving day is finally here.

My big sister is leaving home, taking her husband and twins with her. Even if she is leaving the dog behind.

It's weird to think she won't be around any more. She's been on the other side of my bedroom wall my whole life.

In a funny sort of way, I think I'm going to miss her.

Although I won't miss being woken up at 1 a.m. by the babies. Or 2 a.m. Or 4 a.m. Or 6 a.m. Last night was not a good night.

Dad's so happy he's practically skipping around the house. And I'm sure I've heard him mutter "one down, two to go" more than once. Flipping charming, no?

Mum, on the other hand, is a mess. Worrying and flapping and fretting – and doing her best not to cry. I caught her burying her head in the washing machine earlier, attempting to hide her sobs.

I give her a hug. "Come on, Mum, they're only moving to the other side of town, it's not that far. Only a short drive in the car."

"I'm just not sure I'm ready for them to leave," Mum sniffs. "And I'm worried how Amber's going to cope by herself. You know what she's like…"

"I know, but people have babies all the time and manage," I try to reassure her, even though I can totally see why Mum's freaking. Amber with one baby by herself would be bad enough, but two? She's way outnumbered.

"I can't believe my little girl is leaving home," Mum says, dabbing at her eyes with a raggedy tissue. "My nest is starting to empty."

"But you've still got two of us left," I say. "Although please don't call me a little girl, or I may be forced to kill you."

"I know," Mum says. "And it'll be lovely to spend more time with you and Harry. I can help you with your homework, and we can go on girls' days out, and have movie nights… ooh, that's cheered me right up. It'll be great, won't it?"

Instantly she seems to be happier, while I'm left slightly horrified. The thought of mother/daughter bonding time isn't all that appealing to be honest. Yikes.

"What will we do together first?" Mum says.

"Er, let's chat about it later," I say. "I think I can hear a baby crying."

"You can?" Mum says, dashing off.

I can't. But they cry so much, there's a pretty good chance there's wailing going on somewhere.

Amber wanders past with a hairbrush, which she stuffs into one of the bags.

"Do you want to give us a hand, Amber?" Dad asks, hefting several boxes and turning a funny shade of purple as he realises they're heavier than they look.

"I will, in a minute," Amber says vaguely. "But right now you're doing a wonderful job."

"All this is never going to fit," Dad says, as he returns for a lamp, a suitcase and the twins' play gym.

"We can come back for a second trip," Mark says. "Who knew Amber had so many shoes?"

Dad rolls his eyes.

It takes well over an hour to jam stuff into the two cars, and even then it's obvious they're going to need to come back. The baby stuff alone takes up most of the Volvo.

"Right, we're going to drive this lot across town,"

Dad says to me and Harry, slamming the boot.

"You two going to be all right here?" Mum says. There's no way we could go with them even if we wanted to, every spare centimetre is crammed full.

"Sure," I say.

"Keep an eye on your sister," Mum adds.

Amber comes over and puts her hands on my shoulders. Then she pulls me close into a hug so tight I can barely move and starts to sob.

I think I'd be more upset if I could actually get some oxygen. At the moment all I can think about is the fact my lungs are getting seriously crushed.

"Um, Ambs?" I gasp. "I can't... really... breathe."

Amber pulls away, leaving a snot trail on my shoulder. Gross. My lungs expand gratefully.

"I really am going to miss you," she says.

"I'll miss you too," I say. And I mean it. Sure my sister is bonkers but she's a lot of fun to have around. And she has a lot of cool clothes to borrow. And what am I going to do without her make-up stash to raid?

"The girls are going to miss having their favourite aunt around, too," Amber adds mournfully.

"Hey!" Harry says from behind her phone. She's filming everything, of course.

"Sorry. Joint favourite aunt," Amber amends.

190

"We'll come and see you soon," I say.

"Bye!" Harry says. "Don't hug me," she warns, as Amber advances on her.

"Bye, guys," Mark says, giving me a quick hug and slapping a high five with Harry.

"Amber, are you *sure* you can look after the babies by yourself?" Mum asks.

"Course I can," Amber says. "I've been doing it for weeks, haven't I?"

"Well, I *have* been around to help you out if you've needed it," Mum says tactfully. "And you don't do any cleaning or laundry while you're here, you've got me helping you out with that. It might be a shock to the system when you're totally by yourself. And are you sure you're going to be all right with the cooking?"

Amber laughs. "Luckily melon and tabasco sauce don't take much preparation."

"Yes, but you're not going to be on that diet forever, are you?" Mum says. "And Mark might want to eat at some point."

Amber waves her hand breezily. "Mum, you're so sweet. But of course I can clean. And cook. The babies and I will be okay."

Mum looks deeply sceptical. As well she should. I don't think I've *ever* seen Amber do any cleaning. I'd be astonished if she even knew what a hoover was, let alone how to turn one on.

"Look, I tell you what, we'll have you all over for supper," Amber says. "We'll need enough time to unpack first." Her eyes fall on the calendar hanging on the noticeboard. "What about... ooh, Bonfire Night's not that far away. Why don't you come over and we'll have a little party, some food and fireworks."

"That sounds lovely," Mum says, "but are you sure? It could be a lot of work."

"No it won't, it'll be easy-peasy. Could you give Uni her bottle?" Amber says, thrusting the baby at Mum. "I need to paint my nails. Thanks, you're the best!"

"Amber, we're leaving!" Mark says.

"Won't be long," Amber calls. "And Uni needs feeding."

Does my sister really not see the irony in how she's behaving, letting Mum do everything for her? Really?

Mum stares after her, shaking her head. "I hope she's going to be all right, I really do."

"Well, we'll soon hear about it if she's not," I say. "I'm starving. What's for tea?"

"Whatever you can find in the freezer," Mum says. "Oh, listen to that dog, would you?"

Crystal is seriously unimpressed at being abandoned

and is sitting in the doorway, howling at the top of his doggy voice, refusing to move, so everyone trying to get in and out trips over him on the way past.

It's ages before Amber finally returns and gets into the car.

"Happy unpacking," I call after them.

As I wave them off, the wail of a baby disappearing into the distance can be heard from the open window of Mark's Micra. Harry's filming them leave.

"I'm getting her bedroom," Harry says, turning the camera off.

"No way," I protest. "We've been through this. I'm older, if anyone's getting it, it should be me."

"But I'm going to be at home longer than you," Harry says, with infuriating logic.

"Yeah, well, the parentals said neither of us can have it."

"We'll see," Harry says.

As I enter the house, I'm struck by how quiet it is. Just me and Harry. It's weird. I'm so used to having tons of people around, with loads of hustle and bustle. I guess this is what it must be like to live in Danny's house. It's only Danny and his dad at their place, so Danny has more peace and quiet than he knows what to do with. He loves the chaos of our place, the big weirdo.

I grab a bowl of cereal and head upstairs, spooning cornflakes into my mouth.

"Er, Suzy," Harry appears on the landing from Amber's bedroom. "You have to come and see this. You won't believe it."

I follow Harry into my sister's room. It's completely empty – the wardrobe's bare, the bedding stripped, toiletries gone – all except for one thing.

Chichi is in the middle of the floor, bundled up in her coat and hat, strapped into her car seat. Her big blue eyes blink a couple of times in confusion, and then she starts to cry.

"They forgot Chichi?" I ask in alarm.

"Yup," says Harry. "Don't ask me how. These people are about to be entrusted with full-time solo care of their kids." She sighs. "Do you want to ring Mum, or shall I?"

CHAPTER SEVENTEEN

We're in the middle of English, reading aloud from *Romeo and Juliet*, when there's a knock at the classroom door. Everyone looks up in relief, glad to get a break. Shakespeare makes everyone's heads a bit melty.

Chloe, one of the girls from the year above, comes in to talk to Mr Patterson, who then gestures to me.

"Suzy, there's a delivery for you at reception."

I'm confused. A delivery? What kind of delivery?

"Oooh, what do you think it is?" Millie whispers.

"Mr Groves wants to see you about it," Chloe says.

"I don't see why this can't wait until break," Mr Patterson says. "We're in the middle of a lesson."

"Mr Groves said he needed to see Suzy immediately," Chloe says.

"Fine," Mr Patterson sighs. "Off you go. Amy, please take over Suzy's part."

As I wander along the deserted corridors, I'm still trying to figure out what the delivery can be. I wonder if it's something from Danny? Maybe he's sent me flowers! He knows I've been majorly stressed over all this party stuff lately, perhaps he's done something to try and cheer me up.

Yeah, I know it's majorly unlikely, but I can't think of anything else. My mind has drawn a total blank.

When I arrive at the reception, Mrs Clarke, the receptionist, points me in the direction of Mr Grove's office. "He's waiting for you."

"And is the delivery in there?" I ask eagerly. I can't wait to see what it is.

"Yes," Mrs Clarke says, doing her best not to laugh. She fails.

Huh. Well, that's weird. What's that all about? There's nothing funny about a bunch of flowers that I know of. So maybe it's not flowers after all. In which case, what on earth has been sent? I tentatively knock on the door.

"Come in."

Mr Groves looks up from his paperwork and inhales. "Suzy. Thank you for coming. I'm hoping you can explain the meaning of this?"

When I see what he's pointing at, I gasp. In the

corner of his office is an enormous stone statue of a Greek god. It's muscly, and all it's wearing is a laurel wreath on its head.

The statue is all kinds of naked.

Why is Mr Groves making me look at that? I immediately avert my gaze to avoid any kind of eye contact with its, y'know, *thing*.

"Well?" Mr Groves says.

When I finally speak, my voice is all croaky. "Um, I'm not sure I understand?"

"This was delivered to you from the Party Props Warehouse. I don't know if it was a practical joke or what, but I can assure you, I'm not amused. It had better not be for the fundraiser. This is *not* the kind of thing we want at our party."

"Delivered for me?" How did this happen? And what must Mr Groves think of me now? He must be under the impression I'm some kind of pervert. This is awful!

"Get it out of my office," Mr Groves says. "And be warned that this kind of behaviour is deeply inappropriate. If anything like this ever happens again, there'll be serious trouble, do you understand? You're lucky I'm drowning in paperwork today and don't have time to look into this further."

"But I didn't order this," I protest.

"Well, the invoice attached to its leg has your name on," Mr Groves says. I glance at the statue again, but my eyes keep getting drawn hypnotically towards the groin area.

For the love of God, stop staring at it, Suze. That's not helping anything.

"I –"

"Just get it out of here."

"Isn't it really heavy?" I ask.

"It's plastic," Mr Groves says.

Oh God. How am I meant to carry it without touching it *there*? I don't want to be seen wandering through the school grappling with a naked statue!

"Can't I pick it up later?"

"Afraid not. I've got a meeting in half an hour, I need that gone."

"But –"

"I propose you remove it from my office, pronto, and I'll pretend I've never seen it. Otherwise there will be consequences. What's it to be?"

"I'll move the statue," I mumble.

It takes several attempts before I manage to pick it up in a manner that in no way involves me having contact with the crotch area.

I've got to hide it somewhere before the bell goes. I need to get it back to the Party Props Warehouse and explain the confusion, but I really don't want anyone to see me with it before then.

I'm passing the girls' toilets when the door opens and out come Jade and Kara. They're both holding phones.

"Smile, Suzy!" Jade says and clicks, before she and Kara run off sniggering.

Oh come *on*! How do those two always, without fail, manage to see me when I'm at my absolute worst?

I'm staggering up the corridor still trying to work out what to do with this statue when the bell goes. I duck into the stationery cupboard, dragging Nuddy behind me, and text my friends to come ASAP. No way am I letting anyone else see me with this.

In the dark I close my eyes, and lean back against the wall. This is awful. Just awful.

There's a knock on the door.

"Suzy?"

It's Danny's voice.

"What are you doing in there?" Danny says. Jamie and Millie are peering into the cupboard, looking baffled.

"I had to leave English because of this," I say, pointing at the statue.

My friends all crack up laughing.

"What *is* that?" Jamie says.

Danny and Millie can't speak they're laughing so hard.

"Is that what the delivery was?" Millie asks, once she's managed to calm down.

"Yup. It came from the Party Props Warehouse. The delivery had my name on it, but I didn't order it."

"Oh, Suze," Millie says, biting her lower lip and trying to quash her smiles. "Does he have a name? You'll get a reputation hanging out with naked males in cupboards, you know."

"Why did they send it to you?" Jamie asks.

"I don't know!" I shriek.

"Then maybe you should give them a call and find out?" Millie says. "Is there a phone number on that piece of paper?"

She carefully removes the invoice taped to Nuddy's thigh and unfolds it. "Yep, there's one here."

"Will you do it, Mills? Please?" I ask.

"Okay," Millie says. "Are you ever going to come out of that cupboard?"

"No," I say gloomily. "I'm going to stay in here until I die."

"It's ringing," Mills whispers, and then snaps into grown-up professional mode as someone answers. She wanders off, chatting away. I try to stretch out. It's awfully cramped in here, and I'm getting pins and needles in my foot.

"Well?" I say, when Millie returns.

"It's really weird," Millie says, crinkling up her nose. "They said you rang and requested the statue to be sent to school. And that it had to be for today."

"Er, no I didn't!"

"That's what I told them," Millie says. "But they said it was paid for and everything. You've only got it on hire for today, though. You need to get it back to them by first thing tomorrow, or you'll have to pay another day's hire."

"What? How am I meant to do that? This wasn't anything to do with me! Although..."

I remember Jade and Kara and how they'd popped out of the toilets at that convenient moment. Coincidence? I think not.

"I bet it was Jade and Kara," I say gloomily. "They took pictures of me walking down the corridor with it."

"You're kidding. Even for them that's outrageous," Danny says.

"Tell me about it. I'm going to need to get it back to the warehouse after school then, aren't I?" I say. "I don't want to start being charged for being in possession of the flipping thing."

"Can your mum drive you over?" Millie asks.

"Doubt it," I say. "She's got her hands full at the moment. And Dad's at work."

"I would ask my parents, but they're in London again today," Jamie says. "Sorry."

"I could ask my dad, if you like?" Danny offers.

"No way!" I say. The thought of me and a naked statue being in the same car as Danny's dad – yurgh. That's too disturbing for words. Never going to happen.

"I'll text Mum," Millie says. "But if she can't help you, we'll have to get the bus back over. I'll come with you."

"Thanks, Mills," I say gratefully.

The bell rings.

"What am I going to do with this thing?" I say. "I can't leave it here. What if it gets lost? Or stolen?"

"It really is all kinds of naked," Jamie says.

"I've got an idea," Millie says, making a grab for Jamie's bag.

"Hey!" he protests. "What are you doing?"

Millie pulls out Jamie's PE shorts and waves them triumphantly. "Here! Put these on him."

After a short struggle, Nuddy is finally covered up. Thank goodness for that. Although it's going to be mortifying hauling this thing around school with me, at least he's decent.

CHAPTER EIGHTEEN

An update on my life:

I'm trying to juggle the organisation of two big parties, one of which has to be kept a huge secret and requires me to try to manage my mother in the process, who's getting totally carried away and is texting constantly with questions about every minute detail. For the other party I keep getting distracted by having to do jobs like wrestle enormous naked statues onto buses. Thank goodness Nuddy's been returned safely to his warehouse now.

The less said about my day lugging around a Greek god, the better.

I'm still no closer to bringing The Drifting to our school, despite sending more emails and Facebook messages. Nobody ever called back from their management team.

Urgh. This all sucks.

It's no wonder I can't concentrate on the reading I'm supposed to have finished for English later.

Millie comes flying through the door of the IT lab, her cheeks flushed and her eyes sparkling.

"You'll never believe what I just heard!"

"What?" I say. I hardly look up from my phone, Millie gets crazy excited over ridiculous stuff, like enchiladas being served in the cafeteria, or a BOGOF on Jelly Babies.

"You'll never believe what I just heard!" she repeats.

"Hmm?" I'm in the middle of a text to Mum, who's asking how many frozen sausage rolls she should get from the supermarket. I tell her four hundred. It's better to have too much food than too little, right? We don't want people to be hungry.

Who knew that parties required so much effort? I've only ever turned up at them before. Sorting all the logistics to actually make them happen is one big brain-ache.

"Suzy, listen!" Millie snatches the phone out of my hands.

"Hey, I was in the middle of something," I protest.

"It can wait. I just got the best news. The Drifting are doing an appearance on the radio!"

"Um, so?" I don't get what there is to be excited about.

I mean, sure, it'll be cool to hear them interviewed, but it won't get them any closer to appearing at Collinsbrooke.

"Don't you get it?" Millie says. "Don't you know what this means?"

"Uh, no?"

Millie rolls her eyes. "You're so dense. We can wait outside the radio station for them! If we speak to them I'm sure they'll help us out if they can."

"I'm not so sure," I say.

"Well, have you got any better ideas?" Millie says. "We've tried emailing them. Nothing. We tried writing to them. Nothing. We tried calling. Nothing. I honestly think this is our last chance, Suzy. But I'm sure, I'm really, really sure, that if we can only get a chance to speak to them, they'll be able to do something. They seem really nice guys."

Well. When she puts it like that...

"I've seen pictures of people waiting outside the radio station for bands in magazines," Millie says. "There never seem to be that many people. I'm so excited!"

Now I'm starting to catch Millie's enthusiasm.

Maybe this *could* solve all our problems! Sure it's a long shot, but it might work...

"So which radio station are they going to be at?"

"They were saying on the Drifting forum pages that

it'll be one of the London stations. Nobody knows the exact details yet."

"Erm, if they're talking about it on a forum, doesn't that mean loads of people know about it?" I ask, my heart sinking into my shoes.

"Yeah, course they'll have some fans there, but it won't be that many, will it?" Millie says. "It'll be fine, Suze, c'mon."

"Have you talked to the boys about it? Are they coming too?" I ask.

Millie shakes her head. "It'll just be us going. The boys are going to stay at home to try and call into the radio station, just in case we don't get a chance to talk to the band. Which we will. Because this is our last chance. All we've got to do is convince our parents to let us go to London."

The way she says it makes it sound so easy — *all we've got to do is convince our parents to let us go to London* — and then maybe we'll be able to give everyone the party they want.

"Okay," I say decisively. "I'm in."

CHAPTER NINETEEN

"**Have you seen** your dad?" Mum asks, walking into my room and putting a pile of clean washing onto the bed.

"Hmmm?" I say, not really listening.

"Suzy? Have you seen him?"

"Who?"

"Your dad," Mum says in exasperation.

"Oh. No. Have you tried the shed? He's probably avoiding the trick-or-treaters." Dad's always in the shed these days. He spends hours out there, reading in his comfy chair. And, weirdly, Crystal Fairybelle spends all his time with him. The other day I thought I spotted him curled up on Dad's lap, but I must have been seeing things.

Dad would *never* let that happen.

"By the way, Isabella's been trying to talk to you. There was another missed call from her on Skype," Mum says.

Irk. I've kind of been avoiding her.

Isabella's the daughter of Mum's best friend and has only just moved back to the UK from Italy. She came to stay with us over the summer holidays, and it's fair to say that at first we didn't exactly get on. I accidentally threw a bra on her head (as you do) and said something she took completely the wrong way, then she acted all snooty and mean. I even thought she was trying to take Millie away from me.

Eventually we sorted everything out, and I realised that Isabella's actually super nice, and now we're friends. She's moved to London, into this crazy huge house because Isabella and her mum are *seriously* loaded. We've been messaging and Skyping regularly.

Although I really like Isabella now, I've been ignoring her calls lately.

Because I'm not sure I want to hear all about her fantastic house and fabulous new friends and the fact she's probably been out spending a huge ton of cash when my life is so utterly poo.

I feel really bad for thinking such mean things, though. Just because I'm having a rubbish time, doesn't mean I should take it out on other people, and Isabella's not had an easy ride lately either.

"I'll try to call her back later," I mumble, knowing full well I probably won't.

"Don't forget to put that washing away," Mum says, heading out of the door.

"Um, Mum," I say. I've been trying to figure out how to convince her to let me go to London. "There's something I wanted to ask you."

"Is it about your dad's party?" Mum says. "I'm so excited, it's going to be great! But there's still so much to do: we need to sort out accommodation for people who want to stay over, put together a list of places they can stay, and I'm still waiting to hear back from the musicians – honestly, these people have no sense of urgency. And then there's the cake: we really need to decide what kind of design we want, and what flavour it should be and, of course, how many tiers. I've got a list of jobs for you to do; Harry's useless, and Amber's too busy."

"Great," I say weakly. "But I didn't want to ask you about the party. I, um, was wondering if I could go to London for the day with Millie?"

"London?" Mum frowns. "Why do you want to go to London?"

"To go and see The Drifting," I say. "They're doing this radio interview and Millie and I want to be there. Please, Mum? Please? Pretty please?"

"They're going to let you on the radio?"

"No!" I say in exasperation. "But we can wait outside."

Mum smiles. "I remember I did that for Duran Duran once. It was one of the best moments of my life, and I only saw the top of John Taylor's quiff."

"So I can go?"

"How are you planning on getting there?"

"Um, train I think..."

Mum shakes her head. "I'm not happy about you getting the train by yourself all that way."

"Okay. If we find some other way of getting there, can I go?"

"We'll see," Mum says.

Aaargh! That's nearly a yes!

I bash out a text to Millie.

> **Mum says I cn cum 2 LDN bt can't go on d train. Excitement!!!!**

A reply comes back instantly.

> **Amazes!! I'll ask Mum f she cn driV us.**
>
> **Jamie, dan + me havN a mvie nyt 2nt. Scary films. U in?**

I read the text and shudder. As much as I don't want to be stuck at home on Halloween, I really, *really* don't want to be stuck in a cinema that's showing terrifying movies. Besides, Dad banned me from watching them ever again because he got fed up of me waking him up in the middle of the night to check there wasn't a crazed axe-murderer lurking behind the bathroom door.

Typical, though, the one night my boyfriend can be persuaded to watch something other than *Star Wars*, and it's films I hate.

As there's no way I'm going to be joining my mates tonight, I guess that means a night on the sofa. I could do my maths homework, of course, but who am I kidding? At least I won't have to fight Harry for the TV, she's usually off out trick-or-treating with Dad on Halloween.

Blimey, if Mum goes with them I might even have the whole house all to myself. That hasn't happened for yonks. It's still weird without Amber and Mark and the twins living here. Quiet. Although that's partly because Dad's not shouting so much any more that he's trodden in a dirty nappy, or tripped over a teddy bear.

I immediately start plotting what I'm going to do with my night in.

First, I'm going to cook that pizza Dad hid at the bottom of the freezer. Unlucky, Dad, you can't fool me. Especially when you've hidden it underneath the choc-ices I've disguised in a box of reduced-sugar healthy-living orange lollies.

Mwah-ha-ha-ha.

So. Stolen pizza and TV… I seriously miss our

Netflix subscription. It got culled in the money-saving panic following Amber's wedding and hasn't yet been reinstated. Still, Amber's left loads of her DVDs behind in the cupboard, so maybe I'll find something good there. Something feel-good and funny, without a vampire or zombie in sight. Something that won't give me bad dreams for the next month. I'll have to remember to turn the lights off so the trick-or-treaters don't keep bothering me...

Yeah, I know, I'm a spoilsport. But it's a night to myself! Perhaps I'll leave the tub of sweets outside, then they can help themselves.

After my TV marathon, maybe I'll take a bath; Mum's got some lush new bath oil that she snuck into the house and thinks I haven't seen.

And then I can curl up in my PJs and read my new magazine.

Oooh, it sounds like heaven. Relaxing has not been on the cards much of late.

I head down to the kitchen to see what time people are going out. I arrive at the same time as Dad, who comes through the back door, letting in a huge gust of cold air. He *has* been in the shed, I was right. Crystal's trotting at his heels.

"Did you fancy going out one night later this week?"

Dad's asking Mum. "I was reading about this great new film, looks hilarious…"

"Hmm?" Mum's bum is sticking out of the freezer. She'd better not be going near that pizza.

"Well, Jen?" Dad says.

"What? Oh, um, not this week, sorry. Harry might go with you, is there something you could see with her?"

Dad pulls a chair up to the table, and sits down with a harrumph. "I don't want to see a kids' film. Besides, Harry's always off Skyping that Ant, and now you're turning me down too. Nobody's got time for me any more."

He actually looks proper dejected for a few seconds before he starts flipping through *What Car?* magazine.

"This convertible looks fantastic," he muses, disappointment clearly forgotten.

"You're not getting a two-seater," Mum says, removing herself from the freezer and closing the door firmly.

"You haven't even seen it yet. It's got four seats," Dad protests.

"I don't need to see it. Whatever it is, you're not getting one," Mum says.

"What time are you taking Harry out?" I ask, grabbing a box of popcorn from the cupboard and throwing a packet into the microwave.

Mum straightens up. "I wanted to talk to you about that."

I narrow my eyes suspiciously.

"I was hoping you'd take Harry trick-or-treating."

"What? Why?" I say, my heart sinking. Slowly the dreams of my quiet, relaxing night in are starting to evaporate.

There's a ring on the doorbell. "Wait here," Mum says, grabbing a huge tub of sweets from the side. I reach out to grab one as she passes, but she bats my hand away.

"Trick or treat!" comes the chorus from outside.

"Why do I have to take Harry?" I ask, when Mum returns.

"Amber called about ten minutes ago," Mum says. "She sounds frantic, Chichi and Uni haven't stopped crying all day and she and Mark were wondering if I could go over and cook them tea while they're walking the babies around, so they can actually get something to eat. I thought there was some leftover stew in the freezer, but I can't find it anywhere."

Dad's magazine shoots up to hide his face. Ah. He ate the stew then.

"Anyway, Dad and I are heading over, we'll have to pick something up from the supermarket for them on the way."

"Dad could take Harry instead," I say.

Dad perks up at the thought of an excuse to escape two screaming babies. "I'd be happy to."

"No way," Mum says firmly to him. "We need all hands on deck. Suzy can take her. Harry really wants to go tonight and I don't want her to be disappointed. She was really upset when I told her it might not be happening."

"But, Muuuuum..." I complain through a mouthful of popcorn. "That's so unfair. And I've got so much to do, you know with everything I've got on..." I look at her meaningfully.

"You've been working very hard, give yourself a night off," Mum says. And I can tell she genuinely thinks she's being kind. When actually the thought of escorting my sister around the neighbourhood to get wired on sugar and additives sounds like hell on earth.

"I was going to give myself the night off with a movie," I say.

"Trick-or-treating won't take long, you'll still have time for your film when you get back," Mum says, as Harry walks in. "Harry, you can go out tonight after all."

"I can?" Harry says, doing a little hop of excitement. "Am I going with Dad?"

"No, Suzy's taking you," Mum says.

Harry wrinkles up her nose. "Oh."

"Look, I don't want to go either," I tell her.

"I know you'll have fun once you're out," says my deluded mother. "You'll both have a great time."

"Okay," Harry says, clearly realising that trick-or-treating with me is better than no trick-or-treating at all. "I'll go and get changed. What are you going as, Suzy?"

"I haven't got a costume," I say.

"You need to dress up," Harry says, turning round. "I'm not going if you're not in fancy-dress."

"Well, then, I guess it's decided, we're staying here," I say. "If anyone wants me I'll be hanging out on the sofa, watching my film."

"Nooooooo!" Harry says. "Okay, okay, you don't have to dress up. Please come with me, please!"

"Do you know, I think I've got something you could wear," Mum says thoughtfully. "Wait there a minute, I'll be back in a tick."

She returns a few moments later with a plastic packet tucked under her arm, smiling triumphantly. "Here you go. Now you can properly enter the spirit of things!"

Oh no. Oh no, oh no, oh no.

It's a werewolf costume.

A *werewolf*.

And the picture seems to suggest there's a furry

hood, complete with ears, two gloves with huge claws, a tail and what appears to be a hairy chest wig.

Is she seriously expecting me to go out dressed in that? I mean, really? Surely not even my mother's that insane? But look at how she's smiling at me, all proud and happy that she's found me something to wear.

"Why do you even have this?" I ask, stalling for time.

"Oh, I've had it for ages," Mum says, pulling it out of the plastic and shaking it. A load of hair falls to the floor.

Brilliant. Not only am I destined to be a werewolf, I'm a werewolf with mange.

"I got it for your father to wear to a fancy-dress party before Harry was born," Mum says. "He refused to put it on. If I recall, he went as a hotdog instead."

"Yeah, because that's less embarrassing," I mutter.

"Try it on," Harry says. "I can't wait to see what you look like."

"C'mon, Suze, it's Halloween," Mum says, as she sees me hesitating. "It's dark outside and it's not like you'll see anyone you know."

I shake my head. How do I allow myself get roped into these things? I pull the chest wig over my head and fasten on the hood, before slipping on the gloves.

Mum and Harry crack up. As I catch sight of myself in the mirror, I start to laugh, too. I look utterly ridiculous.

"Arooooooooooooooooooooo!" I howl, throwing back my head.

"Do it again!" Harry begs.

"Arooooooooooooooooooo!"

And then I see Harry's filming.

"Harry! Turn that off!"

"But you look so funny," Harry giggles.

Ah well. In for a penny, in for a pound. And on the plus side, the hood hides my crazy hair. "Will you help me with my tail, please, Mum?"

There's a sentence I never thought I'd say.

As Mum fusses way closer to my butt than I'm entirely comfortable with, I still can't quite believe I'm doing this. But it's Halloween. And nobody will ever know. If I'm going to have to do this, I might as well have a laugh in the process.

"Growl for me," Harry says, still practically falling over with laughter.

"Harry, you've not stopped filming. Turn it off or I'm not taking you," I say. I may be trying to embrace the whole werewolf thing, but there are limits.

"Growl!"

"Grrr," I say, waving my claws around. "Now turn that *off*." Harry leaves the kitchen just as Mum's advancing towards me with Harry's face paints.

"Whoa, what are you doing?" I say.

"You need some make-up. A nose, and maybe something on your eyebrows."

"Oh, for goodness sake, can't we just go?"

"Just the nose then," Mum says.

Before I can duck out of the way she thrusts a brush at my face.

"Aaargh!"

I don't dare twist away through fear of having brown streaks all over my face and ending up looking like a mangy werewolf that's been rolling in poo, or something.

"Keep still, I'm not going to be long," Mum says.

Next time I look in the mirror, I've been given a dark brown nose, with a line leading down to my upper lip, and my eyebrows have expanded significantly.

What do I look like? I seriously can't believe I'm going out in public dressed like this. But I suppose at least nobody will recognise me. *I* hardly recognise me.

Harry walks into the room dressed as Draco Malfoy. Her hair is slicked back, and she's all in black, with a cape swishing out behind her. She's even fashioned a broomstick out of a cane she's nicked from Great Aunt Loon (it's got a 'Property of Meadow Park Nursing Home DO NOT REMOVE' sticker on it).

"Now, don't let Harry eat too many sweets," Mum

says, as she ushers us towards the door. "You know she gets hyper if she's had too much sugar. Here's your treat bag, off you go."

"Can I take some eggs? Or flour?" Harry asks.

"Absolutely not," Mum says.

"Toilet roll?"

"No!" Mum says. "You're not vandalising people's houses."

I swish my tail around by way of goodbye.

I'd actually forgotten how much fun trick-or-treating was, although you'd never hear me say so out loud. There are groups of small kids walking the streets with their parents, all looking super cute in their costumes; I've lost count of the number of little girl ballerinas and fairies and boy bats and pumpkins we see being herded along. Harry's got a pretty good haul of sweets so far. Which means I don't think it's going to be too much longer until I can convince her to go home. This hairy hood is giving me a head sweat. Plus, it's way itchy.

"Let's go here next," Harry says, pointing at a huge, gothic house. It looks really creepy.

"We can't, there aren't any pumpkins outside," I say.

"Yeah, but you wouldn't live somewhere like this unless you liked scary stuff, would you?" Harry says, and she's off up the drive before I can stop her.

"Harry, come back!" I shout. But she's not listening. She's busy knocking on the door when I finally catch her up.

We stand there for what feels like ages.

"Come on, there's nobody in, let's go," I say, trying to tug Harry away, but she starts knocking again.

And then the door is flung open.

"Think you can get me with your trick or treat?" an extremely angry man says "I've been caught out by you terrors before. Coming around demanding sweets. I'll give you a trick you won't forget..."

And with that he produces a bucket. Harry, with more foresight than me, darts out of the way, but I only realise as the water's flying towards me what's about to happen.

I gasp as the freezing-cold water soaks through my fur and clothes and makes contact with my skin. I'm *soaking*.

The man has disappeared back inside, slamming the door behind him. The letterbox clatters and we hear an angry "Now clear off my property before I call the police!"

"Wow," Harry says.

"I told you we shouldn't have gone there," I say, starting to shiver.

"I didn't know he'd be such a grouch, did I?" Harry protests.

"We're going home," I say. "I'm frozen."

"Aw, c'mon, Suze, you're not that wet," Harry says. "Just a bit on your head. Your ears are kind of limp, and maybe your chest wig looks a bit soggy. Can't we stay out for a bit longer? Please? Pretty please?"

"Nope," I say firmly. "You've got loads of sweets already."

"Oh, okay," Harry agrees reluctantly. She yawns as she's saying it, so I know she's getting tired, even though she'd never admit it.

We turn and start the walk home, the streets now emptier of trick-or-treaters than earlier; I guess all the little ones have been taken to bed. Harry and I are walking alongside each other; she's jabbering away non-stop, having hoovered about a third of her sweets already and buzzing on a sugar high.

"Look at that!" Harry gasps, grabbing at my furry arm.

I look where she's pointing and she's right, it's a seriously impressive decorated house. The person who lives there obviously goes in for Halloween in a big way. There are several pumpkins, all carefully carved, lining the path to the house. There are black paper bats stuck to the windows next to the front door, and the bushes and trees have been decorated with cobwebs. There are some little glowing ghost lamps by the doorsteps and an inflatable vampire.

"Please can we knock there? Please?" Harry begs.

I'm shivering now and suspect my wet werewolf look isn't the best. "Harry, I really want to go home."

"Just here. Just this one and then we can go home. I promise I won't ask to go anywhere else."

"Oh, all right." It's easier to give in.

Harry gives an excited twirl of her broom and runs up the path to the front door, where she jumps out of her skin and gives a little scream.

"What is it? What's wrong?" I say, as Harry comes racing back towards me.

"There's a creepy butler on the porch," Harry says, dragging me towards the house. "I thought it was real for a moment. You have to come with me and see."

To the side of the door, hidden inside the porch, is a life-sized butler, standing with his eyes closed, holding a tray of drinks. It is incredibly realistic. As I peer closer, the eyes ping open and a robotic voice says, "Come inside for the fright of your life."

I jump out of my skin. "Aaaaaargh!"

Harry's falling about laughing. "That's what made me jump, too," she squeals, delighted she's managed to catch me out.

"That is one of the creepiest things I've ever seen," I say, as the front door creaks open.

And when I see who's standing there, my heart feels like it stops altogether. It's far and away the scariest thing I've seen all night. Way worse than that butler.

Because standing in the doorway is Kara.

Oh no. Oh no, oh no, oh no.

I had no idea this was her house. Otherwise there's no way in hell I'd have come anywhere near it.

Maybe she won't recognise me. After all, I'm covered in half a ton of synthetic fur and dodgily applied face paint.

"Did the butler get ya?" Kara says, laughing.

Figures she'd get her kicks out of scaring people half to death.

"He's fantastic!" Harry says.

I want to tell my sister not to talk to Kara, not to interact in any way, shape or form because she is much more evil than anything Halloween can conjure up, but I can't. I'll only give myself away.

"Oh, I nearly forgot," Harry says. "Trick or treat!"

"Hey, look, it's Harry!"

A young girl wearing a cat costume has pushed past Kara's legs and is beaming at my sister. Harry grins back.

"Is this one of your friends?" Kara asks.

"Yeah, it's Harry Puttock from school!"

I see the cogs turning in Kara's brain. "Puttock?" she says, before turning to me. "Then..."

"This is my sister, Suzy," Harry says happily. "She's a werewolf. Isn't her costume brilliant? It looked better earlier, before a man threw water on her."

Kara's eyes widen. "Oh this is too, too good... wait here while I get the Halloween treats."

"Harry, we need to go," I say, tugging urgently at my sister's arm.

She shakes me off crossly. "I want to wait for my sweets. I bet they're going to be really good ones."

"Harry," I say warningly, but then Kara's back.

"This is definitely a treat," she says.

Then she holds up a phone and snaps my photo, before thrusting a tub of sweets at us.

"Happy Halloween," she says, grinning with glee.

CHAPTER TWENTY

"**There aren't** enough words in the world to describe how much I don't want to go into school today," I say to Millie, as we walk along the road.

"You should have come and watched films with us," Millie says, then sees me glowering. "Sorry. Not helpful."

"How do Jade and Kara always manage to catch me in such stupid situations?" I ask. "It just keeps happening. I bet that photo's all over the internet by now."

I'm feeling proper down. The party planning is going terribly. There's still no reply from The Drifting, or their record company. And now I've been photographed *again*, while being humiliated, *again*.

I just make it too darn easy for them.

"I completely understand where you're coming from, but honestly, I'm sure it won't be that bad," Millie reassures me. "I'm not saying Kara won't have shown anyone the photo she took, but it's not like the whole school will see it, is it? It'll just be a few stupid people, like Jade and Zach, who we don't like anyway. Who cares what they think?"

I do, I think quietly to myself, although I don't say it out loud. And yes, I know I should be better than that. I really shouldn't care about Kara and Jade.

"Look, they'll laugh about it for a bit and then they'll forget about it," Millie says.

"I hope you're right."

Why did I agree to go out in that stupid werewolf outfit? Why?

"Cheer up," Millie says. "It's the weekend tomorrow and we're off to London, remember?"

We meet the boys by the corner shop on the way to school. Jamie's already stuffing a sausage roll into his mouth.

"Didn't you eat breakfast?" Millie asks.

Jamie nods as he swipes the pastry crumbs away from his mouth with the back of his hand. "I wanted a snack."

"I don't know where you put it all," Millie says.

Danny gives me a hug. "Hey, you. You okay?"

I shrug.

"What's up?"

"She's stressing about the werewolf thing," Millie explains as we start to walk in the direction of the school.

"Suze, worse things have happened and you've survived them. Like the time —"

"All right, all right, I don't need reminders," I say, interrupting him.

"The worst that can happen is that she's shown some mates the pictures," Danny says.

"That's exactly what I told her," Millie says, as we join the crowds entering the school gates as the bell rings.

I might be being paranoid here, but it looks like everyone's staring at us.

I shake my head. This whole Kara thing has got me more rattled than I thought.

But there's definitely a group of people over there pointing. And those guys are laughing...

I'm not so sure I *am* being paranoid now.

"Uh, what's going on?" I ask, as one of the kids from the year below barges past, turning round to laugh and point in my face. There's no missing that.

"I don't know," Millie says.

"People are acting weird, right?" I ask. "It's not me imagining things?"

A piece of A4 paper blows across the tarmac, and then another. There's something printed on it, but I can't see what. Actually there are loads of them. These things are everywhere. Jamie makes a grab for one. "What the —?"

"What is it?" Millie asks, trying to take it from him.

"Nothing!" Jamie says hastily, holding the paper out of her reach. Millie reaches for another piece flying by and her eyes widen in alarm.

"Oh no…"

"What?" I say.

Millie clasps the paper tightly to her chest. "It's nothing. Let's go to registration."

"What's going on with you two?" I say. Has everyone taken a weird pill this morning or something? Why is everyone acting so completely crazy?

I grab at a piece of paper.

"Suzy, don't," Millie says, but it's too late.

On the paper are four photos of me. In one I'm wearing the werewolf costume from last night, looking bedraggled and startled. Another one is of me from earlier this year, when I bumped into Jade in a department store, trying on the ugly bridesmaid's dress Amber made me wear, which was way too huge around the bust area. There's one of me lugging the enormous naked statue through the school. And the kicker – me dressed in a towel and cardigan, looking absolutely mortified as I'm paraded out to wait with the rest of the school during that fire alarm.

My chest tightens and my heart thumps as I stare

down at the images. I can feel tears threating to fight their way out of my eyes.

A selection of my most embarrassing moments, set out for everyone to see. It's like I've come to school wearing only my knickers. I feel totally exposed.

And everyone must have seen these pictures. *Everyone.*

I blink the tears away quickly, so I can read the text.

SUZY PUTTOCK – ORGANISING YOUR FUNDRAISING PARTY!

Then, underneath the photos, it says:

DO YOU REALLY THINK THIS GIRL CAN GET THE DRIFTING TO OUR SCHOOL? THINK ABOUT IT... THIS PARTY'S GONNA BE A DISASTER!

I've got no idea what to say. I can feel my friends huddling around protectively.

Well, there's no prizes for guessing who did this. I know exactly who took all of these photos. Jade and Kara.

I mustn't cry. I mustn't. That's what they want.

But this is so completely humiliating.

"Oh God. Oh God, oh God, oh God," I say.

It's all I can manage. Over and over again.

"Suze, it's okay," Danny says. His voice is tight and angry. "We won't let them get away with this."

"Everyone's seen it. Everyone," I say.

And as we walk inside, it's obvious that I'm right. The pictures are everywhere. Mrs Morgan and Mr Patterson are striding around, taking them down from the walls.

"Come with me to the toilets," Millie says. "You can have a good cry there, get it all out of your system and then we can figure out how to fight back."

"Murder's still illegal, right?" I say, attempting to make a weak joke.

"Yeah. Fraid so," Millie says. "But we'll come up with a Plan B, don't worry about it."

Right when you think things can't get any worse, Mrs Morgan spots me.

"Ah, Suzy, can you come with me, please?"

Just what I need.

Although, actually, this morning, unless I'm very much mistaken, there's sympathy in her eyes. It's kind of hard to tell, though, under all that mascara. Her eyelashes look like spiders' legs.

"Um..."

I don't even know how to respond. It's like my brain's completely scrambled.

"I was taking her to the toilets," Millie says, trying her best to save me. "She's a bit upset."

"I can imagine," Mrs Morgan says. "I know it can't have been very nice coming into school to see this. I'd like to have a quick chat with Suzy. Millie, you're in the same registration group, aren't you? Go and tell your tutor that Suzy will join you in a bit."

Reluctantly, Millie walks off down the corridor, shooting me a sympathetic glance as she hitches her day-glo pink satchel up over her shoulder.

"Let's go into the staff room," Mrs Morgan says. I follow her in and hover awkwardly. It's weird being in here; I haven't seen it from this side of the door before. There's a random selection of brown furniture, posters on the walls and a kettle and a lot of cups on a shelf against one wall.

"Hot chocolate?" Mrs Morgan says, filling up the kettle and switching it on. "It's good for shock."

I can't even bring myself to speak. Instead I nod dumbly.

"Do you have any idea who might have done this?"

I stare at the floor, deliberately avoiding all eye contact.

Of course I know who did it. But there's no way I'm going to say anything.

"Hmm. Well, I can see why you might not want to answer that. I have suspicions of my own…"

I look up to see Mrs Morgan staring at me intently. "There have been quite a few problems with the party lately, haven't there?" she continues gently. "Losing the props budget, nobody volunteering for anything… Don't get me wrong, I don't think it's anything we can't sort out, but it's been hard work for you, hasn't it? And you certainly seem to have been covering for a lot of the other committee members who haven't been doing their fair share."

She noticed? I'm astonished. I thought she was too busy reminiscing about her RADA days.

"Suzy, I'm trying to say this sensitively," Mrs Morgan continues, handing me a mug of hot chocolate. "This has obviously been very embarrassing, and I don't want you to feel that you have to keep going with it all, staying in the full eye of the storm organising the party, as it were. You can take more of a back seat, if you'd prefer."

I think about it. All the stress would go away. All the problems. I wouldn't have to work with Jade or Kara any more.

It's tempting. Oh so tempting, to say, yes, I want out.

And maybe I *should* quit. I could hand the whole thing over to Jade and Kara — they could do the party they wanted all along, with their red carpets and their awards ceremony and annoying Saturday-night celebrities.

But that would mean they'd win.

That would mean Jade and Kara would get what they wanted all along and their bullying would have succeeded. And we've worked hard to try to make this party a success. And yeah, okay, we've not done that well so far, but we're trying. And there's still time. Besides, what would I tell my friends? I don't want to let them down.

I shake my head. "No, I don't want to leave the committee."

"Are you sure?" Mrs Morgan says.

I take a deep breath. "I'm sure. I know this party is going to be a success."

"Okay. And I don't want you to worry, the Head will definitely be getting involved in this whole situation," Mrs Morgan tells me. "This kind of behaviour isn't acceptable, and we don't tolerate bullying here at Collinsbrooke. There will be repercussions for the people who did this."

Mrs Morgan must know it's Jade and Kara. She might be daft, and way too obsessed with all things thespy, but she's not a complete idiot. She's seen how they've been over the last few weeks. And there's not many people in the school who are that nasty.

"If you do find out who did this, you know you can always come and talk to me. And do you know, I've got some friends who work on a music TV channel, I don't know why I didn't think of them sooner, I wonder if they've got access to any costumes? Leave it with me, Suzy, and I'll see what I can do. Enough is enough, I'm not going to let anyone ruin this party of ours."

Wow. Mrs Morgan sounds properly feisty. And I do feel a smidge relieved that it sounds like, at last, we're going to get some proper help. As much as I hate what Jade and Kara have done, maybe this is the very faint silver lining to it all.

"I'll keep you posted. You can go back to registration now," Mrs Morgan tells me, helping herself to a biscuit. "And don't worry about anything. Between us we'll get it sorted."

I let myself out of the staff room and stand in the now empty corridor.

All I can do is hope we make contact with The Drifting in London. Because now, more than ever, I need to prove Jade and Kara wrong.

CHAPTER TWENTY-ONE

When Millie approached her mum, Clare, about getting the train to London, apparently her reaction was even worse than my mum's. I don't quite know what they thought would happen to us on a just-over-one-hour train ride, but Clare's decided to drive us instead, which is brilliant, because that meant Mum had to let me go. Clare's going to drop us off at the radio station where The Drifting are doing their interview, meet her friends for a coffee at a nearby café, then pick us up at lunchtime. We're not exactly sure how long The Drifting are going to be in the building, but hopefully that should give us enough time.

"You can just drop us here, Mum," Millie says, as the car edges its way through the morning traffic at a speed even a snail would sneer at. We're both shifting nervously, desperate to get out. I've been to London a couple of times before and always love staring at the city skyline, watching the crowds of people on the pavements and trying to spot the famous landmarks. But today, I'm too distracted to do any of that.

Despite the stern talking-to I gave myself earlier, my tummy's fizzing with nerves and excitement. We could actually see the band today! Talk to them! I can't believe this might actually happen… I'm refusing to think too much about the fact we also need them to come and play at our school to save my butt. That's way too stressful. Right now I'm trying to stay focused on the fun part.

Clare indicates and pulls the car over. "Get out as quick as you can, girls," she says, over the sound of furious honking from a black taxi behind. "I'm not supposed to stop here. I'll see you later, okay? Good luck!"

Millie runs round and pops the boot, grabbing something from it.

"What's that?" I ask.

Millie grins. "I made a banner." She waves the A3 piece of card at me — on it she's written: 'I LOVE YOU NATE! STOP AND TALK TO US!'

"Thought it might help," she says, sheepishly, as Clare finally manages to pull back out into the traffic and the car moves off.

Then Millie and I are left in front of the London Radio building. It's huge, stretching up towards the clouds high above our heads.

Millie stares across the car park. It's packed, but there are hardly any people to be seen. "See? I told you! There's nobody here!"

It's not until we get round the corner, searching for the main entrance that we see them.

Oh God.

There's an enormous crowd, at least two hundred people, held behind a barrier. In front of the barrier are several burly men, each about the size of a small house. Or at the very least a bungalow.

"Maybe they're not here for The Drifting," Millie says weakly. But the banners waved by girls proclaiming things like 'NATE, I LOVE YOU!' and 'MARRY ME, LIAM!', plus the girls wearing The Drifting T-shirts, badges and holding camera phones, suggest otherwise.

Some of the girls are really dressed up, in tiny bikini tops and denim bum-hugger shorts. Despite the fact it's autumn and freezing cold out here.

A group of four girls sprint past us, screaming, and join the crowds. "Are The Drifting here yet? Have you seen them?" they holler.

I want to cry. The boys were right to stay at home.

They're never going to notice Millie and me. It just won't happen. Even if we do manage to push our way to the front of the crowds, they're not going to stop and have time for a chat.

"What are we going to do?" I say quietly.

"Don't give up yet," Millie says, grabbing my hand and running forward.

"What time did these guys get up to be so near the front?" I say.

"Some of them camped all night," one of the boys standing nearby says. He shakes his head. "I wanted to give them a demo I'd made, but this is hopeless." He stuffs the CD into his jacket pocket and wanders off.

Even if I stand on my tiptoes I'm still struggling to see anything. I've got a view of the backs of lots of people's heads. If I jump in the air, I can just about see the doors... but no way are we going to be able to talk to the band. We're too far away.

"What time are they coming?" Millie says, tapping the arm of a girl in front of us.

"Any time now," the girl says, hopping up and down. "I'm so excited. Oh God, I think I'm going to actually pass out if I see Liam in the flesh. I totally love him. Like, so much."

"Look, I've got a back-up plan," Millie says to me.

"You have? What is it?"

"I wrote them a letter explaining everything," Millie says, taking a red envelope out of her pocket. "In case we couldn't get near enough to talk to them in person. Which we still might be able to – maybe everyone will leave when they go in. If we hang around until they come back out we might be able to talk to them then."

"What about the barriers...?" I begin, but my words are drowned out as suddenly people start screaming.

I've never heard noise like it. There's shrieking and people shouting and yelling the names of the band. All because a black minibus has driven up nearby.

The doors open. I can't see exactly who it is from my frantic jumping, but it's definitely not anyone I recognise. The crowd sags in disappointment as the man who exits waves at us, shouts "Sorry to disappoint you!" then flashes a pass to get inside the building.

But then another minibus pulls up. The doors slide open, the crowd starts screaming again, and this time, there's no doubt it's them. Around me, everyone's going nuts. I jump up and down manically, trying to see through the forest of arms waving phones, posters, banners. I get a brief glimpse of a baseball hat, and what I think is the tip of Nate's waving hand, and then we see them properly as they head up the steps into the building. I grab onto Millie's arm as we jump and scream too, forgetting for a moment that we didn't get to talk to them, because we're so excited to catch a glimpse of the boys in real life.

It's so weird to see them, these people who've only existed to us on TV screens or posters before. Millie's screaming so hard I don't think she's even breathing properly – she's got a humongous crush on Nate Devlin, the lead singer, and seeing him in the flesh is blowing her mind.

It's *The Drifting*. The Drifting are standing right there in front of us!

It's kind of weird how normal they look. Just like ordinary people. And a bit shorter than I'd imagined.

They turn and wave before they go inside, then the door swings shut and they're gone.

Around us girls are crying and hugging their friends. The boys amongst them are trying to look like they're way too cool for such hysteria, but I can tell they're pretty excited by it all too.

"That. Was. Amazing," Millie says, sighing happily.

Around us, a few members of the crowd are leaving, but most of them seem to be staying put. And then the excitement of what we've seen wears off and I remember exactly why we're here. We need to talk to

The Drifting. Or at least get a message to them.

For the next hour we stand in the cold, hoping that the crowd is going to disperse. But no luck.

"I've just had a text from Jamie, they didn't manage to get through on the phone-in. I'm going to have to do something drastic," Millie says. "We'll never get to them like this. I'm going to try and get down the front."

Before I know what's happening, Millie and her banner are shoving through everyone, leaving me standing helplessly at the back.

I wait for what feels like forever before the band come back out. This time they stay a little longer; I can't see properly but I guess they're signing autographs and posing for photos. I can only hope that Millie's made it to the front.

The band eventually leaves and everyone starts to drift away. I scan the crowd, starting to get a bit nervous – after all, right now I'm currently stuck all by myself in the middle of London. And that's a teensy bit scary.

Eventually I see Millie's bright red jacket and sag with relief.

"Did you manage to speak to them?"

Millie shakes her head. "'Fraid not."

My heart sinks.

"I'm sorry," Millie says, giving me a big hug.

"It's okay," I say quietly. "At least you tried."

"Those girls at the front were hardcore. Not surrendering their spaces for anything or anyone. But I did pretend to feel faint to get the attention of one of those minder guys, and gave him my letter. He said he'd give it to the band for me... if we wait until everyone's gone we can ask if he did it or not. Mum's not coming back for another twenty minutes."

Soon we're the only two left standing in front of the building, and the minders are dismantling the barriers.

"I gave the letter to that guy," Millie says, pointing. She runs over.

The man looks up. "The band have left," he says shortly. "And no, I can't get you their phone numbers or their email addresses. I work for the radio station, not The Drifting."

"I gave you a letter for the band," Millie says. "It was in a red envelope. Did you manage to give it to them? You said you would..."

The man reaches into his jacket pocket and pulls out a bundle of letters, pictures and postcards. Millie's red envelope is easy to spot amongst them.

"But you said..." Millie's voice trailed off.

"I say whatever I have to, to keep things under control," the man says. "I get given all kinds of junk."

He turns and throws the handful of papers into the bin. Millie's letter disappears with them. "Sorry," he says, shrugging.

That's it then. Our last chance, blown.

The Drifting won't be coming to our school. It's time to accept that I'm finished at Collinsbrooke.

Game over.

CHAPTER TWENTY-TWO

"**Everyone ready?**" Mum says chirpily.

"Yes!" Harry squeals, running down the stairs at top speed, phone in one hand, videoing as she goes.

I wish I could be as excited as Harry about Bonfire Night. But to be honest, the last thing I feel like doing right now is celebrating anything.

Maybe it's time I started looking into boarding schools in Timbuktu, or something. I bet they've never even heard of The Drifting there.

"Where's your dad?" Mum asks.

I shrug. "Shed, probably."

Mum shakes her head. "Honestly, he's never out of there these days. I thought he'd miss the TV, but apparently not. Can you go and get him please, Suzy? Tell him we're ready to go."

Outside, fireworks are already exploding in the sky,

even though it's still pretty early.

I've put my hand out to pull open the shed door, when I hear Dad inside, speaking softly to someone.

"There, there, it's fine, it's nothing to worry about…"

Eh? Who's he talking to? Especially in that voice. I hesitate. All sorts of things are going through my mind. Dad's not in there with another woman, is he? Oh God. My stomach's actually churning at the thought. Too gross for words. And what about Mum? Oh, poor Mum, busy planning him a surprise party, roping us all in to do things for him when he's off canoodling with someone else. What if they get divorced? Aaaargh, this is horrible!

I take a deep breath. Rein it in, Suze. You're getting totally carried away.

But even so, I'm still not charging in there. Just in case.

I go round the side of the shed and cup my hand to the glass, peering inside. Then a firework lights up the sky above me in a shower of pink and I get a better view. I can't see anyone apart from Dad. So who was he talking to then? Is he on the phone to someone? It doesn't look like it…

Dad glances up at the window and jumps out of his skin.

"Aaaaaargh! Who's that?" he yells, leaping up from his chair. There's a horrified yowling noise.

I rush to the door and charge in. "It's me!"

Dad clasps his hand over his chest in shock. "You almost gave me a heart attack. What on earth are you doing, sneaking around?"

"I, um... I heard you talking to someone. I was trying to see who it was."

Dad looks sheepish. "Oh. That."

"So who was it?"

Dad clears his throat. "Um. It was the, er, dog."

"The dog?"

I'm seriously confused.

"Come here, boy," Dad says, making a clicking noise.

Out of the corner of the shed, tummy so close to the ground he's practically belly-crawling, comes Crystal Fairybelle. Dad picks him up and cuddles him close, stroking his head affectionately.

"Er, what's going on with you and Crystal?" I ask. "You two are always together these days. I didn't think you liked him?"

Dad immediately puts his hands over Crystal's ears. "Don't say that," he hisses. "The dog was scared, weren't you?"

Dad holds Crystal up in the air, and Crystal licks at

his nose affectionately. "The fireworks were terrifying him. I was only trying to make him feel better. Us boys have got to stick together, haven't we?"

Who is this man, and what's he done with my father?

"What did you want, anyway?" Dad asks, still stroking Crystal, who's wriggling with delight.

"Um, Mum says we're leaving soon for Amber's."

At the mention of Amber's name, Crystal Fairybelle pricks up his ears and starts whining, struggling frantically to escape Dad's clutches.

"Whoa, whoa!" Dad says, putting him down onto the floor, where Crystal runs and starts scratching at the door to be let out. As soon as it's opened, he races off towards the house.

"I think the fireworks have really unsettled him," Dad says, following me towards the back door where Crystal's now sitting whining. I'm about to turn the handle when Dad puts his hand on my shoulder.

"Um, there's something I wanted to ask you," he says. "It's about your mum... she is okay, isn't she?"

"Why are you asking me this again?" I say, slightly defensive. I don't want to accidentally give anything away. There's no way he can find out about the surprise birthday party now. Not after all the work we've done. Mum will go mad!

"It's just she's seemed, I don't know, very distant lately. I'm a bit worried about her. Has she said anything?"

"She seems absolutely fine to me," I say.

"Right. Maybe it's only me she's being weird around then."

"Maybe!" I say brightly, and open the door.

"There you are," Mum says, shoving her purse into her handbag as we come into the kitchen. "Were you in the shed again?"

"He was hanging out with Crystal," I say, ignoring Dad's ferocious scowl.

"I thought you hated that dog," Mum says.

"That's exactly what I said," I say, grabbing my coat.

"I wasn't hanging out with Crystal," Dad protests, as Harry walks in.

"Don't you hate the dog?" Harry says.

"Will everyone stop saying that!" Dad shouts. "I was in the shed. Crystal was in the shed. Crystal got scared by the fireworks and I picked him up, trying to make him feel better. That's all!"

"Seemed like more than that to me," I say, deliberately stirring. It's proper funny how wound up Dad's getting by all of this.

"Right, are we all ready?" Mum says, jangling the car keys. "Let's go... We need to stop at the shop on the way to pick up some sparklers. Harry, put Hagrid back in his cage, please."

"Aww, I wanted to show Amber and Mark a new magic trick I've been practising," Harry says.

"You know how Amber feels about Hagrid being around her babies," Mum says. "Put him back, quick as you can, please. And you're not coming, either." Mum directs the last comment at Crystal Fairybelle, who's still sitting hopefully in front of the door.

The dog stares up at her mournfully.

"I mean it. You're not coming."

Crystal turns his gaze to Dad.

"No can do, Sonny Jim," Dad says. "Off to bed."

Crystal actually sighs, and then skulks away, passing Harry on the way back into the hall.

"Are we finally ready?" Mum says.

I'm about to shut the door behind us when the phone starts ringing.

"Oh for heaven's sake, who's that?" Mum says.

"Leave it," Dad says, but Harry's already run back to pick it up.

"It's Angie, from Aunt Loon's nursing home," she tells us.

"Stop calling her that," Mum hisses, picking up the phone.

As we wait around it's clear from Mum's end of the conversation that we're going to be doing a detour via the nursing home to visit Aunt Loon. Ugh. That woman's a nightmare. Annoyingly Mum feels really responsible for her as she's practically the only relly left in her family. Aunt Loon rings – or rather, gets her helper to ring – all the time, complaining about something or other. And people say teenagers are high-maintenance – they've got nothing on stroppy old ladies.

"I promised Aunt Lou some magazines," Mum says when she gets off the phone. "I meant to drop them in earlier, but didn't do it because I got held up at work. Apparently she's kicking off, you know what she's like. We'll have to pop in. Poor Angie sounds terribly upset."

"Ugh, that woman," Dad says, rolling his eyes. "She terrorises those carers."

"I know, I know, she's impossible," Mum says. "But she's old, and I don't want her to have another bad night. I'll drop these bits in, it won't take long, then once she's calmed down we can go on to Amber's."

"Okay, okay, fine," Dad says. "But we're already running pretty late."

"Well, at least it'll give them a chance to get supper ready," Mum says. "Guaranteed they'll be running later than us."

So we stop at the nursing home. Mum dashes in with the magazines, and is inside forever, finally returning to the car looking flustered.

"Sorry, she insisted on looking through them with me, telling me she'd missed me and that she hadn't seen me in such a long time," Mum explains, clipping in her seatbelt.

"You shouldn't let her guilt-trip you like that," Dad says, as he pulls out of the car park.

When we finally arrive at Amber and Mark's house, over an hour later than we said that we'd be there, we ring the doorbell and stand outside for ages waiting.

"Aren't they in?" Dad says, frowning. He reaches forward and presses the bell again.

Then, suddenly, the door flies open and Amber's standing in front of us.

"Shhhhh!" she hisses, flapping her hands wildly.

I hardly recognise her, she looks so awful.

She's wearing slobby joggers and a T-shirt that's covered in what can only be baby puke. Her hair has been scragged back in a clip, strands falling all over the place, and there are huge bags under her eyes. And she's not wearing any make-up. I don't remember ever seeing her without mascara and lippy before.

"What are you all doing here?" Amber says.

"Er, you invited us over for supper?" Mum says. "I'm sorry we're so late. Are you all right? You look... um..."

"Rough as a badger's bottom," Harry suggests helpfully.

Amber makes a face, and then sees the phone Harry's holding up. "Are you trying to take a photo?" she shrieks, grabbing for the phone. "Don't you dare!"

"I'm filming my life story," Harry says, ducking out of the way.

"Stop it," Amber says, turning to Mum. "Make her stop!"

"Put the phone away, please!" Mum says. "I mean it," she adds firmly, seeing that Harry's about to protest.

"I didn't think you were coming until tomorrow," Amber says. She huffs a piece of hair out of her eyes.

"We did say Bonfire Night," Mum says.

"Isn't Bonfire Night tomorrow?"

A huge rocket goes off behind me and explodes in the sky with an enormous bang. And then from inside the house comes a furious crying.

Amber's shoulders slump. "Oh God, they're awake again."

"Can we come in?" Dad says.

Amber moves aside and we all shuffle through the tiny stairwell, past the buggy and a teetering tower of unpacked cardboard boxes into the lounge.

It's nice here. Or at least it would be, if it wasn't such a tip. There's stuff chucked everywhere. There are more cardboard box towers in here; it doesn't look like much has been unpacked. There are also baby clothes, muslins, bottles, nappies, changing equipment, toys and half-drunk mugs of herbal tea all over the place.

Dad's tripped over the baby gym when Mark emerges from the kitchen looking seriously frazzled. He's holding Uni, who's screaming at the top of her voice. She's usually the quiet one.

Mum rushes over. "Shall I take her?"

Mark hands her over gratefully. "Thanks. We didn't know you were coming tonight. Are you just passing through?"

"You invited us for dinner," Mum says. "It's Bonfire Night, remember?"

Mark slaps his forehead with the palm of his hand. "We totally forgot. I'm so sorry. Things have been a bit fraught round here today."

"So we see," Dad says, gazing around.

Mark collapses onto the sofa, putting his head in his hands.

Everyone looks at each other, not really knowing what to do.

Well, this is all kinds of awkward.

Mum walks Uni back into the kitchen for a bit and eventually her cries die down, just in time for a high-pitched wail to come down the stairs.

"Oh lordy, that's the other one. Why won't they stop crying?" Mark says in despair. He takes a deep breath and pushes himself up to standing.

"I'll go," Dad says. On the way to the door he successfully avoids the play gym this time but stands on a stripy cow that lets out an indignant squeak. He reappears a few minutes later, holding a very grumpy Chichi.

"I'll go and make a start on dinner," Amber says. "Markymoo, why don't you give me a hand?"

"Harry, set the table, please," Mum asks.

Harry grumbles a bit but does as she's told.

A few moments later, Amber's calling us through.

There are a few spaghetti hoops on each plate, and that's it. And I mean a few. Like, about eight. It looks like Amber's split a single tin of hoops between the six of us.

"Is this it?" Dad says. His tummy growls loudly.

"You're bringing in the toast, right?" Harry says.

"We don't have a lot of food in," Amber says apologetically. "I've been doing the banana and avocado diet this week. You can have some avocado with it, if you like?"

Mmm, spaghetti hoops and avocado. Excuse me while I chunder.

"Amber, you need to eat properly," Mum says. "Stop these ridiculous diets. You need to eat well now you've got the girls to look after."

"But I'm still trying to lose my baby weight," Amber protests.

Mum shakes her head. "You're not fat. Don't be ridiculous. It'll come off when it's good and ready. Nine months to go on, nine months to come off."

"Is this really all we're having?" Dad says. Mum gives him a glare.

We finish our food in about two mouthfuls. Mum eats hers a hoop at a time, trying to eke out the meal, but even she finishes in under a minute. *And* she's holding a sleeping Uni so she's doing it one-handed.

"Pudding?" Amber asks.

"There's pudding?" Dad asks, cheering right up.

His face falls when Mark returns to the table with a Curly Wurly broken into small pieces.

"There's only five bits," Harry says. Opposite me, I can see her secretly filming everything.

"I'm not having any," Amber says, popping a chunk of banana into her mouth.

This is the most hilarious dinner in the history of the

world ever. Who seriously serves spaghetti hoops and Curly Wurly?

"Don't you have any other food in?" Mum asks. "Nothing at all? Mark's not on the banana diet, is he?"

Amber's eyes fill with tears. "The babies have been crying all the time… and I tried to go out today but then one pooed and then they needed feeding and then they pooed again and then we all fell asleep."

"They haven't been sleeping very well," Mark adds. "Uni always used to be pretty good, but they're waking each other up all the time at the moment. This week has been awful."

"Right, that's it," Mum says. "I knew I should have been helping more."

"I can do it," Amber protests.

"Of course you can," Mum agrees. "But I can still give you a hand. Now, first thing tomorrow I'm going to go to the shops to pick up some shopping and then I'm coming to help you unpack your things and sort the house out a bit. I'd also like you to think about making an appointment with the doctor, to go in and chat things over."

"But…" Amber starts to protest, but Mark cuts in.

"That would be great. Thank you. Ambypamby, you need a hand while I'm at work. You're the best mummy in the world, but we need to eat properly. And I can't keep knocking over the boxes all the time. What if one falls and crushes one of our princesses?"

Amber looks horrified.

"Okay, Mum. If you don't mind coming that would be great. Thank you."

"I'll see you tomorrow then," Mum says. She nods decisively and pops her piece of chocolate into her mouth.

We're all so starving we go via the drive-thru on the way home.

CHAPTER TWENTY-THREE

As I walk through the school gates, I'm thinking hard. I've been thinking a lot lately. About how this is all a complete mess and I can't see any way out of it. We've got nothing organised – no props, no band, nothing that even vaguely resembles a party. Rumours have even started circulating since the leafleting that the party's not going ahead. Mrs Morgan said she'd help us, but I haven't heard anything from her for days.

I think we're almost at the point where we're going to have to confess that The Drifting won't be coming. We tried. We tried so flipping hard, harder than I've ever tried at anything else in my life before, but we failed.

Because after emails, Facebook messages, phone calls and even a try at a face-to-face meeting, all attempted contact with The Drifting has amounted to nothing.

And as if that wasn't bad enough, Jamie told us this morning that there was a note left out on the breakfast bar reminding his mum to call the estate agent back in London about a property. It looks like there's a very real chance he could be leaving Collinsbrooke. Millie's a mess.

"Uh, Suzy?"

I'm snapped out of my daydream of gloom by April the Goth. To be honest, she's one of the last people I want to see right now. I've been trying to keep a low profile from the other committee members.

"Hi," I say weakly.

"Um, I saw those flyers," April says.

Is that why she's stopped me, to tell me that? Because let's be honest, who didn't?

"It was Jade and Kara, right?" April goes on. "My friends heard it from some other kids."

I shrug. I'm not going to start snitching. Everyone know – it's not like I have to start blabbing.

"They're just so horrible," April says. "I feel so bad for what they did to you. You've been trying your best. They're only jealous because you said that you could get The Drifting to the school and beat their idea."

Yeah, yeah, I think, wondering how fast I can escape. Although I know April means well.

"Everyone's been seriously impressed with how you've handled things," April continues. "I'd have never come back to school again if they'd done that to me."

"Thanks," I say, smiling weakly.

"I wanted to quickly talk to you about something," April says. "I know there's been problems with the budgets and stuff, and we don't have much to spend on the party. I don't know if you know my friend Louisa?"

I rack my brains and eventually realise who she's talking about. Louisa is so shy she's practically invisible. She's not in any of my classes, but I have seen her with April a few times.

"Er, yeah, I think so," I say. I still don't have a clue what Louisa's got to do with me. Or with Jade and Kara.

"Her mum's a set designer," April goes on. "A good one. She's worked in the theatres for ages, proper stuff, like in the West End. Lou told her mum what's been going on, and how nasty Jade and Kara have been to you, and Lou's mum wondered if you wanted to borrow four thrones. You know, for the judges to sit on?"

I can hardly believe what I'm hearing.

"Are you serious?" I ask.

Okay, so it's only four fancy chairs, but it's a start. One less thing to worry about.

April nods.

"That would be amazing!" I say. "Thank you so, so much. I can't wait to tell Millie."

"No problem," April says. "And my dad said he'd still donate that tablet from his shop, you can use it for the raffle, or for a prize for the best act."

"You're kidding?" I stare at her in delight. This gets better and better!

"No problem," Amber says. "I'm really sorry for not doing more, we all are. Jade and Kara kind of made it clear we weren't allowed to help you guys and there'd be trouble if we did."

"They what?"

April shrugs apologetically. I should be more shocked, but to be honest, I wouldn't put anything past those two.

"We should have all stood up to them earlier. But better late than never, right? We're going to work together to make this party unbelievable. I've spoken to the others – Ryan, Zach and Max were being rubbish but Sophie and Eve are in. I'll have a chat to you at the next meeting about what you want and let Lou's mum know," April says.

Well, that's good news at least. At least now the room will have *something* in it.

To my surprise, that's just the start. Everywhere I go, people are stopping me. Seems everyone's heard the rumours that Jade and Kara were behind the flyers, and also that they were blackmailing people not to help out with the party planning. Some want to say how sorry they are about it all, but others are offering great things for the party. Loads of people are volunteering to do the judging. Someone else has said their cousin will come and DJ for us after the singing competition. And lots of people know businesses that can donate more amazing prizes for the raffle.

To my amazement, all of a sudden it's looking like the party might not be a total disaster after all.

Seems that Jade and Kara have peed off a lot of people, and now everyone's had enough. Especially when it looks like they're putting the party that everyone's been looking forward to so much at risk.

So at long, long last, things don't seem so doom-laden. Except for the part about The Drifting, of course. That's still a nightmare. But the rest of the stuff seems to be coming together really well. And maybe – just maybe – we'll be able to have a good party without The Drifting. If only we could brainwash everyone and make them forget they were ever supposed to be coming.

"Emergency meeting!" Millie says, grabbing my arm.

"What?"

"Mrs Morgan's called an emergency meeting," she says.

* * *

"Right then," Mrs Morgan says when we're all there, staring around the table with a steely look. Even Jade and Kara look a bit alarmed. "It's clear that I've taken my eye off the ball regarding this party, but as we haven't got much time left, that's all going to change. Suzy has been working very hard to manage and organise things for us —"

There's a snort from Kara and Jade's end of the table.

"And it's become clear to me that she's been working under very difficult circumstances and without the support of a lot of you," Mrs Morgan says firmly. "All of this is going to change. As I'm sure you're aware, Suzy has been the victim of a very nasty slander campaign. While we're yet to track down the perpetrators, I want us all to start pulling together to make this party the best it can be. Now, Suzy. Could you give us an update into what's happening, please?"

For the first time since this whole sorry mess started, I don't feel like I want to be sick when I start talking through the party arrangements. As of today, we've now got music backing tracks, a DJ, thrones and a caterer.

"That all sounds wonderful," Mrs Morgan says, nodding.

"How's the stage coming on?" I ask Jamie and Danny.

"Um, well, there's still a bit left to do, painting and stuff," Danny mumbles.

"But it will be finished for the party, won't it?" says Millie, eyeballing them fiercely.

"Yup," Jamie says hastily. He knows better than to say anything else.

"Jade and Kara have been sorting the decorations," I say.

"And how's that going?" Mrs Morgan asks.

"All fine," Jade says. "Nothing to worry about."

Let's hope they're telling the truth. Somehow I doubt it.

"Can we get a bit more detail than that?" Mrs Morgan presses. "What are the decorations going to be?"

"It's going to look great and it's all under control. All in keeping with the music theme. My mum's on the PTA, she knows what's going on," Jade says breezily. "It'll all be sorted for the party and we'll get there early to get the room looking fantastic. Don't worry about a thing."

"Right, okay," Mrs Morgan says, although she sounds unsure.

"Um, we still need to get some costumes for people to wear for when they're performing," I say nervously. "We've been struggling to get anyone to lend them to us."

Mrs Morgan taps a pen against her teeth thoughtfully. "I haven't heard back from my friend yet, but I'll keep chasing. Apart from that, it sounds to me like everything is coming together brilliantly. I know we haven't discussed The Drifting's attendance, but I get the impression Millie and Suzy are handling that and it's all under control. Give me a call if you need anything, girls, okay? I'm really looking forward to seeing them."

Oh yes. The Drifting.

The sick feeling returns to my stomach. Because it doesn't matter how great the rest of the party is, The Drifting is what everyone really wants.

And they're not going to be there.

CHAPTER TWENTY-FOUR

Lack of The Drifting apart, it's actually looking like we've got a pretty decent event lined up at the school now. I still don't want to be there for it, because I'm pretty sure I'll be lynched when the band don't show, but hopefully people will be slightly less angry than they would have been with no band *and* an entirely rubbish party.

There's so much still to do, and not forgetting Dad's birthday party as well. I'm about to get cracking with some of my to-do list when Isabella's Skype avatar starts flashing and bleeping on the PC screen.

I can't avoid her forever. I hit the video answer button, and arrange my features into a smile.

"Whoa, what's up?" Isabella asks.

"What do you mean?"

"Something's going on with your face," she says. "You look like you haven't slept in forever."

"Wow. Thanks."

Isabella's not exactly known for her tact. If something's on her mind, she doesn't have a filter to stop it coming out of her mouth. She starts laughing. "Noooo, I didn't mean it like that. I just mean… what's up?"

I sigh heavily.

"C'mon, spill," Isabella says.

So I start to explain to Isabella what's been going on. About how nasty Jade and Kara have been, and how I opened my mouth and said things I shouldn't have, and made promises I couldn't keep, and how everything's gone all sorts of wrong and even though everyone's started pulling through for me, it's still not going to be what they're expecting. There's hardly any time left now until the party and I'm going to have to show up and face the music and endure eternal humiliation and I'll probably get booted out of school for lying to the teachers.

Isabella listens carefully, interjecting with the occasional 'uh huh' or 'wow'.

"So, that's what's been going on," I conclude, miserably.

Isabella looks thoughtful.

"Say something!"

"You know, you can't let Kara and Jade win," Isabella says. "Especially with all your history. They want you to be freaking out and feeling horrible, but it sounds like you've arranged a really amazing party for everyone. Okay, so it's not going to be as good as if The Drifting were there but people can't really be expecting them to come, can they?"

I shrug.

"I don't even want to go to the party," I say. "I'm going to give it a miss."

"You have to go," Isabella says firmly. "I mean it. No matter what happens you can't give Jade and Kara the satisfaction."

"I don't have anything to wear, and everyone will be horrible."

"They might not," Isabella says. "And I bet Millie's got something you could borrow. Or Amber. Look, the party might not be as bad as you think. Promise me you'll go. Promise me you won't let those bullies win."

I stare at her.

"Promise," Isabella says. "You're better than this. Your party sounds fantastic!"

"Okay, I promise," I say. I figure Isabella won't know what I end up deciding to do anyway.

"Good. It does sound like it's been a complete nightmare, I – hang on, Mum's calling me. Yeah?" she shouts over her shoulder.

Behind Isabella I see her bedroom door open and Caro walks in.

"Sorry, sweetie, are you on Skype? Didn't realise. We need to leave in five minutes, okay? Is that Suzy you're talking to? Hi, Suze! All okay with you guys? Your mum well?"

"Yep, we're all good," I say.

"I'm sorry, I've got to go," Isabella says, as Caro leaves the room. "But I'll give you a shout if I come up with anything that might be helpful, yeah? Don't give up. The answer's out there somewhere, you've just got to find it."

"Thanks." I smile weakly, and then Isabella's gone.

I collapse face forward onto the keyboard.

"Hey, careful!" Mum says from behind me.

I sit up, pushing my hair back from my face.

"Everything all right?"

"Yeah," I lie.

"Good. Just be careful with the PC please. We can't afford a new one. You'll never guess what I've found for your dad's party," Mum says. "A photo booth! You hire them and they have silly props to wear, and people get their photos taken in them. It'll be brilliant!"

"I thought we were doing this party on a budget, Mum?" I say.

Mum flaps her hand around. "Ooh, shhh. It'll be fine. It wasn't expensive." She hesitates. "Well, not *that* expensive. And it'll pay for itself."

"How?"

"Because you can't put a price on people having a good time," Mum says firmly. "Now, your dad and I are popping out for a bit. We're going to a show at Aunt Lou's home; they're performing songs from the wartime years."

I snigger. "I bet Dad's delighted."

"He's not exactly overjoyed, true," Mum says. "But singing is good for you. Lowers the blood pressure and has all sorts of other health benefits. He'll enjoy it once he gets there."

Somehow I doubt it. Especially because Aunt Loon's best friend Margy has taken a real fancy to Dad. She gets dead flirty whenever he's around, keeps stroking his arm and winking. Mum finds it absolutely hilarious. Dad... well, not so much.

"You can come along if you like," Mum offers.

"No thanks, I'm good. Are you taking Harry?"

"She's got a science project to finish. She's under strict orders not to leave her room until it's done."

That means I sort of get the house to myself. What a result.

It'll give me a chance to go through some of the outstanding jobs I've got to do for the parties, and catch up on homework. I'm way behind.

I'm halfway down the stairs when the doorbell rings. Ugh. Who's that?

"Surprise!" says Danny.

"I'm confused," I say. "What are you doing here?"

"Surprising you," Danny says. "Are you going to invite me in, or what?"

"Uh, yeah," I say, standing aside. "We didn't have plans, did we?"

Danny leans forward to give me a kiss. "I thought you could use a night of distraction," he says. "So I brought snacks – crisps, with dip, and the biggest bag of chocolates they had in the shop, plus a movie."

I open my mouth, but Danny gets in first. "It's not *Star Wars*, don't worry. I chose something I hope we're both going to like – it's a comedy."

My insides go all squidgy. My life may be in meltdown, but my boyfriend's still pretty amazing.

"I wish I could, but I can't," I protest. "I've got so much still to do for the party…"

"No," Danny says. "You need a night off."

"But –"

"But nothing."

272

I think about all there is still to do. Playlists and checklists and... arrrgh! But Danny's right. I do need some time out.

"Okay, thanks," I say, wrapping my arms around his waist to give him a big hug.

"Your parents are out, right?" Danny says.

"Yeah, they've gone to see Aunt Loon butcher some war songs."

"Sounds like a treat. And Harry?"

"She's here. But she's working on a science project and has been banned from leaving her room until she's finished."

Danny grins. "Fantastic!"

We grab some drinks and head through to the lounge, where Danny chucks his coat onto the chair, then rummages through his backpack before throwing over a huge bag of Minstrels.

Last time we attempted a romantic evening, it all went horribly wrong. Danny rocked up with a *Star Wars* DVD (possibly the least romantic movie in the history of the world) and then Harry ended up gatecrashing the whole thing. A romantic evening for three doesn't really work so well.

As the opening credits come on I start to relax, and I even laugh at some of the stupid stuff happening on the screen. This is the first time I've felt even remotely chilled in weeks. This was just what I needed. My boyfriend is the best.

I cuddle into his side and he kisses the side of my head. I turn to look at him and he lowers his lips onto mine for a long, tender kiss.

"Mmmm," I say, as Danny pushes my hair away from my face and stares into my eyes.

Then I see a movement in the doorway.

"Harry, what are you doing?" I say, absolutely furious as I jump to my feet.

"Nothing," Harry says, giggling.

"Were you filming us?"

"Maybe."

Gah. There is no torture in the world evil enough for my little sister. She's such a freaking nightmare.

"Give me that phone," I demand.

"No," Harry says.

"Gimme. Now. I mean it," I say, holding out my hand.

"No chance."

"Then at least delete the video," I order. "Danny, help me out here."

Harry loves Danny. Like, proper loves him. I know full well she'd swap me for him in a heartbeat. If he's on my side I might be in with a chance of that footage not getting spread all over the place.

"Hiya, Harry. You need to do what Suzy says and delete that," Danny tells her.

"Aw, but, Danny..."

"No buts," Danny says. The tips of his ears have gone pink. Apparently the threat of a film of him kissing me going public is what it takes to get him to act all forceful. "It's not cool to film people without them knowing about it. And if you do, they have to give their permission for you to use it. Which neither Suze or I will. So delete."

"Oh all right," Harry grumbles, crinkling up her nose and pressing a few buttons. "It's gone."

"Don't you have homework you should be doing?" I ask pointedly. "Mum said you weren't to leave your bedroom until you'd finished it."

"All done," Harry says.

"Really?" I so don't believe her. If she's telling the truth, I'm a water buffalo. "You going to show me?"

"I "

Harry's saved from having to come up with an excuse by the doorbell ringing.

I'm cursed. Seriously. Who's here now? Are Danny and I ever going to be left in peace? We have a movie to watch, people!

"Do you have to answer it?" Danny asks.

I peep out of the corner of the curtains, and my heart sinks when I see it's Amber and Mark standing outside, each with a car seat containing a baby.

The way my big sister's been lately, I can't leave her standing on the doorstep. She might have a total meltdown.

"It's Amber," I say.

"I think I'll make a move," Danny says.

"No, don't leave," I beg. "Please, they might not be staying long..."

The doorbell rings again, for longer this time.

"I'll get it!" Harry shouts. She opens the door and I can hear Amber and Mark coming inside. Uni and Chichi are with them, but for once they don't seem to be crying.

"Hi, you two," Amber says, coming into the lounge. "How's it going? Ooh, you've got the new film with thingy in – look, Mark, it's that movie Conni G was going on about in her last column. Is it good?"

"I don't know, we've hardly got to watch any of it yet," I say through clenched teeth.

Amber bends to unclip Uni from the car seat.

"Shouldn't they be in bed?" I ask.

Mark rolls his eyes. "Bedtime's horrible at the

276

moment. They refuse to sleep. So we've given up."

"The colic medicine from the doctor should hopefully help them settle," Amber says. "Would you like a cuddle with your Aunty Suzypoos, Uniwoo? I know you've been dying to get a snuggle-wuggle, haven't you?" Amber coos, lifting Uni into the air.

"No, Amber, it's —"

I don't get a chance to finish my sentence before Uni's deposited into my arms and Amber's collapsed onto the sofa with a sigh of pleasure.

"I'm so tired," she says. "Where's Mum and Dad?"

"Gone to see Aunt Loon singing," Harry says.

"Oh yeah, that's right," Amber says. "That's a shame. I wanted to see Mum, and tell her how I got on at the doctor's."

"Is everything okay?" I ask. I'm a bit distracted by Uni, who's giving me an enormous, gummy smile. Talk about cute! That's the first time she's done that. The babies are actually pretty adorable now they're more smiley and not screaming all the time. I'm sure Amber and Mark would disagree, but that's the brilliant thing about being an auntie, isn't it? I just get to be there for the good bits, and hand them back when they get too loud.

"Yeah, Mum's been bugging me to go and see the GP for ages. Because of the stress of the babies and stuff," Amber says. "The whole mothering thing has been harder than I thought it would be. The doctor told me I need to stop the dieting, I'm not getting enough nutrients or something and it's making me ill."

"I've said all along you're beautiful the way you are," Mark says, leaning over to kiss her cheek.

"The doctor also gave me the contact details for a twins group, so we're going to go and make some new twinny friends, aren't we?"

As Amber snuggles into her husband, I realise my sister seems happier than I've seen her since the babies were born.

Danny clears his throat and shifts awkwardly from foot to foot. Amber's probably getting a bit too personal for him. This sort of stuff makes him majorly uncomfortable. "Um, I'm going to go."

"Don't leave on our account," Mark says, putting Chichi across his chest. "We're not staying long."

"Nah, you're all right," Danny says. "Nice to see you all."

I pass Uni to Harry and then follow him out to the hall where we stand, staring at each other dejectedly. "We don't have much luck, do we?" Danny says.

"You can say that again. But thanks so much for doing this."

"I'll see you at school, yeah?" Danny pulls open the front door. Then he pauses, and looks back. "Suze…"

"Hmmm?"

"I wish there was a way I could make everything better. Whatever happens, though, you know it'll all work out, right? And I'll be here for you, no matter what."

My insides melt at his words. He doesn't say stuff like this very often.

He wraps his arms around me as I snuggle into his chest. As I look up at him, he smiles sweetly, then lowers his head to mine. His lips are soft, and he tastes faintly of chocolate.

"Night," he says. I watch him walk down the path, feeling better than I have for ages.

CHAPTER TWENTY-FIVE

IT'S THE MORNING of the parties and I've not slept. At all.

I've spent the entire night staring up at my ceiling, tossing and turning. I tried counting sheep. I tried focusing on calming seas. I tried deep breathing. I tried every flipping thing I could think of but I couldn't nod off.

I've just got too much going on, my brain won't stop buzzing.

Because not only is it Dad's party later, today is also the day of The Party Of Doom Where The Drifting Won't Show and Everyone Will Kill Me.

We had our last committee meeting yesterday, and Mrs Morgan has suddenly stepped up, turning into a total drama stresshead and getting everything whipped into shape (I think she finally realised her reputation was on the line if the party didn't work out and there was a distinct possibility she'd never be allowed to organise any plays ever again). We've worked our butts off, coordinating everything.

But however hard we've worked, at the end of the day it's going to be a room without The Drifting in it. And people are counting on seeing the band. That's what they bought their tickets for, after all.

Oh God. My stomach flips over.

I know the rest of the party will be amazing, we've worked super hard to make that happen, but what if it's not enough?

At least by tomorrow it'll all be over, I try to reassure myself.

Yeah, like your life, the niggly voice reminds me.

My phone vibrates with a text. Millie.

CaL me asap.

She answers on the first ring. "Have you had the radio on yet?"

"No."

"Then brace yourself." Millie sounds unusually flat, and I'm suddenly wide awake, wondering what's going on. "I've got bad news and more bad news. Jamie's just called: he overheard his parents talking about a flat they've put an offer in on. It looks like they're moving to London. They were lying, after all."

I can tell from her voice she's trying not to cry.

"Oh, Mills, no! That's awful. But what's that got to do with the radio? They haven't announced he's moving on air, have they?"

I'm way confused.

"That's the other bad news. The DJs on most of the stations have been talking about the fact that The Drifting have announced a gig in South America, to support the victims of that mudslide there last month."

"So?" My brain is struggling to keep up.

"The gig's tonight," Millie says glumly.

Tonight.

So that means everyone knows I've lied. Even though some people have suspected it for a while, now it's confirmed. The Drifting definitely won't be coming to our party.

"It's all over the radio stations and the music channels as well as Facebook and Twitter and the fan forums."

"I can't do any damage limitation," I say desperately. "I just don't have time. It's Dad's birthday party today. Mum will freak if I'm not there."

"Leave it with me," Millie says. "I'll speak to the others."

"How are we going to get out of this?"

"No idea," Millie says. "No idea at all."

As we end the phone call, I want to cry. There's no getting away from it now. Everyone knows I lied.

In the hours before we leave for Dad's party, Mum hits new levels of crazy, levels not seen since Amber's wedding earlier this year. It's astonishing Dad hasn't figured out what's going on. Mum's spiralling. Literally, it seems — when I attempted to brave the kitchen for breakfast earlier, she was standing in the middle of the room, turning round and round in slow circles. I think she was looking for something, but even so, I backed away before she'd seen me, figuring I'd grab my toast later, when she'd gone. I'm trying to lie low as much as possible, wondering what damage limitation Millie and my mates are up to.

It's not long now until we have to leave. Mum's told Dad that we need to get some things for the patio and have to go to the garden centre. All of us. The costumes have been packed in a bag in the boot, we'll get changed when we get there. Even Mum couldn't think of an excuse good enough to convince Dad that we needed to dress up as eighties throwbacks for a trip to investigate bulbs and potato sacks.

On the way, we'll be passing the scout hut. Harry will

say she thinks she left her coat there and can we all go in and help her find it?

Mum's convinced it's foolproof. I'm not so sure, but we'll see.

"C'mon, Crystal," Dad says, as we all pile into the car.

"Why are we taking the dog?" Mum asks as Crystal jumps into her footwell.

"Because he gets lonely at home by himself," Dad replies.

"Is he wearing a new collar?" I say, peering forward for a better look. Crystal's not wearing the usual pink studded one Amber loves. Instead, he's got a smart brown leather one on, with a little silver bone dangling from it.

"Er, yes. I bought it," Dad says with a cough.

I open my mouth, ready to start taking the mickey, but Mum's stress gene kicks off again.

"Let's get going!" she says. "We don't want to be late!"

"For the garden centre?" Dad says.

"Let's just go," Mum says.

After fifteen minutes, we're approaching the road that the scout hut is on. This is Harry's cue...

Nothing happens.

I try to get her attention, but she's gazing out of the window.

Come on, Harry, focus!

I knew it was a mistake making her such an integral part of the plan. The child is not to be trusted.

Mum gives a little cough. And then another. Then a proper *ahehehehem*, trying to get Harry to look up.

"Are you all right, Jen?" Dad asks. "Frog in your throat?"

Mum laughs, nervously. "Er, yes, something like that. Sorry."

The scout hut is getting nearer. Nearer...

I reach over and punch Harry's thigh.

"Ow!" Harry exclaims. "What the —? Mum, Suzy hit me!"

I eyeball her meaningfully, pointing subtly outside, trying to get her to understand what's going on without making Dad suspicious.

"Suzy, pack it in," Dad says.

"Yeah," Harry says, then sees me pointing, clocks where we are and eventually realises what I'm up to. "Ohhhhh!"

Finally!

"Any more hitting and you'll be grounded," says Dad.

"Er, don't worry about it," Harry says. "It was my fault, actually. Can you stop here, Dad? At the scout hut?"

"What? Why?"

"I forgot my coat last week and need to pick it up," Harry says.

"Aren't you wearing it?" Dad says.

"Not this one, my other one. Please, Dad. Please?"

"No," Dad says. "We'll do it on the way back."

And with that, he drives straight past the scout hut.

"Chris, you're going to need to turn around," Mum says.

"What?"

"Just do it!" Mum shrieks, totally losing her cool.

Dad looks all kinds of startled and hits the brake. There's a furious honking, and I think the car behind only narrowly avoids rear-ending us.

"It's just a damn coat," Dad mutters, after we've turned around without causing any more carnage and are pootling down the other side of the road, back towards the scout hut.

Mum's sitting in the passenger seat, doing some deep breathing.

The car pulls into the car park and Dad comes to a stop. "There you go, Harry. You'd better come back with that jacket. I don't want to think about what will happen to your mother's blood pressure if you don't."

"Um, I'm going to need help looking for it," Harry says awkwardly.

We hadn't discussed what she'd say at this point. Oh no! Emergency! Emergency! We've left Harry to freestyle the most important part of the plan!

"We'll all help you find it," Mum says. "Come on, Chris."

Dad's still grumbling as we cross the car park and enter the scout hut. "Where do you think you left it? In there?" He points to some double doors.

Harry shrugs. "Maybe."

Dad shoves the door open.

"Surprise!" comes the shout from the assembled crowd. Dad jumps about six feet in the air and stares around in astonishment, his mouth flapping open and shut like a goldfish. He can't take his eyes off the people gathered around him – most of his friends and relatives are there, all in costume, and there's Aunt Loon, down at the front dressed as Margaret Thatcher, in some kind of motorised wheelchair.

I've never seen so many badly dressed people in one place before. Fluorescent leggings, headbands and lurid eighties make-up a-go-go.

The entire room has been completely transformed and looks astonishing. It may have cost a fortune but it was totally worth it. There are drapes over the walls, so it's almost like being in a marquee, tables and chairs surround the dance floor, and a huge disco ball and lights are shining and spinning. In the corner is the photo booth, which people are already spilling out of, laughing their heads off. There's a huge table laden with food, and there are lifesize cut-outs of eighties celebs dotted around that people are taking selfies with. It looks fantastic.

"Happy birthday!" Mum says.

Dad's still speechless.

"Aw, you brought Crystal along. Hiya, baby boy. Say something, Dad!" Amber says, stepping forward dressed as Kylie Minogue. She's wearing a weird hat, which is all brim and no top, with her hair, which she's curled, pulled through it. She's got Chichi in her arms. For once Chichi isn't crying. In fact, she looks positively angelic as she gurgles and grins at everyone. She and Uni have been dressed up as Smurfs, with little blue circles on their cheeks (using organic baby-friendly face paints, as recommended by Conni G), while Amber seems totally relaxed, standing next to Mark, who's come as Michael Jackson.

Dad swallows. "Is this... is this all for me?"

"Yes!" everyone shouts.

"And this is what you've been up to? Why you've been so distracted lately?" Dad says.

"Yes!" Mum tells him.

Dad looks completely relieved. "I thought... I thought... you'd gone off me because I was getting too old..."

"What?" Mum sounds aghast.

"Nothing," Dad says hurriedly. "I was being daft. But you do know it's not my birthday until tomorrow?"

"Which makes it an even bigger surprise," Mum says.

"I can't believe you did all of this." Dad still sounds dazed.

"Well, believe it," Harry says, giving him a huge hug as Mum beams. "We think you're ace. We wanted everyone to know it."

"Where are your costumes?" someone yells.

"They're in the car," Mum says. She passes me the car keys. "Go and get them, would you, love? Once we're all dressed, this party can really get started!"

In no time, we're all in our costumes. I've gone for a generic eighties vibe – leggings, baseball boots, tutu and fluorescent top with my ponytail right on top of my head, tied with a scrunchie. Dad's Indiana Jones, and Harry's some weird rodent called Roland Rat she discovered and instantly fell in love with when she was Googling the eighties.

"Why aren't you putting on your outfit, Mum?" Harry asks. "We don't even know what you're dressing up as yet."

Mum smiles mysteriously. "I'll put it on in a minute. Just before the band starts."

Aunt Loon rolls up in her wheelchair. I'm not sure she's that great with the steering; it's juddering about all over the place.

"Since when has Aunt Loon been in that?" I whisper.

"The nursing home is lending it to her for the day," says Mum. "Since that fall she had she's not been as steady on her feet as she was. They're trying to encourage her independence."

"Oh, this stupid damn thing," Aunt Loon mutters, wrestling with the electronic wheelchair controls.

"What seems to be the problem?" Mum says, bending down to help. She fiddles with the lever. "There you go."

"I hate fancy-dress parties," the Loon mutters darkly, not thanking Mum. "Who are you meant to be?" she asks, looking me up and down.

"Just an eighties girl," I say.

"A what?" she shouts, cupping her hand behind her ear.

I repeat myself.

"Hmm," she says, disdainfully. "You could have made a little more effort."

Ugh. She really is the worst.

"Do you want to put on your video montage?" Mum asks Harry hurriedly. She gives my back a quick, reassuring rub.

"Oooh, yeah!" Harry says, and runs over to where a giant projector screen has been set up ready.

"Can I have your attention, please," Mum says into the microphone. "Harry has been spending the last few months filming the run-up to this party as a tribute for her dad. If you could all look this way, we'll watch it."

"Happy birthday, Dad," Harry says. "Hope you like it!"

As the film begins to play, it's quickly obvious that Harry's managed to capture an awful lot of Puttock family life over the past few weeks. There's me, half-asleep, staring out of the window at Dad and Ian building a shed, and later on, howling in my werewolf suit. There's Amber and Mark dealing with a screamy, angry Chichi while Uni looks on, then a shot of the four of them sleeping soundly on Amber's bed, and another of them moving out. There's Mum frantically trying to do all the catering and banner-making for the party, getting blue paint all over the carpet, while Dad was holed up in the shed. And there's Crystal Fairybelle, stealing the babies' comfort blankets — none of us knew what had happened to them; Harry's such a cheeky monkey for not saying anything! – and then we see her following Dad around, and a shot of Dad, taken when he clearly thought nobody was about, cuddling the dog and scratching it tenderly behind its ears. People laugh.

The last scene is of Harry grinning at the screen, and holding a banner that says 'Happy Birthday, Dad!'

I glance at Dad. Unless I'm very much mistaken, it looks like he's trying hard not to blub.

Behind me, the band strike up a few notes, and people start to clap and cheer as they turn round. When we see who's up on the stage, everyone gasps.

Except me.

Because I want to disappear into a hole in the ground.

I thought my parents had hit their maximum embarrassment potential when Dad entered a talent competition back in the summer, dressed in gold hot pants, riding a unicycle and playing a trombone.

But nope. Mum's decided to give him a run for his money.

She's wearing a practically transparent white lace corset top, a white skirt, white heels and white elbow length gloves. Around her head is an enormous white bow, and she's got on a belt buckle reading 'Boy Toy'. There are chunky gold crucifixes round her neck, and she's striking a pose as the opening notes to Madonna's

'Like a Virgin', the song she's been listening to constantly all over the house for weeks, ring out.

She really can't dance but I can see she's doing her best to get a routine going (as much as I can see, anyway – I've got my hands over my eyes), but her lip-syncing's pretty good. She must have been practising all those times I heard this song play.

She could have picked a different song, though. Mortifying doesn't even come *close*.

Dad's loving it and almost killing himself laughing. "See this, Suze?" he says. "This is one of the reasons I love your mother. She's always been up for a laugh."

He's cheering louder than anyone, and puts his fingers to his lips to let rip a deafening wolf whistle.

I can't help myself. I start to giggle. I haven't laughed at anything in such a long time, and it feels really good. And for a few minutes, I allow myself to forget about everything else and just get swept up in the craziness that is my mother dressed in the world's skimpiest lace outfit, prancing around to a Madonna song.

If she wasn't so utterly embarrassing, I might even tell her that she doesn't look half bad. Mum's got a pretty good figure for someone her age.

"Thank you very much!" Mum says, blowing kisses as she finishes the song with a flourish, and everyone gives her a huge round of applause. "Now, planning this huge surprise hasn't been easy, and I couldn't have done it without help from the rest of my family, but in particular, Suzy has helped out loads. Come up here, Suze!"

As everyone claps loudly, I walk onto the stage and smile sheepishly. Mum gives me a big hug, and as she pulls me close, whispers in my ear: "I've got you some Bojangles vouchers as a thank you. I know you've had a lot on, but you've been a star helping with all this. Look how happy your dad is!"

She pulls away, and says to the crowd, "Thank you all for coming to help my husband celebrate his forty-fifth birthday. Happy birthday, Chris!"

"Happy birthday!" everyone echoes as Mum jumps down from the stage.

Dad grabs her in a huge hug, and then they're kissing.

Oh dear God, my eyes. This is actual snogging, in public, with tongues.

"Wow, they're really going for it," Harry murmurs.

I have to look away before I barf.

"Good one, Mum," Amber says, who's obviously a lot cooler with our parents swapping saliva than I am. "I'm going to say something now. I've got a surprise for Dad too."

Amber gets up onto the stage holding Uni and takes

the microphone. There's a loud squeal of feedback and Amber drops the mike in alarm. Uni jumps in her arms then crumples up her eyes as if to cry. Amber quickly puts her over her shoulder and pats her back. By some miracle, the scream we're all waiting for doesn't come. Amber smiles with relief and tries again, bending down apprehensively to pick up the microphone.

Actually, now I come to think of it, the babies seem really chilled. I haven't heard them cry once the whole time we've been here.

"I'd like to say a very happy forty-fifth birthday to my wonderful Daddy Bear," Amber says, smiling. The parents have finally unlocked their lips and are standing with their arms wrapped around each other.

The room 'awwwws' as one.

"I'm really lucky having two such amazing parents," Amber continues. "They've always supported me in everything I've done, especially lately, since having the twins, and I couldn't have wished for better."

Mum and Dad exchange a sappy look.

"Now, where's Markymoo?" Amber says, scanning the room. "Mark, come up here with Chichi, please."

Amber beams as Mark joins her on the stage, Chichi held peacefully in his arms. "Aren't our babies the most gorgeous?"

Mark slips his arm around her waist and the pair of them beam happily out at the crowd, the very picture of a happy family. If a happy family consisted of Kylie Minogue and Michael Jackson with two baby Smurfs, that is.

"Daddy, we'd like to sing you happy birthday and the twins are going to join in too," Amber says.

"What's she talking about?" Dad mutters. "They can't talk, let alone sing."

Amber and Mark start to sing, very badly and out of tune, bobbing around with the twins who seem completely baffled by the whole thing. They get another big clap once they've finished.

"Happy birthday!" Amber says. "From Marky and me, and Uni and Chichi. They love their Grampy!"

Dad raises his pint in her direction.

"Seems like they've really got things together," Dad says. "What a relief. And it's great Amber's finally getting her independence and they're living in their own place, making it work. I thought for a while there they weren't going to be able to do it."

"They've done brilliantly," Mum says in agreement.

"Now, we haven't given you your present yet," Amber says. "And you'll get your proper gift tomorrow, on your actual birthday. But here's a little warm-up present for you. We've got an announcement to make…"

"Oh God, *now* she's pregnant," Dad mutters, clamping Mum's arm with a vicelike grip.

"She can't be," Mum says, but even she looks freaked.

"We're moving back in with you!" Amber says. "Now you can see your grandchildren every single day. Isn't it wonderful news?"

Mum screams with delight. "My baby's coming home. And my baby's babies. Oh, this *is* wonderful news! I'm so excited, I can't believe it."

As Amber, Mark and the twins get another huge cheer, and Mum rushes off to dish out kisses and cuddles, Dad looks like he's about to hyperventilate. Or pass out. Or maybe both at the same time. He's doing a weird snorty breath through his nose, trying to keep calm.

"They can't be coming back, we've only just got rid of them. Not enough space in our house…" he mutters.

"Well, Daddy, what do you think?" Amber appears with an absolutely enormous smile on her face.

"I'm… I'm… I don't know what to say."

"I told you he'd be blown away," Amber says happily to Mark.

"We're really looking forward to coming back," Mark says.

"I'm delighted," Mum says. "I'm going to be able to

help out much more now the party's out of the way. Much more time to spend with my delicious grandchildren."

"That's great, Mum, thanks," Amber says. "We need you!"

"But what about your friend's house?" Dad manages to get out. "What happened?"

"We had a call from Josh a couple of days ago," Mark says. "Australia's not worked out and he's really homesick. So he's coming back. Next weekend, in fact. He offered for us to stay there with him, but that would be crazy, there's too many of us and we've got too much stuff."

"Of course that would be crazy," Dad says, shaking his head slightly. "Too many of you, and too much stuff..."

Amber sighs happily. "Coming home. I can't wait."

And actually, although I never thought I'd admit it, it will be nice to have her back. And the twins. I'm looking forward to hanging out with them more, especially now they've stopped crying all the time.

"We do have a plan for a deposit, Chris," Mark says, seeing Dad's not exactly delighted by the news. "Amber's agreed she's going to stop spending so much on the girls' clothes, and I've had a pay rise, so I hope we'll be able to afford our own place before too long."

"Great," Dad says weakly.

"Now we'll be able to look after Crystal again,"

Amber says. "I've missed my puppywup loads."

Dad pauses. A strange expression flashes across his face. "Um. About that. You can come home on one condition. Me and the dog, well, we've bonded of late. Man to man, you know how it is. So, Amber, I'd, er, be grateful if... if the dog and me, could, er, still hang out sometimes."

Amber shrieks with delight. "Daddy! You've fallen in love with Crystal! Of course we can share him. I found this darling pink coat online I want to order, you can help me choose all his clothes now!"

So much for her spending less.

Dad drains his pint, tucks Crystal under his arm and staggers off in the direction of the bar, shaking his head. "Don't worry, mate, I won't let her dress you in any more of those ridiculous outfits," he says to the dog. "Triple whisky, please, neat," he orders.

"I always knew he liked the dog more than he let on," Mum says knowingly.

A few hours later, everyone's danced, eaten and sung themselves into a stupor. We've been having so much fun it's hard to believe it's still the afternoon, but now our time's up and we're getting ready to leave the scout hut, gathering up plates of food, presents and cards, and packing everything into crates to go back in the car.

A couple of huge men have come to take away the photo booth. And I get an idea.

"Er, excuse me, but has this thing only been hired for a couple of hours?"

"Nah, love," one of the men reply. "It's an all-day thing. It's paid for up till midnight."

"In that case, I don't suppose there's any chance you could take it to Collinsbrooke School, is there?" I say. "We're doing a fundraising event and this would go down a storm."

The man looks at his mate. "We don't usually do a double pick-up. What's the event for?"

"Our headteacher, Mrs Cooper is leaving, and we're raising money for a recording studio in her honour."

The man starts to laugh. "Old Cooper, I remember her, she was head when I was a kid. Didn't take too kindly to those stink-bombs we let off in her office, though. Can't believe she's been there so long. Cooper was a legend. Yeah, it's no problem to drop this off there for you."

"That's fantastic, thank you so much!"

I run back over to where my family have almost finished stacking plates of sausage rolls and slightly curling sandwiches.

"That was a great party," Dad says, a huge smile on his face. He stumbles and cracks up laughing.

I'm starting to suspect he may be the teensiest bit tiddly.

"Are you glad we surprised you?" Mum says. "I know you said you didn't want a party…"

"I didn't. But that one was fantastic," Dad says.

"Look out!" There's a shout from behind.

People are scattering left and right.

It's Aunt Loon. Advancing at speed in her wheelchair.

I guess Dad's reactions are a little slowed from the alcohol, because he doesn't manage to move out of the way fast enough. Aunt Loon hits him from behind at speed.

Dad totters and wobbles unsteadily, then ends up sitting on Aunt Loon's knee as they collide into the tables and chairs, knocking them over like skittles.

Food flies everywhere, there are crisps, bits of cake, sausages and sandwich all over them.

"Oh my goodness," Mum says, rushing to help Dad up after they finally come to a stop. "Are you both all right?"

"I did warn you to get out of the way," Aunt Lou mutters crossly. "It's the stupid steering on this thing. Get off my knee, would you?"

"That was brilliant! I got all that on film!" Harry says, delightedly. "I'm going to post it on YouTube. If it goes viral it'll make a fortune. I'm going to be rich!"

CHAPTER TWENTY-SIX

Back home, I'm trying to decide what to do about the school party. It's not long now; it was always going to be a tight turnaround after Dad's bash. I really don't want to go. I know I owe it to my friends to be there but it's the last thing I want to do. I've been trying to get hold of them ever since we got home to get an update on everything, but their phones have been permanently unavailable.

I'm mainlining one of Dad's birthday presents – the biggest box of chocolates I've ever seen – when there's a knock at the door. When I open it, Mrs Green is standing there with a huge parcel in her hands.

"This arrived while you were out," she says, smiling as she hands the box over. "The courier left it with me. Apparently he had firm instructions it had to get to you today."

I assume it's a birthday present for Dad, but when I check the label, I'm surprised to see it's addressed to me. There are stars and flowers and hearts round my name and address, which is written in funky purple glitter pen.

I frown in confusion. What's this? Who's sending me a parcel?

Unless… maybe it's a bomb. Maybe a crazed Drifting fan from school heard they weren't going to show and wanted to get revenge.

And now Mrs Green is holding it. What do I do? I can't let our elderly neighbour get blown up.

I shake my head slightly. What am I like? Of course it's not a bomb. I do not appear to be reacting well to all the stress. Even so, when I take the parcel, I bend my head towards it briefly, to see if I can hear any ticking. It *seems* okay.

"Thanks," I call, as Mrs Green heads off down the path.

"No problem, dearie."

Carrying it carefully inside, I place the parcel down on the floor.

"Ooh, what's that?" says Harry, bounding up to have a look.

"It's for me."

"Who's sending you enormous presents?" she says in disbelief.

I shrug.

It's tempting to offer to let her open it, in case there's something horrible inside. But I won't. After I've tracked down the scissors, I carefully slice through the brown tape. Harry's watching out of the corner of her eye. It's *so* obvious she's trying not to look interested, when really she's desperate to know what it is.

I pull away the outer wrappings, and inside is a beautiful white box tied with a silky white ribbon.

I extract the box and gently untie the bow. As I lift the lid, I'm still confused what this is all about. It's fabric of some kind... a beautiful turquoise colour. I reach to lift it out and it tumbles down to reveal the most stunning dress I've ever seen. And I'm a girl that doesn't do dresses. It's floor-length and V-neck, with ruching to one side, and a delicate scattering of beads round the neckline. I don't recognise the name on the label, but I don't have to. It's obvious this dress is very, very expensive, most likely designer. Underneath there's a gorgeous pair of oyster-coloured heels, still with labels on, and a bottle of expensive-looking hair serum.

"Why's someone sending *you* this stuff?" Harry asks.

"No idea," I say.

"There's a note at the bottom of the box!" Harry picks it up. 'Isn't that Isabella's handwriting?'

"Hey, give that here," I say, snatching the paper from her hands. It's been folded into four, and my name is on the outside, surrounded with more doodles.

Dear Suzy,

Surprise! I know you don't want to go to the party at school, so here's a little something to make it more bearable. This is one of my favourite dresses, I got it a couple of months ago from a Covent Garden boutique. I'll take you there one day, promise.

You can still look great even if you feel rubbish on the inside, right?

The dress is on loan, so look after it! But the shoes I'm giving you as a gift. I hope I remembered your size right. And the hair serum is supposed to be amazes – thought you'd want to try it.

Lots of love,
Isabella xxoo

I'm absolutely speechless. I can't believe she would do this!

"Why did Isabella send you a dress?" Harry asks.

"To wear to the school party later. Only I'm not going," I say, putting the lid back on the box sadly. Such a pretty dress. And such a shame I'll never get to wear it. I won't feel right keeping the shoes Isabella sent if I don't wear them tonight, so they'll have to be returned too. I hope she kept the receipt.

"Why not?" Harry asks. "Don't you have to be there? Didn't you organise the whole thing?"

I shrug. "Not really feeling in a party mood," I say.

Harry screws up her nose. "You're weird."

I take the box and carry it upstairs, stashing it first carefully under the bed, then realising there's a chance Crystal will pee all over it if I leave it there, so I slide it onto the top of the wardrobe.

Then I collapse on the bed, fold my hands behind my head, and stare up at the ceiling. Yep, that same ceiling I spent hours staring at when I couldn't sleep last night.

You can never get too much of a good ceiling, I find.

I don't move when I hear the doorbell, or when I hear Harry talking to someone in the hall. Then I hear footsteps up the stairs, before a knock on my door.

"Who is it?" I say grumpily.

"Me," says Millie. She drags Murphy, her enormous and un-tameable dog, into the room behind her. Oh brilliant, that's all I need, her insane canine eating the entire contents of my room.

"Did you have to bring him?" I ask.

"Yup," says Millie. "We're off for a pre-party walk, aren't we, Murph? No, we're not walking yet. Sit! Sit!"

As Murphy starts to whine and pull frantically at his lead at the mention of the word 'walk', Millie's left wrestling the giant beast, pushing at his hindquarters to try to get him to lie down. It only takes about ten minutes.

"Finally!" Millie says, clambering onto the bed and kneeling on the end, facing me.

"How are you doing?" I ask. "You know, with the whole Jamie thing."

I still can't believe Jamie's moving.

It breaks me up every time I realise he's not going to be hanging around with us anymore. And if I feel like that, Millie must be *devastated*.

Millie shakes her head. "Can't think about it. Not today. Got to get through the party. If I think about it too much I'm going to fall to pieces, so let's not talk about it, okay?"

"Okay," I say, but I give her a hug. She squeezes me back gratefully.

"So, how was your dad's party?"

I shrug. "Great, actually. He loved it. Apart from the

part where Aunt Loon mowed him down, along with almost taking out half of the other party guests."

"What?!"

"Yup. She's got a mobility scooter and pressed the wrong button. Those things can move way faster than you'd expect."

"Hilarious! Is everyone okay?"

"A couple of bruises and minor cuts, and Uncle Jim sprained his ankle when he jumped out of the way. Oh, and the leftover cake didn't make it. But otherwise, yeah. Harry's ecstatic. She got it on camera; she's hoping the video goes viral and makes her a ton of money."

"Smart kid. Anyway. How are you doing?"

"About as well as someone who is going to be hated by her whole school in a matter of hours. I'm going to get slaughtered now people know there's no way The Drifting are going to be there."

"Jamie, Danny and me have been spending most of the day contacting everyone we can think of," Millie says. "Most people are still coming later, you know. Despite everything."

"Thanks, Mills. You guys are the best," I say. "Does everyone hate me? I bet they're only coming so they can attack me in person."

"Um, overdramatic, much?" Millie says. "Nobody's

going to attack you. It's going to be a great party, people are looking forward to it."

"Don't they feel let down?"

Millie's phone pings with a text message.

"It's Jamie," Millie says, pulling her phone from her bag. "Wondering when we're going to get there. We need to get a move on, there's loads that needs doing."

Oh, help. Millie's assuming I'm still going. I'm just going to have to come out with it and tell her.

"Um, about the party," I say. "I don't think I'm going to go."

Millie stares at me in horror. "You *what*? What are you talking about?"

"I don't think I'm going to go," I mumble again.

"Okay, I'm going in with some tough love," Millie says. "You don't get to bottle out of this. Seriously, you don't. You helped plan this party. You helped put it all together. You've done most of the work. And yes, things went wrong, but you've managed to pull it back, and at least everyone knows The Drifting won't be coming now. But you need to be there to make sure it's the best it can be, because even without the band it's still going to be epic. I can't wait to see everyone all dressed up, it'll be such a laugh. And the raffle prizes are amazing; we're going to make a ton of money."

"But —"

Millie holds up her hand to stop me. "I know you messed up about The Drifting. And everyone else knows it too. I'm not saying you won't get any snarky comments, and Jade and Kara will probably have a few people onside being horrible, but you can handle that. You've dealt with worse and got through it. It's not going to be more unpleasant than appearing half-naked dressed in only a towel in front of the whole school, is it?"

"Thanks for the reminder," I mutter.

"That was pretty funny, though," Millie says. "And the picture of you as a werewolf…" She gives a little snort. "I so wish I'd seen you in that costume."

"Shut up," I say, but I'm starting to smile.

"It'll be fine," Millie says, leaning over to wrap me in a huge hug, and I know she's not annoyed with me any more. "You've got me. You've got Danny and Jamie. You've actually got tons of other people who want to have fun tonight. It will all be great. Trust me, okay?"

"I —"

"Stop," Millie says. "No more. You're not allowed to say anything else. In fact, all you're allowed to do is come and give us a hand, because there are things that need doing and you don't get to ditch us now. I'll drop

Murphy back home and meet you there."

Millie's phone plays a chirpy tune. She reads the display and then turns the phone to show me. "Another text from Jamie. They really need us."

I'm going to have to do this, aren't I?

"All right, I'm coming," I say, taking a deep breath.

"Yay!" Millie says. "Decided what you're wearing yet? We're getting ready at the school after all the setting up's done, right?"

"Isabella sent me a designer dress and shoes," I say, pointing up at the wardrobe.

"She what?" Millie shrieks. "Oh my God, I am so totally and utterly jealous! She didn't send me anything. You're so lucky. You have to show me. Immediately!"

As Millie coos and fusses over the dress, I start to tell myself maybe it won't be so bad. Maybe it will all be okay. And if all else fails, I'll hide. Or buy a disguise for the rest of my school year.

CHAPTER TWENTY-SEVEN

I pause outside the double doors that lead into the gym and take a deep breath.

"Ready?" Millie asks.

"I think so."

"Good," Millie says, "because there's something else I need to tell you."

"You do? What?"

"When Jamie texted earlier, the reason he wanted us to come so urgently is because Jade and Kara haven't shown."

"What? I thought they were due here hours ago!" Apart from the thrones April sorted, and the stage, they're the ones supposed to be providing all the decorations for the hall!

Mille nods her head, biting her lip. "Uh huh."

"So we have nothing other than the thrones and stage? At all?"

"I don't think so."

OMG. And we still don't even know if there are going to be any costumes. Mrs Morgan was still chasing her friend yesterday, trying to get an answer.

"Let's go in and talk to the boys and find out the score," Millie says.

Could things get any worse? Actually, I really shouldn't tempt fate by asking that.

As I push open the door and take in the scene in front of me, my heart sinks into my shoes. Actually it sinks into my shoes and tunnels on downwards.

The trestle tables for the food are in place, and so is the stage, which looks utterly fantastic – the boys have done a brilliant job. They've painted the wooden wings purple, and they're covered in black musical notes and silver stars. There are purple velvet curtains on either side that they've borrowed from the drama department, and it all looks very dramatic. Over in the corner, there's a guy I assume to be the DJ busy setting up all the equipment we need for 'The Star Factor' to happen, like the mikes and the buzzers. The photo booth has been placed against one wall. There's also a huge projection screen, ready to show Mrs Cooper's farewell photo montage, a load of empty tables, four gold and purple thrones in the middle of the room and the banner we made in art, which reads 'Goodbye and Good Luck, Mrs C! Thanks for everything!'

But that's it.

There is nothing else going on.

The place still looks like a gym hall.

Oh no.

Oh no, oh no, oh no! This is worse even than the terrible parties the PTA throw for us, which have limp streamers and balloon animals.

What are we going to do? People are going to be seriously unimpressed when they see this.

And the local paper's coming to record the whole thing for posterity. Apparently they're still covering the event, even though they know The Drifting are a no-show.

Danny and Jamie are talking to Mrs Morgan in front of the fire doors, along with April, Sophie and Eve. Nobody else has turned up. They all spin round when we enter.

"Finally, you're here. I've got to go and make a few calls," says Mrs Morgan, seeming proper frazzled. "I've been trying to catch up with the caterers all day. They're not answering their phones."

"The caterers aren't the only ones not answering their phones," Danny and Jamie say as we join them.

"Kara and Jade aren't, either."

"They so planned this, didn't they?" I say. "They had no intention of ever doing any decorating. They wanted to make us look even worse than we already would when The Drifting didn't show."

We stare at each other hopelessly.

"I don't know what we're going to do," I say. "It's not long until the party starts, and we haven't got enough time to go to the shops, they'll be closing soon."

"Maybe people won't notice," Sophie says. "We've got the stage and the judges' chairs, with the lights dimmed it might not look too bad..."

"People have paid a bomb for their tickets," Millie says. "They're going to notice. At least your stage looks great."

"Yeah, you did a brilliant job," I say.

"Glad you like it," Jamie says. "We were up pretty much all night finishing it off."

"Thanks for the thrones, too, April," I add. "It's great you managed to sort those for us."

"At least I could do something to help," April says.

"Hello?" There's a woman I don't recognise peering round the double doors.

"Can I help you?" I say suspiciously. The last thing we need is more hassle. And everyone in this gym seems to have problems coming out of their ears at the moment.

"Do you want Mrs Morgan?" Millie says, much more politely. "She's had to go and make some calls. She'll be back in a minute."

"Okay, thanks," the woman says, smiling. "I'm Anna, I've got the costumes for tonight?"

I let out a small scream of joy and run over. "We didn't know if you'd be able to come!"

Anna laughs. "You wouldn't believe how many release forms I've had to sign to take these. Took forever. Now, I've got two rails of outfits in the van. Julie – sorry, that's probably Mrs Morgan to you – has said she's happy to supervise them, making sure they get put back after every song. Not that I don't trust you, but y'know. We have insurance, so don't look so worried," she says, seeing the look on my face. "And in all honesty they're probably never going to get used again, they've been gathering dust in our props cupboard, but it's better to be safe than sorry."

"Thank you so much for lending them to us," I say. "We really appreciate it."

"No worries. Can someone give me a hand to get the rails out?"

"Yeah, we'll get the boys to help," Millie says,

sending Danny and Jamie after Anna.

"At least we have costumes now," Millie says. "And costumes worn by actual famous bands and singers, so it's not all bad. And you know, later, when it's dark, maybe nobody will notice the lack of decoration. I'm sure the DJ has got a disco ball and some coloured lights or something. I can get Jamie to stand on the stage flicking a torch on and off if he doesn't."

As Danny and Jamie return, helping Anna with the clothes rails, Millie runs over and starts rummaging through the outfits, squealing with delight.

"These are fantastic," she says. "Everyone's going to look so good! Check out this wig. And these glasses! Just brilliant. It's going to be amazing."

"Happy to be able to help," says Anna. "These things are always so much more fun if you can get people dressing up. It really adds to the atmosphere, gets people in more of a party mood. Um, I hope you don't mind me saying this, but aren't you leaving it quite late to start the decorating?"

"There's kind of been a decorating disaster," I mumble.

"How so?" Anna asks, frowning.

"A couple of girls on the committee were supposed to be in charge, but they've let us down," I explain.

"That's a shame," Anna says.

"That's Jade and Kara for you," Jamie says. "We're pretty sure they did it on purpose."

Anna looks shocked. "But why would they do that? Why would they want to ruin the party for everyone?"

"It's a really long story," I say. "But, uh, they kind of have an issue with us."

"They didn't like the fact everyone picked our idea for the party and not theirs," Millie adds. "It didn't go down too well."

"Well, that's not on," Anna says. Then she looks thoughtful. "Do you know, I might be able to do something. Give me a minute, I'll make a quick call."

"We're quite tight on time," I say nervously.

"I won't be long." Anna smiles reassuringly, finds a number in her phone and wanders off, chatting.

My friends and I look at each other, then shrug. Who knows what Anna's up to?

"So I spoke to my friend who co-owns Party Props," Anna says when she returns.

My face falls.

"Don't look like that," Anna says. "She told me about what had happened with you lot and spoke to her business partner, and they're happy to help out now they know I'm here and that the props are needed for a charity do. They're going to lend you some stuff for free. They figure they'll get some good publicity out of it, especially as the local paper's coming along to cover tonight. Just make sure you mention the Party Props name if they send a journalist to interview you, okay?" Anna checks her watch. "My friend shouldn't be long. Back in a minute!"

We wait nervously for Anna to come back. When she finally returns, she's got another woman in tow, both dragging huge boxes and bags behind them.

"This is Jojo. She's got some drapes for the walls," Anna says, opening one of the huge boxes. "There's more stuff in the van, we couldn't carry everything."

"Guys, can you go and get the stuff?" Millie says. "People are going to be arriving really soon."

Jamie and Danny immediately run off, followed by April, as we watch Anna pull out some gorgeous purple velvet drapes from the box.

"We thought we could hang these around here..." Anna says, deftly scrambling up the wall bars to hang the drapes. "Jojo, you get the other end..."

Even a few drapes around the walls have made a huge difference. It doesn't feel quite so school gym with the hoops and bars covered up.

Millie and I push all the freestanding equipment out

and shut it into a classroom. Nobody wants a pommel horse at a party.

We'll have to remember to move it back after the party's done. Nobody wants a pommel horse in a science lab, either.

By the time we return, it's looking pretty fantastic. The lights are dimmed and the DJ's lasers are flashing, drapes are up, the tables have been covered in cloths, and the huge gold microphones we'd coveted in the Party Props warehouse are standing each side of the steps up to the stage, which are now covered in a red carpet. The judges' chairs are carefully positioned and there are some large silhouettes of instruments hanging around the place – guitars, drum kits, mike stands and keyboards, as well as glittery stars hanging from the ceiling

"This is incredible, thank you so much," I say in awe.

"Not a problem," says Anna. "I've also put in a call to one of my other friends who should be here in a bit... ah, here she is!"

A woman walks in, hefting a huge balloon arch behind her. Sophie and Eve rush over to give her a hand.

"What's this?" I say, eyes wide with amazement.

"My friend Ali supplies these to weddings. This was

used yesterday — seems a shame to waste it, doesn't it? And Ali said she'd got a load of leftover balloon centrepieces for your tables, too," Anna says.

I stare, open-mouthed. I can hardly believe what I'm seeing. In only a few minutes, the room has been completely transformed, and it hasn't even cost us a penny! People will be blown away when they see it. Even better, with all the ticket sales, plus the raffle tickets we'll sell, we should make a ton of cash by the end of the night.

"I can't thank you enough," I say quietly to Anna.

Anna laughs. "Happy to be able to help. You kids are going to have enough stress and hard work next year with GCSEs and what not, so have a good time while you can. I was bullied at school. We can't let people like Jade and Kara win, can we?"

Millie gives me an excited smile, and grabs me into a big bear hug. I squeeze her back happily.

"We need to set up the table with the raffle prizes," she says. "Then I think we're ready to go!"

Jamie's phone starts to ring. He grabs it from his pocket, stares down at the display, then says, "I've got to take this." He disappears off into a corner, talking at top speed.

"What's going on with him?" Millie asks.

Danny and I shrug. I don't really have time to think about Jamie now. I'm surprised that I actually feel loads better than I thought I would. Okay, so The Drifting aren't going to come. But at least the party isn't an entire washout. If I end up getting grief I'll go home, but hopefully everyone else will still enjoy themselves.

It won't be that bad, will it?

The look on Mrs Morgan's face as she approaches says otherwise.

CHAPTER TWENTY-EIGHT

"What's the matter?" I ask.

Because Mrs Morgan is *freaking*.

"I've finally got hold of the caterers and they can't fulfil all of our order. The drinks are fine, but apparently the person who was preparing the food came down with a sickness bug and they can't risk infecting everyone."

Seriously?!

Is everything going to go wrong here? This must be the most cursed party in the history of the world.

"The food is the most important thing!" Jamie says, who's returned from his phone call and is looking horrified.

Do you know, I just can't get stressed about anything else.

"I've got an idea," I say. "Let's get pizza. Why don't

we ring Hannah at Bojangles, and see what she can do? She won't be able to do it all by herself, the kitchen there's not big enough for the quantities of food we'll need, but she knows of loads of other cafés around the place who might be able to help us out."

"Pizza?" Mrs Morgan says, wrinkling her nose. "But we spent so much time choosing all the food. What about those darling cupcakes with the musical instruments iced on the top…"

"I know, it's a shame, but I don't think we've got any other options, have we?" I say. "At least it'll keep everyone happy. Everyone in the world likes pizza."

"Well, okay then," Mrs Morgan says. "I'll go and make a call now."

As she trots off, Jamie grabs my arm. "Can I talk to you and Mills? I've just had some news and it's kind of urgent, I –"

"Not now," Millie says. "Suze and I have got to get ready. C'mon, you!"

Even though Jamie is still trying to get our attention she drags me off to the toilets, where we do the quickest change of our lives.

I feel amazing in Isabella's designer dress and heels. Okay, I can hardly walk in them, but that's a minor detail. And the serum she sent! Oh raptures, my hair is behaving and looks amazing, all ringletty and princess-like. I don't want to sound too braggy, but for once, I actually look pretty okay.

Millie looks beautiful too in her short pink prom dress with a netted skirt, accessorised with bright yellow heels and colourful jewellery.

"Ready?" she asks, smiling.

"As I'll ever be."

We walk back out into the hall, and I do another double-take when I see how stunning it is now it's been decorated properly. We did this! Surely people might go easy on us when they see how hard we've worked?

Danny's spreading musical note confetti all over the tables when I walk over and touch his arm.

"That looks great," I say.

He spins round, and when he sees me his mouth drops open.

"Wow," he says, before his lips stretch into a big grin. "Look at you."

We stand for a moment, smiling shyly at each other.

"You look completely gorgeous," Danny eventually says.

"Thanks," I say. "So do you." Danny's changed into smart jeans with a shirt over a t-shirt and looks sexier than I've ever seen him before in my entire life.

Swoon.

"Did Jamie catch up with you?" Danny asks.

"Um, not yet," I say. "He tried to speak to me and Mills earlier."

"Yeah, you need to see him, it's urgent. He said he's got good news for us."

"He has? I could use some."

I'm trying to hunt Jamie down when I bump into the judges instead.

"Suzy!" Jamie calls a few minutes later, as I'm deep in discussion over competition rules.

"Hang on a minute," I say distractedly.

"But I need to talk to you."

"Yep, let me sort out these guys and make sure they know what they're doing, then I'm all yours."

"But I really need to tell you something. It'll be quick, I promise."

"Jamie, I can't right now, I've got to get a running order organised. I'll be with you in a sec, okay?"

After the judges are sorted, I'm about to go and find Jamie when the photographer from the paper arrives and wants to take photos of us. Then the DJ grabs me to check over his playlist and make sure I'm happy with it. Across the room, I see Millie and the other committee members rushing around, just as busy as I am.

326

Jamie tries again and again to talk to me and Millie, but we've got no time to stop. It's full on, trying to get everything sorted before the party's due to start. But we're determined that, despite the lack of The Drifting, and Jade and Kara's best efforts to sabotage us, our party is going to be out-of-this-world amazing.

Finally the four of us get a moment together, and Jamie's about to start talking when up walks Mrs Cooper. Jamie's face falls. Mrs Cooper claps one hand on my shoulder, and one hand on Millie's.

"I want to say thank you for doing such a wonderful job. You've worked ever so hard. This is the best send-off I could have asked for. I hear there've been a few teething problems, but I must say, you've risen to the challenges beautifully and I'm extremely proud of you all. We're going to make a lot of money, so well done!"

Jamie tries again to say something, but he's interrupted by Mrs Cooper.

"Look, people are coming in! Let's get your party underway!"

People have started to arrive in droves, and Mrs Morgan herds Jamie and Danny backstage to start organising the acts. Jamie looks agonised as they go.

Although there's some muttering about The Drifting and some dark looks being sent in my direction, everyone coming in seems up for a party. There's a lot of exclaiming about the props and the costumes and everyone seems to be genuinely impressed with the room and the set-up. Zach and his mates skulk in, looking sheepish, but I'm watching the door for Jade and Kara. When they eventually arrive, I can tell from their expressions that they're astonished by what we've done, and also *seriously* annoyed. They cover it up by sneering at everything.

Grrrr.

But ha! They must be livid.

I decide to ignore them and allow myself a flicker of satisfaction as I gaze around. We made this happen! Despite everything, and no thanks to certain people, we've done a pretty good job. Go us!

Behind me, Mr Groves has walked up the steps onto the stage and is trying to get everyone's attention.

"Everyone! I'd like to say something. Simmer down, please… Welcome to our fundraising evening. We hope you're having a good time. As you know, we're here because of Mrs Cooper, who's sadly retired. Hers are big shoes to fill, but I hope I'm doing her justice."

Mr Groves looks around the room at this point, clearly expecting whoops, cheers or some kind of feedback. Instead there's silence as everyone stares at him.

Awkward.

"Ahem," he coughs. "Right, well, if I could invite Mrs Cooper up here, let's give her an enormous cheer to say thank you for all the hard work she did for our school."

There are cheers that nearly raise the roof. Mainly because she's gifting us a recording studio, I expect, but Mrs Cooper was a pretty great head. Loads better than Groves, anyway.

"Now, we've put together a montage of pictures of your time here," Mr Groves says, and the photos start to flick through on the screen. They start from way back in the eighties, where Mrs Cooper was all big curly hair and shoulder pads, and go through the years all the way up to today. She's done so much during her time here!

"Thank you, Mrs Cooper!" Mr Groves says, when the montage has finished. "Let's give her another hand."

Once all the applause has finished, Mr Groves starts talking again. He's loving the sound of his voice this evening. "Now, the singing competition will kick off in the next hour or so, I know we're all looking forward to that, and don't forget to buy your raffle tickets, there are some fantastic prizes on offer. I've got my eye on that flatscreen TV. We've got our party committee to thank for this great evening, so I'd like you to help me thank them. Up here, all of you!"

There's actually a pretty big round of applause as we troop up onto the stage. Not as big as the one for Cooper, and okay, there are a few boos, but the claps are definitely louder.

"We knew you were lying," Jade hisses as she and Kara follow behind me. "The Drifting were never going to show."

I just ignore her.

"Where's Jamie?" I whisper.

"Dunno," Millie says. "He dashed off a minute ago."

"And, before 'The Star Factor' kicks off, I'd like to mention the other star of the hour, Mrs Morgan," Mr Groves says.

Mrs Morgan walks onto the stage, smiling broadly.

"I know some of you were expecting The Drifting to be here," Mr Groves continues. A few boos ring out around the hall. I feel my cheeks turn pink and I stare down at my feet. I'd very much like to disappear, right here, right now.

"As you know they've been approached to do a charity gig for survivors of the mudslide in South America," Mr Groves says. "So although it's obviously very disappointing not to see them perform tonight, the gig they're doing is for a very worthwhile cause and –"

He stops talking as Jamie dashes up the steps, waving

something in his hand. It looks a lot like a USB stick.

"What is it, Jamie?" Mr Groves doesn't look very pleased at being interrupted.

Jamie beams triumphantly as he passes us. "Wait until you see this," he mutters, then puts his hand over Mr Grove's microphone as he talks to him quickly. Out on the dance floor, the crowd are getting a bit bored, shuffling and talking amongst themselves.

"Well, this is certainly unexpected," Mr Groves says, looking puzzled, after Jamie's finished. "Jamie's got something he'd like to show us."

Jamie fiddles around with the computer, inserting the USB stick and pressing a few keys. The projection screen turns blue, and then the words 'The Drifting' fill it.

He turns to the crowd and smiles triumphantly. "The Drifting may not have been able to appear here in person tonight, but they recorded this for us instead."

Huh? What's he talking about?

My breath catches in my throat as the film starts to play, and there, on the huge screen, blown up to larger-than-life size, is Nate Devlin, lead singer of The Drifting smiling at us all.

My heart stops. Oh my God. I don't believe this!

"Hello, Collinsbrooke!" he says.

What the —?

Down below, people have started cheering, grabbing onto each other with delight. The noise level in here has gone through the roof.

"Shush, or you'll miss what he's got to say to us!" Jamie bellows into the microphone.

He turns up the volume so Nate can be heard over the din.

Nate continues: "I know you were expecting to see us at your school tonight, and I'm really sorry we can't be there."

At this point the camera pans back to reveal the rest of the band, with their instruments. A few girls let out muffled shrieks, and start jumping up and down.

A quick glance to the side reveals Jade and Kara are *not* happy. They look like they've been sucking on lemons.

"When we heard the news about the mudslide, we knew we had to support those affected, especially as our drummer has family out there," Nate continues. "We didn't want to leave you guys in the lurch, though, especially after your committee had worked so hard to get things organised. So we're going to play some of our biggest hits for you. This first one's for Suzy and Millie. Hope you enjoy it, girls!"

Oh. My. Actual. God.

Nate Devlin said my name.

Nate Devlin said my name!

And then they break into 'Ready', their first big hit. Everyone in the hall starts whooping, and then they're all going nuts on the dance floor.

As Millie clasps my hand, I'm still too flabbergasted to move.

Jamie darts over and gives us a huge smile.

"What the...? How did you...? What's going on?" I finally splutter.

"Why didn't you say something?" Millie says, going to give Jamie a wallop on his chest. He ducks out of the way, laughing.

"I have been trying! I wanted to tell you we might have things sorted, but I didn't know it would definitely go ahead until a few minutes ago – we've had a nightmare trying to get the data transferred. This has literally only just been delivered. Anyway, every time I tried to talk to you earlier, someone kept pulling you away. But how mind-blowing is this?"

"So mind-blowing," I say, still unable to believe what's happened. People are dancing and laughing as the music plays.

Even some of the teachers are joining in. Urgh. My eyes. Some things a girl really doesn't need to see.

"I still don't understand how you managed to pull this off," Millie says, as the song comes to an end and everyone's clapping. It sounds like her voice is coming from the end of a long tunnel. It's all so surreal. I feel like I'm in a dream.

It all worked out okay! It all worked out!

"Look at her, she's a complete space cadet," Danny says. He puts his arm around me and gives me a squeeze, kissing the side of my head. "Bit of a shock, right?"

"You can say that again," I say, finally managing to get my vocal cords working. Relief is surging through every part of my body, and my knees are trembling. The Drifting actually made an appearance at our party! And okay, so they weren't here in person, but they spoke to our school! And now they're playing – for us!

"You know Mum and Dad have been working up in London a lot?" Jamie asks. "Well, their top-secret project was for The Drifting!"

"Shut up!" Millie and I chorus together in disbelief.

"Not really?" I say. "And they didn't tell you?"

"They couldn't," Jamie says. "They had to sign all sorts of scary legal documents and confidentiality agreements and would have got into a whole heap of trouble if they'd said anything. You still need to keep it quiet, okay? They've designed the cover of the new album!"

"No way!"

"I know," Jamie says. "Mum and Dad's names are even listed in the credits. Who'd have thought the olds could ever end up doing something so cool? They had to do loads of pitches and stuff before they won the work. Probably helped that The Drifting's PR manager is an old friend of theirs from university..."

"Oh my God!" Millie exclaims.

"Yeah. Anyway, when you told Mum what you'd done, Suzy, apparently after they'd won the contract she talked to her friend, who spoke to the band and explained everything, especially the bit about people blurting out promises they couldn't keep..."

I blush. "Sorry."

"Don't be sorry. None of this would have happened otherwise!" Jamie says. "You wouldn't believe how tight it's been to get organised. This didn't even get filmed until this morning, the band did it just before they got on their private jet to South America! The PR manager was really keen for them to do it to get some positive publicity, mainly because of those rumours about them fighting and stuff. This story is hitting the papers tomorrow."

"They're not splitting, are they?" I ask. I have to check.

Jamie shakes his head.

"I can't believe you didn't say anything," Millie says. "Suzy's been so stressed!"

"I was trying to!" Jamie protests again. "You wouldn't stop and listen! I'm so sorry, Suze, I didn't know myself until today. My parents weren't sure if they were going to be able to get it done on time, and they had to be extra careful. If word had got out about them working with The Drifting they could have been fired, and they've got loads more work lined up with them, which, incidentally, is worth a bomb. Want to hear some more good news?"

"There's more?" Danny says.

"We're not moving," Jamie says, his face widening into an enormous smile. "My parents just told me what's been going on."

"You're not?" Millie shrieks. "Oh my God. Oh my God!"

"So what was the deal with all the property details? And the conversation about buying a flat up there?" Danny asks.

"They *were* thinking about it," Jamie says. "Because they've been working in London so much, and they'll probably get tons of new contracts on the back of this Drifting thing. Luckily they decided it wouldn't be fair on me, taking me away from you guys and making me change schools at the start of GCSEs. They're buying a flat up there to use instead – their offer was accepted earlier today, but we're keeping the house in Collinsbrooke."

This evening can't get any better. Jamie's staying. The party's a success. Even The Drifting are here.

"So happy," Millie says. "So, so happy."

"Yeah, me too," Jamie says. "Now, let's focus on The Drifting for a bit, hey? Although we'll totally be watching this again later. Look, Nate's going to talk again."

Up on the screen, there's another Nate close-up. Millie sighs dreamily. "Is there any way your parents can fix it so we can meet them, Jamie?"

"I'm working on it," Jamie grins. "Now, shush. The man's got something to say."

"Hope you enjoyed that," Nate says. "Before we get cracking with some more songs, I've heard you're fundraising for a school recording studio. See this guitar Liam's using? It's coming your way. You can auction it and hopefully raise a ton of money."

The rest of what he's saying is drowned out in the screams from the crowd.

Mrs Morgan walks over and pats me on the back. "This is wonderful. You've all done such an incredible job. I'm so proud of you."

"I couldn't have done it without these guys," I say. "They're the best. It was Jamie, really."

"But you've all worked very hard and pulled together as a team," Mrs Morgan says. "Well done."

"Just glad everything turned out the way it did," Jamie says, his eyes sparkling as he grins at me.

Out in the crowd, I can see Jade and Kara. Absolutely raging doesn't even come close.

"Shall we go and dance?" Danny shouts, over the drums and guitars.

"Yeah!" we all agree.

"Good one, Suzy," someone says, as we walk across the hall.

"Yeah, never thought you'd be able to pull it off. Nice one," says Zach.

Zach! Even Zach's impressed with what we've done! I almost fall over with the shock, but manage to hold it together enough to stride past, giving him a quick smile.

"You look fantastic, love your dress," someone else adds. Everywhere we go, people are saying nice things about me and my friends.

"Everyone thinks you're pretty amazing, you know that, right?" Danny whispers in my ear.

I just grin happily.

338

At the edge of the stage, I see Mrs Morgan talking to Mr Groves.

"Kara, Jade, could you come here for a moment, please?" he says, leading them to the side of the hall.

Millie and I sidle a bit closer, eager to hear what's going on.

"Mrs Morgan tells me that you were in charge of providing the decorations for this party and you didn't show up this morning," he says. "She says that none of these decorations were organised by you."

Jade and Kara stare at him, their faces sullen.

"Well? Is that true?"

Kara gives a half shrug and Jade pulls out the winning smile she's used countless times before to get herself out of trouble.

"Sir, I think there's been a misunderstanding. The company that we used didn't deliver the stuff we needed and —"

"But you didn't let anyone know what was going on and you weren't answering your phones, is that correct?"

You can see the cogs whirring in Jade's brain as she desperately tries to think of a way out of this one.

"Um, well, we were…"

"I don't want to hear any more lies," Mr Groves says. "You and Kara were very irresponsible, leaving Mrs

Morgan completely in the lurch. You had an obligation to her, and to the rest of the committee, and you let everyone down. Now I don't want to say that you did it on purpose —"

Jade opens her mouth to protest but Mr Groves holds out a hand to stop her. Jade and Kara have both turned a particularly beautiful shade of purple.

"Under the circumstances, I have no choice but to ask you to leave the party," Mr Groves says.

"But, sir —" protests Kara.

"That is so unfair!" storms Jade. "It wasn't our fault."

"Even if that's the case, not letting people know what was happening, and not helping to sort out the problem, certainly was your fault. I'm very disappointed in you both. We're also still investigating those malicious flyers from a few weeks ago, and discovering who took those pictures, so you might want to think whether there's anything you'd like to own up to. Now, get your coats. I'll ring your parents to come and pick you up. You can wait for them outside my office. I'll be having a further discussion with you both on Monday morning."

They're being kicked out? Seriously? And getting into a whole heap of trouble with it? Just when I thought this night couldn't get any better!

Jade shoulder-barges past, muttering insults, Kara

following behind.

As soon as they've gone we burst out laughing.

"Can't say they didn't deserve that," Jamie says. "But don't gloat for too long, Nate's up again."

"To finish off, we're doing 'All I Can Think of Is You'," Nate says on the big screen. "Sounds like you've got a great night lined up, so enjoy the rest of it. Have fun, everyone. Maybe we'll come and pay a visit to that recording studio one day. We could come and open it for you, if you like."

More screams echo around the gym.

As the familiar notes of 'All I Can Think of Is You' ring out around me, I don't think I've ever felt so happy.

"They're playing our song," Danny says, grinning.

And he's right. It's the one Danny dedicated to me at Amber's wedding just before we got back together. I have such happy memories associated with this music. I wrap my arms around Danny and Millie. Jamie joins in, and then we're dancing together in a cluster, arms round each other, singing crazily at the tops of our voices.

I'm at a brilliant party, wearing a great outfit, and even my hair's behaving itself. Jamie's staying. Nobody wants to kill me. I have the best friends *in the entire world*.

Everything worked out, thanks to my amazing mates. I still can't believe it, and I'm not even quite sure how it happened, but it did.

I throw back my head to sing along with Nate, not caring that I'm out of tune. I'm too happy to care. We're all laughing and giggling uncontrollably, bumping our hips into each other, as we dance around in our group of four.

There's no mistaking it.

From being what I thought would be one of the worst days of my life, this evening has turned out to be one of the best.

Yep. Right now, life is pretty darn great for me, Suzy P.

And it's definitely time to party.

ACKNOWLEDGEMENTS

First, a special mention for Chloe Yandell, who bid in a charity auction to be included in these acknowledgements. Here's to you and your lovely girls, Mia, Erin and Isla. I'm going to mention Eddison too, because I don't want him to feel left out. (One other thing – there's a posh lemonade in the fridge for you should you pop by.)

Thank you to the wonderful teams at Templar and Hot Key Books, with a special mention to Tilda and Debbie, as well as the others in editorial, publicity, marketing, design, and everyone in all the other departments who worked to make the book happen.

Thank you to Ade, who is always the most amazing support, I really truly couldn't do this without you. You rock. Oliver needs a mention too, as does the so-far-nameless-kicky one who'll be making an appearance into the world at around the same time as this book does.

Thank you to the people who helped make Suzy possible right from the start, because none of this would have happened without you. Lindsey Fraser, Helen Boyle, Emma Goldhawk and Sara Starbuck, I'm so grateful for everything you did. Group hug!

Thank you to my family and friends for all the support and encouragement you give me. And the Bath Authors. I couldn't forget you marvellous souls.

Thank you to Anna Wilson. She knows why.

A huge thanks to all the bloggers and reviewers who've got behind Suzy and have been so supportive.

And finally, I also can't not say thanks to YOU – for picking up this book. I hope you enjoyed reading it. Do pop by my website, or Facebook page, or Twitter feed and say hello – I'd love to hear from you!

FIVE FACTS ABOUT

ME, Karen Saunders xxx

1) I have a genuine fear of toe socks. They make me feel sick.

2) One of my favourite places in the world is Brownsea Island.

3) My favourite colour of nail varnish is blue.

4) I don't have any pets but would very much like a guinea pig or two.

5) Although Suzy has two sisters, I don't have any of my own. I've got one younger brother.

You can find me online at: www.karensaunders.co.uk

f facebook.com/karensaunderswriter

🐦 @writingkaren

Suzy tweets too: @suzyputtock

Do come and say hello!

DON'T MISS BOOK ONE...

Meet me, Suzy Puttock (yes, Puttock with a <u>P</u>), fourteen years old and a total disaster magnet.

My life's full of ups and downs. My loved-up big sister Amber's getting married and wants lime green bridesmaids' dresses. I'm not happy about that.

But there's this hot new guy, Zach, just started at my school. I am happy about that. Only I've had a boyfriend since forever – Danny.

So now I'm all kinds of confused...

'A hugely entertaining read.' *Cathy Hopkins*, author of *Million Dollar Mates*

'A lively, heart-warming story, sure to put a smile on your face.' *Luisa Plaja*, author of *Diary of a Mall Girl*